THE CINDERELLA MOMENT

JENNIFER KLOESTER

Copyright © 2013 by Jennifer Kloester. U.S. Edition. Originally published in Australia by Penguin Australia.

THE CINDERELLA MOMENT by Jennifer Kloester
A girl spends the summer in Paris masquerading as her bestfriend, but her secrets begin to unravel as she falls in love with a boy who thinks she's someone else.

Edited by Mandy Schoen
Cover design by Stephanie Mooney
Cover art copyright ©2013 by Swoon Romance

For Jean Frere,
with love and thanks,
And for River Dianne,
who understands.

THE CINDERELLA MOMENT

JENNIFER KLOESTER

Chapter One

Angel knew the moment she saw it. The colour was exactly as she'd imagined—a deep midnight blue. She ran her fingers over the velvet, catching it between her palms to test its weight. Just as she'd thought: pussycat soft, but heavy and luxuriant enough to hang perfectly.

She lifted the bolt of cloth down from the rack and carried it to the counter. The salesgirl smothered a yawn. "How much?" she asked in a bored tone.

If she only knew what it's for, thought Angel. "I'll need six yards."

The girl looked at her doubtfully. "That'll be three hundred and eighty-nine dollars."

Please let there be enough, Angel thought, digging into her purse and placing the bills on the counter, her heart beating faster as the roll of cash gave up its twenties, tens and fives, until all that was left was a small wad of one-dollar bills.

She counted slowly: three eighty-two, three eighty-three, three eighty-four . . . She was five dollars short. "Maybe just *under* six yards."

The girl unrolled the cloth and Angel watched in quiet ecstasy as the fabric flowed in great velvet waves across the counter. It was perfect.

***

The uptown bus seemed to take forever. It was a sultry May evening and Angel's legs prickled with sweat under the parcel of fabric on her lap. It'd be hot walking home from her stop, but she didn't care. She'd help her mother with dinner, rush through her homework and get started on the dress. She'd have to go carefully. This dress, more than anything she had ever made, needed to be exactly right, down to the tiniest detail. And when it came time to *cut* the velvet—well, she'd work up to that.

It was nearly seven when she turned onto Fifth Avenue and ran up the front steps of the five-story townhouse. Inside, the marble foyer was brightly lit and she could hear voices upstairs. The hateful Margot by the sound of it, probably berating the cleaner again, unless—had Lily come home early from play rehearsal?

Angel paused for a moment, straining to hear. The first voice reached a new pitch and the answering murmur grew even softer. Definitely Margot and definitely *not* Lily.

It could be Clarissa. Angel hadn't yet met Margot's seventeen-year-old daughter, but she'd *heard* her. Last week, after Lily's dad had left for South America, Lily and Clarissa had fought like cats. Afterward, Lily had come down to the kitchen wing and burst into tears.

Angel and her mother had tried to comfort her, but they'd both known it wasn't the fight that had upset Lily so much as her dad inviting Margot and Clarissa Kane to stay the whole six weeks he was away.

Lily had done everything to convince her dad not to invite them but she hadn't succeeded. And it was only after the fight that Angel had realized how much Philip's decision had upset her best friend. She'd never known Lily to lose her cool like that. Sure, she had a passion for drama, but she could always hold it in when she wanted to. Trouble was, as Lily told Angel later, on that occasion she hadn't wanted to.

In the week that followed, Lily came downstairs so often

to report Clarissa's latest iniquity that Angel suspected the older girl of deliberately trying to start another fight. So far, Lily had managed to refrain from taking the bait, but Angel doubted she'd last another five weeks without biting back.

Angel listened again. The voices were moving away; she heard footsteps, a door close and silence. She sighed with relief and crossed the foyer. As she passed the hallstand she stopped. Thrown carelessly against the antique Japanese cabinet was Clarissa's discarded schoolbag. Books, folders, pens, an iPad, headphones and a crumpled cheerleader's uniform spilled out across the floor beside a black-and-white Moschino jacket.

At least, it looked like one of the latest Moschino designs . . . Angel hesitated, glanced nervously around and, satisfied she was alone, put down her parcel and picked up the jacket.

She cast a judicious eye over the cut and fabric. It was well-made and she noted with approval the even seams and well-fitted lining. The black-and-white look was very much in the Moschino style, but it wasn't Moschino. Angel checked the label and felt a tiny shock of recognition. A flamboyant black CLARISSA told her at once who had made the jacket.

Ever since Lily had told her that Clarissa designed her own clothes and had a part-time job working for the up-and-coming New York fashion designer, Miki Merua, Angel had felt a guilty fascination for her best friend's archenemy. Anything to do with fashion was an irresistible lure for Angel and (despite Lily's regular catalogue of Clarissa's vices) she found it hard to believe that anyone who brought their own dressmaker's dummy and sewing machine to the house could possibly be as bad as Lily made out.

Angel held the jacket away from her—the cut was good and the black panels were a cute idea but something—

Upstairs a door slammed. She stiffened as the staccato

tip-tup sound of high heels on marble came toward her. Angel dropped the jacket, grabbed her precious parcel and fled.

Opening the door to the kitchen wing, she passed through into the safety and familiarity of her own world. There was no gleaming marble here, but over the years Angel had grown to like the bare walls and worn carpet. This part of the house might be austere but it was quiet and these days that was all she wanted.

She walked quickly down the hallway past the long-disused butler's room and the former housekeeper's old room. Angel's bedroom was opposite her mother's at the end of the hall. They were next to the kitchen, which made things quicker in the morning—especially when Philip had guests and there were breakfasts to be delivered upstairs.

Angel frowned. Usually Philip de Tourney's houseguests were pleasant and undemanding, not like Margot and Clarissa Kane. It was incredible: they'd only been in the house a week and already they'd created havoc. No wonder Lily kept staying late at school. Unless . . .

She crossed the hall and entered the butler's old room. Here lay a treasure trove of unwanted things gathering dust. In the center of the room, two large wooden wardrobes and a low table formed a makeshift theatre and standing on the table, with her back to the door, was Lily.

"What do I want?" Angel heard her say. "What motivates me?"

"Fame, money, a movie deal—the usual things," said Angel.

Lily spun round. "I wasn't talking about me!"

"I know, but maybe it's what your character wants."

"No way," cried Lily, jumping down. "Emily Webb is deeper than that." She sat down on the coffee table. "Though she'd probably like a new dress if it was offered."

"Who wouldn't want a new dress?" smiled Angel, holding out her parcel.

Lily's eyes widened. "Don't tell me you finally found it?"

"Look." Angel sat down and parted the paper.

"OMG, it's exactly how you described it—the same color as—"

"—the dress you were wearing the day we met." Angel nodded. "I've always remembered it. It was the prettiest dress I'd ever seen."

"You couldn't have seen many," objected Lily. "You were only six."

Angel smiled. "You're forgetting, I'd seen your mother's entire wardrobe by the time you came down here."

"Yes, and you looked so guilty!"

"I *felt* guilty. We'd only been here three weeks and I thought for sure your dad would tell Maman we had to leave."

"No chance of that. Dad was far more likely to be mad at me for invading Simone's privacy. He'd made me promise not to come down here bothering her."

"And we both know you *always* do what your dad tells you."

Lily gave her a shove. "I do when he's reasonable. Anyway, he likes us being friends. He knows what a good influence you are on me."

This time it was Angel's turn to shove. "Sometimes you make me sound so boring."

"As if you're boring! You just think about stuff. Not like me . . ."

"You do jump in sometimes," conceded Angel.

"Which can be a good thing, right?" asked Lily. "Like coming down here that day and knowing straight away we'd be best friends."

"Even though I was going through your mother's things?"

Lily looked surprised. "You weren't hurting anyone. If my mother had been alive I don't think she'd have minded.

All I wanted was to see the little French girl my dad had brought home with our new housekeeper."

"I'm a quarter American," protested Angel. "Papa grew up in France but he was born here and . . ." She fiddled with the velvet, ". . . he died here."

Lily looked at her sadly. "I'm sorry, Angel," she whispered. "I know you miss him."

Angel managed a tiny smile. "It's okay. He was sick a long time."

Lily put her arm around Angel's shoulders. "I can't believe it's been four months," she said gently. "I wish I'd been here with you when it happened."

Angel shook her head. "You couldn't have done anything. That was the weekend your dad came back from China. Your first real chance to see him since New Year's."

"True, but I would've given up our holiday if you'd told me about your dad."

"I know."

"How's Simone?" asked Lily gently.

Angel hesitated. She still wasn't entirely sure how her mother was coping with Papa's death. He'd been ill for so long. It was ten years since they had come to New York for the surgery they'd hoped would cure him. It had taken months and months of waiting and most of their hard-won savings before Simone had finally accepted that, despite the famous surgeon's best efforts, her husband would never be one of his success stories. It had taken another six months to find a nursing home they could afford for as long as Papa needed care.

In the end they'd had to settle for a place three hours' train ride away in upstate New York. Not that the distance had stopped Simone—it was a rare Sunday that they did not visit Angel's dad. But since he'd been gone, it seemed to Angel as though some part of her mother had gone with him.

She sighed. "You know what Maman's like, she keeps things inside."

Lily nodded. "Yeah, but I thought she might've talked to you."

"She has, a bit." Angel chewed her lip. In the week after his death, Simone *had* talked to Angel about Papa—mostly recounting memories of their life in France when Angel was little, before the accident that ended their happiness.

Angel had been too young to remember the day the tractor had run over Papa, crushing his back and leaving him partially paralyzed. Whenever she asked Maman about it, Simone would always change the subject and talk about how good things would be when Papa was well again. She would never speak about the accident or about having to sell the vineyard or the dreadful months they'd endured with Grandpère before coming to New York. Angel soon learned not to ask.

She had hoped that Maman would tell her things—that she would overcome her sadness and talk to her about the past. Instead, Simone built a wall around her grief and locked it away. She was as loving and affectionate as ever, but she would not share her pain.

Sometimes Angel wondered if she was as stubborn as her mother. She hoped not. It seemed like such a barrier to happiness and more than anything Angel wanted her mother to be happy.

She sighed. Simone had such a fierce pride that it made her impossible to move once her mind was made up about something. Angel shifted restlessly. "I sometimes wish . . ."

"What?" asked Lily.

"Nothing," said Angel abruptly. She stood up and pulled Lily to her feet. "Maman is fine and so am I, but what about you? How's the play going?"

"Good, I think."

"I'll bet it's awesome," said Angel. "And you're going to be amazing in it, like always."

"I'm not always good, Angel," said Lily with a smile. "Remember that awful play I wrote when I was ten?"

"The one where you played all the lead roles and I made those terrible costumes?" asked Angel.

"The costumes were the best thing in it."

"They were horrible!" cried Angel. "I was a total novice."

"I was worse," said Lily. "But look how far we've come since then."

"Sure, but look how far we've got to go."

"We can do it, Angel," declared Lily. "I know we can. I'm going to be a famous stage actress and you're going to be a top fashion designer. It'll happen—you'll see."

"I like your enthusiasm," said Angel, "but I think it'll need more than enthusiasm to get us over the line."

"Nah, it just needs you to win the Teen Couture and me to convince Dad that acting is a real career."

"Shouldn't be too hard," said Angel with a wry smile.

"It'd be a lot easier if he'd stop listening to Margot. Or just stopped seeing her altogether!"

Angel hesitated and then said tentatively, "You don't suppose you could try to like her?"

Lily snorted. "Been there, done that, got burned. Anyway, even if I could bring myself to like Margot, *nothing* could ever make me like Clarissa! She's the most stuck-up, spoiled, self-absorbed, wanna-be-famous-for-all-the-wrong-reasons, queen diva who thinks she's a lot more talented than she is!"

"She must be pretty talented, or she wouldn't have got the job with Miki Merua."

"She got the job because Margot pulled strings, like she always does." Lily scowled. "People don't see Margot the way I do. They think she's marvellous. It's like she's got some weird power that makes people practically fall over themselves to please her. She's even got my dad sucked in."

"Maybe when he gets back from South America, you can tell him—" Angel broke off as Lily's cell phone buzzed insistently.

"Oh, shoot!" cried Lily. "That's Dad now. I'll have to go, it's better reception upstairs."

Angel followed her out the door.

In the kitchen, her mother looked up from cleaning the coffee machine and smiled.

"There you are, Angelique, *ma chérie*." Ten years in New York hadn't diluted Simone's accent and not even her plain housekeeper's uniform could disguise her indefinable air of French chic.

"Sorry I'm late, Maman." Angel hugged her. "But I found it."

Simone stopped cleaning. "Not the velvet?"

"Yes. Wait till you see it."

"Where was it?"

"That little shop in Soho—I don't know how long it's been there but it's everything I'd hoped for." She opened the parcel, cradling the velvet in her arms as her mother reached out to touch it.

"It's beautiful." Simone looked anxious. "Did you get enough?"

"Just. It took the last of my savings, but it's okay 'cause I've already paid for the international courier. The ball gown is the last thing I need to make and there's still three weeks before I have to send everything to Paris." Angel hugged the fabric to her chest. "I'll have to work on it every spare minute but I know I can get it done—I must!"

Simone hesitated, then said, "You know how much I believe in you, *chérie*. I know you are talented and passionate about fashion design, but . . ." She twisted a strand of Angel's tawny hair around her fingers. "Winning the Teen Couture is a big dream, *mon ange*."

Angel's blue eyes were earnest as she said, "I know, Maman, but some dreams do come true."

"Yes, but you're competing with teenagers from all over the world. Young people trained in fashion design, while you've . . ."

"Never even been inside a design studio, I know. But the Teen Couture is my chance to change all that. First prize is $50,000 and a year working in Antoine Vidal's Paris salon." Angel's eyes shone. "Can you imagine? Antoine Vidal—the king of haute couture himself. I mean, he *actually* trained under Christian Dior before setting up his own fashion house and creating the Teen Couture."

She took her mother's hand. "And tomorrow night I might get to see him—all because you convinced Jean-Pierre to hire me as a waitress last summer." Angel hugged the velvet. "Imagine—me in the same room as Antoine Vidal. And maybe, just maybe, I might make the final in the Teen Couture and get to meet him!"

"Yes, *chérie*, I know." Simone's soft brown eyes were sombre as she cupped her daughter's face in her hands. "And I know how much you dream of it all. It's just that . . . you and your papa were so close and now he is gone. I don't want you to be hurt by anything more. Some dreams can be dangerous."

"Not this one." Angel's voice rang with confidence. "I know I probably won't win, but something good will come of it, I'm positive."

Her mother looked skeptical. "I hope you are right, *mon ange*."

Chapter Two

Angel put down her pencil and looked glumly round her room. It was a cozy space with her pillow-strewn bed in the corner, a sewing table beside the big wooden closet, a tall swing-mirror and the trunk she'd found all those years ago.

She remembered that day so vividly. It was the summer she turned six and they'd just moved from their dreary two-room rental in the Bronx to the de Tourney's palatial townhouse. Angel loved her new home and her favorite place was the butler's old room.

She liked to sit amidst the clutter, reading, or drawing in the sketchbook her mother had given her, and imagine what might be in the cupboards and boxes around the walls. Eventually she'd grown adventurous and begun opening the drawers, cupboards and boxes, one by one, exploring the long-forgotten contents. She'd left the big wooden trunk until last.

It had been full of clothes.

Angel had always loved clothes: how they moved and sat and hung. How different fabrics suited different things. She was fascinated by the way an outfit could look good on one person and awful on someone else. She would spend hours drawing in her sketchbook and "fixing" outfits she'd seen in the subway or on the street.

The trunk had been a revelation. She hadn't known whose it was, only that its owner was a woman of taste. In it was a suit made of material that Angel could only think of as a miracle: coral-colored, it had been gossamer light, but fine and warm and soft. It hung superbly and she loved to examine the tiny stitches that held the perfect seams together. It had a label in the neck that she carefully read and for weeks afterwards she'd whisper "Chanel" to herself as though it were a magic word.

There were dresses, skirts, shirts, suits and a coat that was so beautiful it made Angel want to cry. And the fabric—that was what began it—the cloth that was like heavenly color in physical form, some of it silken, some stiff, some soft and some crisp.

Angel had never touched fabric like that. Her dresses were all plain and sensible, the material drab and unyielding. They didn't flow or swirl; they just sat, dull and stodgy with no hope of ever being pretty. She knew it wasn't Maman's fault—Simone did her best—but now Angel's own dresses didn't matter because she had this miraculous chest full of promise.

Of course, it wasn't really hers—not then, anyway—not until six months ago when Lily had given it to her and insisted that she use the contents in whatever way she liked.

At first Angel had protested, pointing out that Philip mightn't approve of her using his dead wife's things, but Lily had just said defiantly, "Dad won't care, and if I want to give my best friend some of my mother's things, I will."

Angel hadn't known what to say. It was such a shock to hear Lily sounding angry with her dad. They'd always been so close—even after he'd started dating Margot Kane. But ever since Christmas something had happened to push them apart—only Lily wouldn't say what.

And that was really weird because Lily never kept secrets from Angel. She'd insisted on giving her the trunk and eventually Angel had given in and set about finding the best use for each precious piece of fabric.

She could see some of the fabric now: tiny pieces of it pinned to some of the dozens of fashion sketches that covered the wall. Four designs stood out.

She gazed at each drawing in turn. The red cocktail sheath had taken her ages to get right, but she'd eventually nailed it. It looked amazing beside the green-and-white silk day dress and the simple navy suit with its pencil-line trousers and short jacket with the white trim. But Angel's favorite design was the hot pink bikini with the halter top and the flirty ruffled skirt—just looking at it made her think of palm trees, white sand and surf.

Angel stretched out her leg and prodded the closet door open with her big toe. She could see the four designs hanging inside, each one painstakingly cut and sewn by hand as the competition rules demanded. From conception through to design and execution, her Teen Couture entries had taken her months. Now all she had to do was finish her final design, then cut and sew a fabulous ball gown.

"If only it were that simple," muttered Angel, spinning round in her chair to consider the hundreds of magazine pictures stuck to the walls. They seemed to stare back at her, mocking her lack of inspiration.

Each picture had taught her something about fashion. Some were daring, most caught the eye, several made her mouth water, but all of them had line, perfect cut and, most importantly, originality. Angel sighed. That was what her design needed.

She gazed at the sketch in front of her. It was of a midnight-blue velvet ball gown, lovely—maybe even beautiful—but still lacking that certain something. She bit her lip. The answer was there, somewhere inside the velvet, just waiting for her to let it out.

"The way a great sculpture is inside a block of marble," she said aloud. "Trouble is I'm not Michelangelo."

"Why would you want to be some old dead Italian guy?"

"Lily!" Angel spun round and immediately saw that her best friend was upset. "You okay? I thought you were talking to your dad."

"I was—for about five minutes—until the connection failed."

"That sucks."

"It does, but that's not why I'm mad."

Angel's eyebrows lifted. "Uh-oh, what's Clarissa done now?"

"Apart from filling the bathroom with a million cosmetics, three hairdryers, a foot spa and a gallon of fake tan? She's told Margot that half the mothers at school are taking their daughters to the Fundraising Gala at the Waldorf tomorrow night so now the she-witch has managed to get tickets and is insisting that I go with her and her detestable daughter." Lily threw herself onto Angel's bed and pulled a pillow over her face.

"But that's awesome!" Angel couldn't conceal her excitement. "Antoine Vidal is showing his fall collection at the Gala. He's guest of honour and you'll be right there . . ."

Lily sat up. "That's great if you care about that stuff, but you know I don't. It should be you watching it, not me. If I thought we'd get away with it, I'd happily swap places with you."

"No, you wouldn't. I'm waitressing, remember? While you're eating your thousand-dollar-a-head dinner I'll be stuck out the back waiting to clear away mountains of dirty plates. I probably won't even see Antoine Vidal—never mind his collection."

Lily looked rueful. "I'm sorry, Angel. I know I'm being ungrateful but it's unbearable to watch Margot schmoozing her way into what she thinks are the best social circles or listen to Clarissa sucking up to anyone connected with the fashion industry because she thinks she's the next Coco Chanel."

Angel grimaced. Lily had told her about Clarissa's burning ambition to own her own fashion design studio and how Margot had spent a fortune at several emerging designers before Miki Merua had offered Clarissa a part-time job. It was hard not to feel a little envious—it must be amazing to have a mother who was rich enough to open doors like that.

"And Margot keeps nagging me about being friends with Elizabeth Montague because she wants to be friends with her mother, Jacqueline. It wouldn't be so bad if Margot wasn't so *good* at it," groaned Lily. "But she is—look at how she's got my dad wrapped round her finger."

"No way—you're the only person who's ever managed that."

"I wish, but Margot seems to have him well-fooled."

"But your dad's so . . ." Angel tried to find the right word. "So *true* and . . . impossible to fool."

Lily gave Angel's teddy bear a fierce hug. "Apparently not, given that he seems to have fallen for her hook, line and sinker."

"You don't think Philip likes her *that* much, do you?"

"What do you think?" retorted Lily. "He asked her to move in while he's away, didn't he?"

"That's because he cares about you, not Margot."

"Oh yeah, then how come he rings her almost as much as he rings me?" Lily held out her cell phone, her face flushed. "She says she's had three calls from him already."

"Oh."

"And there's no point feeling glad that he can't ring her much from South America because he's in remote places, because he can't ring me either." Lily bit her lip. "Dad's left Margot in charge—given her free rein to run the house and order me about." She pushed the teddy bear away. "Every other time he's gone away he's always let Simone look after us." She scowled. "So why not this time?"

"I don't know," admitted Angel. "Did you ask him?"

A shadow fell across Lily's face. "What's the point? He won't listen to me. Look at how he reacted when I tried to tell him about the London Drama Academy."

"But that's theatre school and your dad doesn't think of acting as a real career."

Lily flopped back on the bed. "Tell me about it. I've wanted to go to theatre school in London since I was ten, and now that I might actually get the chance, do you think he'll listen?" She sat up. "But I'll tell you one thing, Angel: if I do get a place at the Academy this summer I'm going to England and nothing and nobody will stop me."

Angel sat down on the bed next to her. "And I'll help you—but right now let's keep Margot happy and decide what you're going to wear to the Waldorf tomorrow night."

Lily smiled and held out her pinky finger. "Friends?"

Angel crooked her pinky round Lily's. "Forever," she replied.

After Lily had gone, Angel sat on her bed and worked on her sketch. She drew until midnight, but no matter how many times she reworked the velvet gown, she couldn't seem to get it right.

Maybe if I sleep on it, thought Angel. She lay back against her pillow and flipped drowsily through her designs.

"Tomorrow." She closed her sketchbook.

***

Angel woke. She'd been dreaming. Lily had been there, and Philip and her mother. Rolling over, she hugged her pillow and groped for the vision. There had been something about a dress. Wisps of the dream floated through her mind and she caught one before it vanished with the rest. Yes. There it was: midnight-blue velvet and . . . something else. Silver, it was silver.

Angel flicked on the light and grabbed her sketchbook and pencil. She bent over the page, her face intent and her strokes certain as she drew.

It was nearly two when she finally laid down her pencil.

Discarded drawings littered the floor, but in her hand Angel held a single sketch. She looked at it for a long time before she turned out the light.

Chapter Three

When Simone came to wake her, Angel was in her pajamas hard at work pinning fabric to her ancient dressmaker's dummy. She moved slowly around the mannequin, concentrating fiercely as she draped and pinned the yards of cheap calico cloth.

As she stepped back to gauge the effect, Angel saw her mother in the doorway, a glass of orange juice in her hand. Simone smiled. "I thought you could use an energy boost."

"Thanks, Maman," said Angel, taking the glass and drinking.

Simone touched the fabric. "You seem inspired."

"I hope it's inspiration. One thing's for sure, pulling it off is going to be a challenge."

"You'll do better with some breakfast in you."

"Okay, I'll just finish pinning." Angel stopped as a bell sounded in the hall.

Simone sighed. "That'll be Margot. She and Clarissa ordered breakfast in bed. I'd better run."

"Don't you dare," commanded Angel. "Remember what the doctor said—the indigestion will only stop if *you* stop rushing around. The she-witch and her horrible daughter can wait."

"You must not call them that, *chérie*. They are Philip's guests."

"I know, but I hate how they constantly ring that bell and keep you at their beck and call. They've only been here a week and already they act like they own the place. I don't get why Philip invited them to stay while he's away."

"He was thinking of Lily. She is growing up and he worries about her not having a mother."

Angel looked at Simone in surprise. It was unusual to hear Maman speak so openly. "Lily doesn't need a mother—she has you."

"I love Lily, but a housekeeper is not the same as a mother."

Angel stabbed a pin into the dummy. "A gold-digging social-climber isn't the same as a mother either."

Simone's brow furrowed as she gently rubbed a pencil smudge off Angel's cheek. "Philip will have his reasons for asking the Kanes to stay. We must make the best of it."

"But—"

Angel was about to list the twenty reasons why Philip had got it wrong when Simone said, "The truth is that Lily would hate anyone who married her father."

"No, just Margot Kane."

"Well, that is Philip's business. Perhaps Lily must learn to accept her father's decisions, whether they are to her liking or not," said Simone.

"But she still has the right to an opinion," said Angel.

"An opinion, yes, but no more than that." Simone frowned. "Sometimes adults must make decisions which their children do not like, but that does not mean their parents weren't trying to do what they thought was best."

"Like you with Papa."

Her mother looked at her sadly, then said softly, "Yes, like me with Papa." She touched Angel's cheek. "Sometimes, *mon ange*, the right decision is not the best decision and the best decision can be impossible to make, no matter how hard you try."

The bell rang again, long and insistent, and Simone hurried away.

Angel threw on her clothes and ran after her. When she reached the kitchen Simone was putting the silver covers over the plates on Clarissa's breakfast tray. As she lifted it, Angel saw her mouth clench in pain. She ran forward.

"Don't, Maman, let me."

She took the tray and heard her mother whisper in French, "*Angelique, chérie, ne m'en veux pas . . .*"

Angel's heart leapt. This was the language of her childhood. She put down the tray and hugged her mother. "I didn't mean to upset you either. *Je suis desolée*—I'm sorry."

As Angel picked up the tray again, Simone said, "Don't let Clarissa upset you. Remember, those that have the power—"

"Make the rules. Don't worry, *Maman*, I'll be . . . an angel."

The tray was heavy and as she climbed the stairs Angel was glad she'd taken it. Her mother's pain was worrying and Angel wished she'd go back to the doctor. She'd only been once and was diagnosed with indigestion. The doctor had told her to slow down and avoid rich food.

Simone insisted she'd followed his instructions, but Angel knew she was often nauseous; only last week she'd heard her retching in the bathroom. Maybe it wasn't indigestion, thought Angel. Maybe it was grief. Maman might have had nearly a year to prepare for her husband's death, but that didn't lessen the pain of losing him. Sometimes Angel missed Papa so much it physically hurt—maybe Maman's pain was the same.

Angel had tried talking to Lily about Simone's symptoms, but Lily's only response had been to suggest they buy her one of the health remedies she'd seen on TV. It wasn't the answer Angel was looking for, but then Lily was never ill, so getting her to understand Angel's worries about her mother was difficult.

Angel sighed. There were times when she wondered how Lily—who easily understood a character in a play—could be so lacking in empathy in the real world. She loved

Lily, but lately she'd found herself wondering if sometimes her best friend wasn't just a tiny bit spoiled.

She pushed the thought away and tried to think of who else she could confide in about Simone.

There was only Philip, but Maman would kill her if she talked to him about personal matters. Even after ten years, Simone still maintained a strictly professional relationship with her employer: she ran the house like clockwork, managed the staff, prepared all the food and met with Philip regularly to discuss household issues and Lily's schedule.

In the early days, Philip would come down to the kitchen to talk and he'd often bring Angel a treat and ruffle her hair and ask her in French how her English was progressing. She'd loved these visits but, after the first few, Maman seemed to find it more convenient to take Philip's instructions upstairs.

That first year at the de Tourneys', Maman would often talk about where they would live once Papa was well again. Angel knew she longed to move on and get a different kind of job, but Philip paid her generously and they needed the money. Papa's surgery had taken most of their savings, but Simone had been convinced that the next procedure would work.

Only it hadn't.

It'd been hard for Simone to accept that her husband would never be well again, and she never seemed entirely comfortable living at the de Tourneys'. Simone never talked about her feelings, but Angel sensed her unease. As she grew older she thought it was probably because Simone's mother had been a cook, whereas Philip's mother was a comtesse. Not that Philip ever mentioned it, but maybe it was hard taking orders from someone you'd been to college with.

Maman rarely talked about her life in Paris before she got married, but she'd told Angel she'd known Philip at university. They'd lost touch after she'd left to marry Yves

Moncoeur but had met again by chance at *Café Un Deux Trois* on Times Square where Simone had been working as a waitress. It was there that Philip had offered her the job as his housekeeper.

As she reached Clarissa's bedroom, Angel suddenly wondered if they'd stay at the de Tourneys' now that Papa was dead.

A sudden surge of sadness rose up inside as she thought of her father. He'd been so frail but he'd made their last days together so precious. She felt a lump in her throat as she remembered what he'd told her.

"I can serve, but I'm nobody's servant," whispered Angel as she knocked on Clarissa's door.

Angel loved this bedroom with its primrose wallpaper and tall windows overlooking Central Park. It was light and airy, with a four-poster bed and a huge armoire from some chateau in France. A pretty mahogany desk stood against the wall with a Louis XIV chair on either side. A blue silk sofa stood at the foot of the bed with a marquetry coffee table beside it.

It was amazing how much mess one person could make in a room that was cleaned daily by a maid, thought Angel. Every horizontal surface seemed to be covered with the belongings of someone very rich and easily bored.

The sofa was hidden beneath piles of discarded clothing, swathes of fabric, drycleaning bags and a pink silk bathrobe. The armoire doors stood open to reveal a collection of designer clothes hanging from its rail while a tangle of socks, sweaters and underwear spilled from its drawers. Two Prada handbags, with price tags still attached, stood on one chair and on the other sat an oversized make-up case, its lid thrown open to reveal an array of cosmetics.

Photographs of famous fashion designers were stuck to the wall above the desk that had almost disappeared beneath a tangle of fabric, cotton reels and sewing things. The coffee table was covered with stacks of sketchbooks and piles of the latest fashion magazines. But most interesting of all was the state-of-the-art dressmaker's dummy in the center of the room. On it hung a partially made silver-and-black cocktail dress. Angel stared. Could that actually be the hand-screened Japanese silk she'd seen featured in *Vanity Fair* three months earlier?

She stepped forward for a closer look and was abruptly recalled to her surroundings.

"Is that my breakfast? It's about time."

Angel swung round to find Clarissa Kane sitting up in bed, polishing her nails and watching her through narrowed eyes.

Even in her nightdress she was striking. High cheekbones, cat-like green eyes and a wide, petulant mouth reminded Angel of the snow queen in her favorite storybook. Clarissa's hair was long, straight, and a pale blonde that must have cost a fortune to achieve. Her eyebrows had been shaped by a master and Angel suspected her eyelashes had been professionally extended. However messy Clarissa might be in her bedroom, she was clearly a perfectionist when it came to her face and hair.

"Well, don't just stand there," Clarissa snapped.

Angel looked around for somewhere to put the tray. Not on the bed, that was a Conran bedspread. Perhaps on the coffee table. She bent down and carefully pushed the tray into the space beside the magazines.

"Not there, you idiot!" cried Clarissa.

Startled, Angel jerked backwards and watched helplessly as papers and magazines cascaded to the floor.

"Great," snorted Clarissa, "clumsy *and* stupid."

Throwing back the bedcovers, she swung her long legs out of bed and stood up. She pointed to the vacant space, "Put it here. And pick everything up before you go."

She strode into the bathroom and shut the door. Angel heard the lock click before the radio started blaring.

She put the tray on the bed and glanced around. Could

she look at the cocktail dress *and* pick up the papers before Clarissa came back?

She decided to risk it. She flew across the room and gently lifted the fabric. The silk slid over her fingers in a sort of whispering rush and Angel's heart skipped a beat. It was amazing. As near to gossamer as she'd ever imagined: light yet strong, and, she suspected, with enough body to make it a joy to sew. She examined the bodice and facing, then picked up the sleeve to look at the cut and set.

The fabric moved sinuously and she imagined how a pair of dressmaker's scissors would sound as they cut the silk. What a great designer could do with such material.

She wondered who the designer was—Miki Merua perhaps. Clarissa had boasted to Lily that he'd agreed to let her sew some of his designs and there were a couple of likely looking folders among the pile on the desk. Angel was wondering whether she had time for a quick peek when a noise from the bathroom sent her scurrying back to the coffee table.

She quickly began picking up the magazines and piling them on the table's inlaid surface. She felt a pang of envy as she gathered the most recent editions of *Teen Vogue*, *Marie Claire*, *Vanity Fair*, *Elle*, *Vogue* and *Harper's Bazaar*—her favorite fashion magazines were a luxury she'd foregone to help fund her Teen Couture entry.

She retrieved the last one and began gathering the scattered papers. To her surprise the pages were covered with fashion sketches.

There were dozens of drawings of every kind of outfit in pastel, pencil and ink. Among them were several sketches of the silver-and-black cocktail dress, each beautifully executed.

Angel stared at the pictures, trying to absorb the designer's vision, then considered the dress on the dummy. She wrinkled her nose, the cut was better than average and Clarissa's sewing was good, but something was not quite right—

Angel looked through the pile of sketches again and frowned. The artist had talent, but not many of the designs seemed original. Puzzled, she leafed through the drawings, trying to recall where she'd seen that off-the-shoulder, slashed-hem evening dress before. And the suit with the short bolero jacket and the tight buttoned legs . . .

Then she remembered. It'd been in an old *Vogue* magazine, in an article about a Spanish designer who'd died years ago.

Angel sat back on her heels. It was the same with nearly all the pictures: the artist could certainly draw and definitely had a talent for copying, but that was all.

Except for the dress on the dummy.

There, at least, the designer had achieved something fresh and new, but when Angel looked at the rest of the drawings she could see nothing original—and not a single idea that she hadn't already seen in one of the major fashion magazines.

She piled the sketches on the table and reached for those near the bed. They were of the cocktail dress and, as she picked them up, Angel noticed the signature—*CK*—and on the next sheet, a flamboyant "*Clarissa Kane*," and beneath it the words: *Teen Couture*.

***

Angel's jaw dropped. Suddenly it all made sense: the sewing things, the dressmaker's dummy, the Japanese silk. Clarissa was entering the Teen Couture. She couldn't believe she'd been so slow to realize it. But it *was* a leap to think of Clarissa—despite her job with Miki Merua—as being like herself: a girl with a passion, who loved to create and who wanted to win the Teen Couture more than anything else in the world.

Of course, Lily had told her about Clarissa's ambition, but stupidly Angel hadn't thought of her entering the Teen

Couture. She studied Clarissa's sketches again and thought of the effort and determination needed to produce so many drawings and five individual hand-sewn garments.

She stared at the unfinished dress on the dummy. The fabric really was exquisite. If Clarissa could make it work, the dress would probably be a contender for the finals.

The bathroom door opened and Clarissa emerged.

"You're still here?"

"Sorry," said Angel, groping under the bed. "Almost done."

"Well, hurry up. I want to get dressed."

Angel grabbed the last errant page and pulled it towards her. She drew it out and found it was attached to a sketchbook. Standing up, she brushed the dust bunnies off the blank page and held it out. "This must be yours."

To her astonishment, Clarissa leapt forward and snatched the sketchbook from her hand. "How dare you touch my things!" she snapped, flipping the book closed. As the pages fell together Angel caught a flash of something red. For a split second she felt an odd sense of déjà vu before Clarissa let fly and the moment was gone.

"How dare you come in here! You shouldn't even be upstairs! You're nothing but a cook's daughter from the kitchen!" Clarissa seized Angel's arm and herded her to the door. "Get out! Get out, Angelique, and go back to the kitchen where you belong!" She pushed her into the hall and slammed the door behind her.

Chapter Four

Angel leaned against Clarissa's door trying to breathe. Her heart was pounding and she was still trying to work out what had just happened when Lily came out of her room.

"My Angel." Lily took her arm and headed for the stairs. "Have you been visiting the evil diva? What did she want?"

Angel thought quickly—if she told Lily what'd happened it'd only make things worse. She took a breath and tried to speak calmly. "Just breakfast in bed."

"Lazy brat."

Angel thought of Clarissa's rage. "I don't think she's lazy. Not where fashion's concerned anyway."

"Oh?"

"Clarissa's entering the Teen Couture."

Lily stared. "You're kidding?"

"That's why she's making that gorgeous silk dress."

"You mean that's her design?" Lily was incredulous.

"Must be."

"I'll bet she had help," said Lily darkly. "It'd be just like Clarissa to cheat."

"I don't think you *can* cheat," said Angel. "The rules are really strict and Antoine Vidal is like a fashion mega-mind—he'd know all the designers."

"Well, if she *is* entering, I hope she suffers epic failure," replied Lily. "And Margot, too. Honestly, I don't get what my dad sees in her."

"Well, Margot *is* gorgeous and Clarissa's a stunner too."

"Looks aren't everything."

"Only attractive people say that."

Lily stopped on the bottom step, hands on her hips. "Really?"

Angel grinned. "Yes. Like people with big blue eyes and long, curly, *naturally* blonde hair. No wonder Clarissa resents you."

Lily punched her lightly on the arm.

"Ow! What was that for?"

"You're the gorgeous one and *you* have style."

Angel laughed and shook her head. "Come on, let's go eat breakfast."

***

"There you are." Simone put breakfast on the table. "You'll have to hurry or you'll both be late for school."

Lily pulled a face. "School. If it weren't for the play I don't think I'd survive the next few days."

"You're lucky you only have days," said Angel. "I have nearly two weeks before vacation and all I want is to be working on my ball gown."

"At least you're busy," said Lily. "Once *Our Town* is over, all I'll be able to think about is the London Academy."

"Shouldn't you have heard by now? Doesn't the course begin soon?" Simone said.

"June twentieth," said Lily. "But you don't hear until a couple of weeks before."

"It does not seem like much time."

"It's not, but the course only runs for two weeks. Mind you, we still put on a full production at the end," added Lily happily.

"It sounds exciting." Simone smiled at her.

"It will be if I get the letter saying I'm in. It'll be *the* most exciting thing ever!"

"*If* Philip lets you go," said Angel.

"I am sure you can persuade him, Lily," said Simone. "But if you cannot, then I am sure he will have a good reason for saying no."

"There isn't any reason good enough," said Lily.

"Then I am sure Philip will give his consent." Simone took off her apron. "I must go. I have errands to run." She looked at Angel. "Dinner will be early so you can get to the Waldorf in plenty of time." She kissed her and then Lily. "I hope your letter arrives today with good news."

"Me too."

Simone wrapped her arms around Lily, and Angel felt a sudden tightening in her throat. She gave herself a mental shake. It was natural for Simone to hug Lily like that— Lily, who had no mother of her own but who always seemed to get everything she wanted. Angel bit down hard on her piece of toast and pushed the treacherous thought away.

The door closed behind Simone and Angel asked, "So when are you going to tell Philip about drama school?"

Lily grimaced. "When I get in."

Angel hesitated and then asked the question she knew Lily didn't want to hear. "Do you think he'll let you go?"

Lily lifted her chin. "He'll have to—it's the London Drama Academy. Two weeks of intensive training with the greatest names in theatre *and* an audition at the end."

"But Philip wants you to go to college here—Harvard or Wellesley or Brown. He'll never let you study overseas— especially not acting."

Lily bit her lip. "I know that's what he says, but if I get in he'll have to agree."

"But what if he doesn't?" Angel knew she was pushing Lily but maybe it was time she realized she couldn't have everything she wanted. A real best friend would help Lily face the facts. In most things Philip let her have her way but a career in the entertainment industry was probably not going to be one of them. Lily had tried everything to persuade him but he remained obstinately resolute. School plays and amateur productions were all he would allow.

"If he won't—" Lily looked mulish. "Well, there's always a way if you want something badly enough."

***

Angel knew she was running late when she arrived in the foyer and found Lily already there. She'd got caught up with her ball gown after breakfast and lost track of time.

"Hurry up, Angel, the bus is coming." Lily had the front door open and Angel could see the bus trundling down the street. She grabbed her coat and was almost out the door when Clarissa's voice stopped her in her tracks.

"Oh, good, it's the kitchen girl. I've left my watch in my room. Run up and get it for me."

Lily swung round, eyes blazing. "Get it yourself, Clarissa. Angel has to go."

"Angel—such a sweet name. But Angel or not, she can get my watch."

Angel put a restraining hand on Lily's arm. "It's okay, I'll go."

Clarissa smiled triumphantly, but Lily wasn't done.

"Angel's not here to take orders from you—"

She stopped as a voice, ice-cold and perfectly modulated, said, "Quarrelling again, Lily? How tiresome."

The three girls turned.

Margot Kane wasn't tall but she was stunning. Looking at her, Angel could see where Clarissa got her looks. Margot's ash-blonde hair was cut into a gleaming cap that perfectly accentuated the superb line of her jaw. Her mouth was wide and full, her nose sculpted to a faint tilt and her violet eyes looked out through the longest, most luxuriant lashes Angel had ever seen. Her eyebrows were a work of art and not the tiniest line dared show itself anywhere on her face. She was the result of tireless dedication to the pursuit of beauty.

Margot surveyed the three girls for a moment before asking coolly, "Are you ready, Clarissa? Lily? The car is here."

"I only need my watch, Mother," replied Clarissa.

"Then we will wait in the car while it is retrieved." Margot stared at Angel, who instantly stepped forward, only to feel Lily's hand on her arm.

"I'll get it, Margot," said Lily. Behind her back Angel felt Lily link pinky fingers with her.

"That won't be necessary. Simone can get it if Angelique has to leave."

"No. I'll go." Angel ran upstairs.

She found the watch and arrived downstairs just as the chauffeur saw Clarissa into the Rolls-Royce.

Lily didn't use the Rolls much. Most days, she and Angel caught the bus together; Angel getting off at the high school and Lily going on to her private girls' school. Clarissa had started there just after Christmas and Lily had been furious when a classmate had told her about the strings Margot had pulled to get her in.

Clarissa was a year above Lily so at least they weren't in the same class but it had proved meager consolation after Clarissa's instant success with the group Lily called "the queen divas." Within a week she was a cheerleader, a member of the yearbook committee and sitting at a center table in the cafeteria. Lily had gritted her teeth and gone out of her way to avoid her.

But she couldn't avoid this morning's ride in the Rolls.

Angel handed the watch through the car window. Clarissa took it without a word.

"Can't we give Angel a lift, Margot?" asked Lily. "We go right past her school."

Margot made a moue of distaste and waved at the chauffeur, "Drive on, Roberts."

As the Rolls pulled away, the first drops of rain began to fall. By the time Angel had put on her jacket it was pouring. She picked up her bag, opened her umbrella and headed for the bus stop.

Chapter Five

It rained all day, which exactly suited Angel's mood. Usually she enjoyed school but today everything seemed to go wrong. Being late meant missing the much-anticipated life-drawing workshop and cleaning the art room instead. As she washed paintbrushes she couldn't help thinking about Clarissa's Teen Couture entry.

If she could pull off that cocktail dress then Clarissa might have a real chance at winning. Of course, Angel hadn't seen the rest of her entry and if those other sketches were part of it, maybe she'd crash and burn. Angel stopped. Why was she wasting time thinking about Clarissa's Teen Couture entry when she should be thinking about her own?

Still, it was hard to push Clarissa from her mind and halfway through biology her distraction proved disastrous. Angel had been imagining what she'd do with that Japanese silk when she knocked over a tray of partially dissected frogs. She spent the rest of the period cleaning up disgusting bits of amphibian guts.

She wouldn't have minded so much if Ryan Davies hadn't seized the opportunity to start calling her "French frog" again. He'd coined the hated nickname in the third grade and tormented Angel with it ever since.

She threw the last frog's leg into the trash with an angry flick. She'd never understood why boys like Ryan got such a kick out of teasing her.

Lily had tried to tell her that boys only teased a girl if they liked her, but that made no sense at all to Angel.

Surely if a boy liked you he'd be nice and not horrible? But that wasn't Angel's experience and it wasn't even as if the boys at her school were the worst.

The prize for the most obnoxious guys belonged to the seniors from the boys-only private school two blocks away. Even Lily admitted some of their so-called banter was over the top—though she still insisted it was how some boys talked when they thought a girl was cute.

Angel had asked her friends at school about Lily's theory, but they'd been divided in their opinions. Taylor had agreed with Angel that most of the guys from the boys' school were just rich, stuck-up jerks, but Katie thought that Lily was right. Either way, boys were still a mystery. Angel sighed, wiped the last bits of frog slime from her fingers and wondered if she'd ever meet a boy she could actually talk to.

***

When she got home from school Angel went straight to her closet and pulled out the big black portfolio case she kept in the back. Laying it on her bed, she knelt down and opened it.

Slowly she went through each folder, looking over her draft sketches and rejected designs, then thumbed her way through the sketchbooks in which she'd drawn all the design details of her Teen Couture entry. Finally, she opened the green folder marked *Final Teen Couture* in which she kept the best sketches of her five designs.

Angel sighed. Her designs were at least as good as Clarissa's and maybe better. She stared down at the picture of her ball gown. Clarissa's Japanese silk *was* extraordinary—maybe Angel needed to rethink her design. She fingered the pieces of blue velvet and silver gauze stapled to the sketch and an idea began to slowly unfurl in her mind. If she could pull it off . . .

Angel pursed her lips, thinking hard. She wouldn't alter this sketch until she was sure she could achieve her vision, but maybe she could draw an outline now. She glanced at her watch. Where had the time gone? She was due at the Waldorf in an hour and she still had to shower and change. She quickly repacked her portfolio, thrust it back into her closet and grabbed her bathrobe.

Twenty minutes later she was ready. Angel eyed herself in the mirror. The catering company was fussy about appearance and tonight they'd be especially picky. She buttoned the double cuff on her freshly ironed white shirt and flicked a thread off her black pants. Her flat black shoes gleamed and the ribbon round her smooth ponytail hung in a neat bow. Angel looked at her watch—time to go. She felt a flutter of excitement—tonight she might actually see Antoine Vidal close up.

"Ready?" Lily appeared in the doorway.

"Wow! You look great." Angel gazed appreciatively at her friend's turquoise dress with its fitted bodice and swirling mid-thigh skirt. Across the bodice and around the hem, waves of tiny crystals glittered like water in the sunlight. Lily's thick blonde hair tumbled down her back.

"I ought to. It's your design after all." Lily touched a crystal. "I wish you were coming with us."

"I'll be fine on the bus."

Lily frowned. "Sure, but it's silly when we're going to the same place."

Angel pushed her gently out the door. "Margot would not agree. You're all guests and I'm just the hired help—definitely not someone to be seen with."

Lily groaned. "Don't remind me. Margot will spend the night charming every celebrity in sight and ignoring everyone who isn't anyone."

Angel grinned. "You almost make me glad I'm just a lowly waitress." She patted Lily's arm sympathetically. "At least you'll see the fashion show. I'd gladly put up with

Margot at her worst if it meant seeing Antoine Vidal's fall collection."

***

It was a bigger night than expected, Angel decided, as she and the other staff waited behind closed doors for the signal to clear away the main course. The Waldorf Ballroom was buzzing with the cream of New York society. While serving the entrée Angel had seen a Karl Lagerfeld gown, two classic Jean Paul Gaultiers, a divine Givenchy creation and a gold, strapless Vera Wang dress that had made her long for a closer look.

Equally thrilling was the discovery that a woman she was serving was wearing Collette Dinnigan. From the first moment she'd seen them, Angel had fallen in love with the Australian designer's intricately beaded tops, vibrant resort dresses and delicate lace gowns. Seeing one up close was a delight. She'd never thought waitressing could be so exciting.

It was disappointing not to be assigned to Vidal's table but not surprising. He was much too important to be attended by a junior waitress. She'd seen him at a distance though, and had been thrilled to see how handsome he was in his perfectly cut tuxedo with two mega-famous film stars beside him, each wearing a Vidal gown. Even from thirty feet away Angel could see how beautifully the dresses were made.

The one blight on the evening was being assigned to wait on Margot's table. Not that she paid any attention to Angel; she was far too busy charming her fellow guests. And she *was* good at it, just as Lily had said.

Angel had watched her while clearing the entrées. Margot had been the center of attention, smiling and laughing, superb in a figure-hugging, coal-black Balenciaga gown with a single blood-red rose at its breast. As Angel collected plates she felt a stab of sympathy for Lily sitting across the table trying not to notice how easily Margot had captivated her dinner companions—even a stern-looking New York congressman had fallen under her spell.

As she served each new course, Angel could see Lily becoming increasingly unhappy. No surprise, given that she was sandwiched between a pompous-sounding author ranting on about the stupidity of this year's Pulitzer Prize judges and the congressman's wife who seemed to think Lily was about ten and in need of advice.

As she cleared the mains, Angel could see Lily muttering to herself and guessed she was reciting lines in an attempt to distract herself from Margot's tinkling laugh and nauseating remarks. "Oh, Senator, *do* tell us what you said to the President."

Even Angel felt like barfing at that.

Things were no better by the time dessert was ending and Angel and Marc, one of the six baristas hired for the evening, wheeled their mobile Barista Bar into position near Lily's table.

Lily looked totally miserable and, rather than eating her profiteroles, had chopped them into tiny pieces, leaving a chocolatey mess in the middle of her plate. Angel suspected she was working out how to escape the Waldorf without incurring Margot's wrath.

A moment later Lily made her way to the Barista Bar and asked Angel loudly, "Can I get an espresso macchiato, please?"

"Certainly," replied Angel. "I'll bring it to your table."

"That's okay, I'll wait," said Lily firmly. Under her breath she whispered, "I can't take much more of this. Clarissa's going on and on about her new portfolio and Margot keeps trying to catch Jacqueline Montague's attention."

"Gross." Angel knew how much Lily hated the thought of Margot getting friendly with the Montagues.

Like the de Tourneys, the Montagues were old money and for as long as Angel could remember Lily and Philip had regularly spent summers with them at Martha's Vineyard and winters skiing in Aspen. Angel had met Elizabeth Montague a couple of times when Lily had brought her home after school. They were in the same class and had known each other forever. Angel had thought Elizabeth seemed sweet, but her mother was a tiger.

She could see her now, talking to the mayor. Tall and elegant, with short dark hair and a wide, vivacious smile, Jacqueline Montague was one of New York's society queens: famous for her charity luncheons, her acid wit, and her ability to elicit information. According to Lily, Jacqueline knew everything about everyone who counted and could make or break a career with a single word.

Clearly Margot knew that, too.

Angel handed Lily her coffee. "Hang in there," she said softly. "The show's due to start in a few minutes and then you can—"

Lily groaned.

"What's the matter?"

"Margot's waving at Jacqueline. *Please* don't let her see," whispered Lily urgently to whatever deity might be listening.

But it was too late and Angel felt Lily stiffen as they watched Jacqueline move towards Margot's table. Angel busied herself polishing the milk jug and pretended not to see Margot light up as Jacqueline paused by her chair.

"Jacqui!" The word was an embrace, but Angel saw the flash of annoyance in Jacqueline's eyes at Margot's use of the more intimate form of her name. Lily had told her that only Jacqueline Montague's closest friends and family ever called her "Jacqui."

Margot rose. "How are you? But I needn't ask—you look marvellous. What a divine dress. Valentino, isn't it?"

Jacqueline nodded.

Undeterred by her silence, Margot said, "I've been meaning to call you ever since the Plaza fundraiser, but what with Philip away, and asking me to look after Lily and run the house and all." Margot gave her tinkling laugh. "Well, you know how it is with teenagers." She waved her hand towards Lily.

Jacqueline's eyes followed the perfectly manicured fingers, saw Lily and smiled. Lily nodded and Angel sensed that it was taking all of her self-control to keep from saying something she'd regret.

"Lily is *such* an adolescent and so headstrong," said Margot.

"Oh?" replied Jacqueline. "I have always found her charming."

"Oh, yes." A faint tinge of color rose in Margot's ivory cheeks. "Yes. She's delightful—though a teensy bit wilful sometimes. Fortunately, living at the house means I can offer constant guidance. And my Clarissa is a wonderful influence." She gestured to her daughter, who smiled modestly.

Angel suppressed an urge to make vomiting noises and instead began polishing the teaspoons. She saw Jacqueline flick Clarissa a glance before turning to Margot with a smile. Angel caught her breath. Maybe she'd imagined it, but for a split second Jacqueline Montague had looked positively *dangerous*.

"So you're staying at Philip's?" she heard Jacqueline ask Margot.

"Yes. He practically begged me to move in while he's overseas. Naturally, in the circumstances, I could hardly say no."

Jacqueline's brows rose. "The circumstances?"

Margot leaned closer. "Of course, nothing's been announced yet." She glanced at Lily, who pretended not to see. Margot lowered her voice, "When Philip returns from Paris, he and I . . . we . . ." She laid a conspiratorial hand on

Jacqueline's arm. "I really mustn't say too much."

Appalled, Angel tried to see Lily's reaction, but she'd turned her head away and Angel could only see a rigid profile. Jacqueline, however, seemed delighted and she patted Margot's hand.

"I quite understand." She smiled. "Darling Philip. So he's in Paris?"

"He will be," replied Margot. "Next month—after South America."

Jacqueline's smile widened. "How wonderful that Philip is going back to Paris at last. He'll be able to visit his mother. How is the dear Comtesse?"

Margot hesitated for a moment then said brightly, "Fine. She's fine. Such a marvellous woman."

"So she and Philip have finally reconciled?"

"Yes. No. That is . . . we hope . . . I—"

Jacqueline cut in smoothly, "Such a pity Lily has grown up without her grandmother's influence. The Comtesse de Tourney is an icon in Paris. Everyone adores her. If only she and Philip were on speaking terms, she could have Lily to stay." She tapped Margot's hand with an elegant finger. "And you know an invitation from the Comtesse opens so many doors."

"Yes. Yes, I had heard that." Margot fiddled with the rose at her breast. "Do you know the Comtesse well?"

"Quite well, we took Elizabeth to Paris for the Versailles Ball last year and saw Elena several times."

"The Versailles Ball." Angel was surprised at the wistful note in Margot's voice.

"That's right," Jacqueline answered. "Of course, you'll have heard of it. It's the climax of the Comtesse de Tourney's famous summer season and where Antoine Vidal announces the winner of the Teen Couture." She touched the diamonds at her throat, "Anyone who's anyone sends their daughter to Paris for at least one Versailles Ball. Elena de Tourney has been running them for years."

"Oh, yes, I—" Margot began, but Jacqueline interrupted.

"Such a pity Philip is estranged from his mother. She created the Versailles Ball, you know. I sometimes think she did it with Lily in mind." The mayor came into view and Jacqueline waved. "I must go. Antoine will be appearing at any moment. Enjoy the collection, won't you?" She nodded to Margot, smiled at Lily and turned away.

Angel knew she needed to hurry. The fashion parade was about to begin and she still had half a dozen dessert plates to clear before she could get off the floor. She could see the catering manager watching as the staff rapidly gathered dirty plates and silverware and headed for the kitchen.

She collected Margot's plate and the congressman's, his wife's, the pompous author's and Lily's. As she picked up Clarissa's plate a passing guest bumped her elbow and Angel watched helplessly as the mess of uneaten profiterole flew through the air and dropped with a chocolatey splat onto Clarissa's pale-blue Marchesa-clad lap.

There was a suppressed yelp as Clarissa stared down at the chocolate staining her dress. Angel saw her furious face and heard the incensed whisper, "You did that on purpose."

"No!" gasped Angel. "I am *so* sorry, I—" The lights had come up on the catwalk and beyond it she could see the catering manager frantically motioning for her to get off the floor. Grabbing a napkin from the table, she dropped it on Clarissa's lap just as a burst of thunderous applause filled the room and Antoine Vidal strode down the catwalk towards her. Angel quickly turned away, but as she moved, something caught her ankle. She felt herself pitching forward and tried desperately to regain her balance.

It was impossible.

At the precise moment that Antoine Vidal, fashion icon and world-famous couturier, reached the microphone, Angel Moncoeur, waitress and aspiring fashion designer, crashed to the floor in front of him.

Chapter Six

Plates and silverware hit the floor with a resounding crash. As she lay among the debris, it seemed to Angel as though the noise would never end, but the deafening silence that followed was worse.

She lifted her head and found herself staring straight up into a pair of sympathetic grey eyes. Antoine Vidal smiled gently and nodded to her right. Someone touched Angel's elbow and helped her to her feet.

The microphone squeaked, the lights dimmed and, as she limped from the ballroom, Angel was relieved to see all eyes turn towards Vidal.

"Ladies and gentlemen, tonight your generosity has raised over half a million dollars for America's homeless youth." Vidal held up his hand to still the applause. "I believe in today's youth. I believe in their energy, creativity and ability to succeed—that is why, six years ago, I created the Teen Couture."

He looked around the room. "I wished to create a competition that would test not only design excellence, but also each entrant's dedication, determination and enthusiasm. This is why every Teen Couture garment must be made with the designer's own hands."

Angel stopped outside the Staff Only door. She longed to stay and hear the rest of Vidal's speech. It was against the rules but she was certain she'd already lost her job so it hardly mattered. She looked back at the stage and was startled to find Vidal's eyes on her. It was only for an instant, but long enough for his next words to burn themselves into her brain.

"Young people need to be both challenged and supported. It takes time to develop skill and years to master a craft. There will always be obstacles, but those who overcome them can achieve extraordinary things."

Angel stepped through the door and heard no more.

***

In the days that followed, Angel decided she was totally sick of obstacles.

As expected, she'd been fired on the spot. She'd tried to explain about being tripped, but her manager wouldn't listen. He was so sure it was her own clumsiness that had caused the catastrophe that by the time she got home Angel had begun to think she'd imagined that brief tug on her ankle.

It wasn't until the next morning she learned the truth.

"It was Clarissa." Lily had come downstairs early, still seething. "You should've seen her, looking all innocent and pretending to be sympathetic."

"I felt something grab my ankle."

"Yes. Her foot—only no one else saw her."

"I don't suppose it would've made any difference if they had."

"Margot made sure of that," agreed Lily. "She was all charm and sympathy, pretending to be so sorry for the poor little waitress."

"That sucks."

"Sure does. I wish my dad had never met her."

"We need to stay out of her way."

"That's the plan." Lily clenched her jaw. "And with any luck, in a few weeks I'll be in London and by the time I get home, Margot and Clarissa will be gone—hopefully for good!"

***

The next week was a struggle. School was manic with end-of-year activities and Angel was unusually distracted. Taylor even went so far as to ask if she was smoking something, which made Angel laugh so much that she felt better than she had in days.

She desperately wanted to be at home working on her ball gown, but she'd promised Taylor and Katie she'd help them pick out their dresses for the dance. They'd spent two afternoons downtown trying on dresses and Angel had eventually managed to talk Taylor out of the strapless apricot number she'd set her heart on and instead found her a gorgeous flame-colored fifties-style dress guaranteed to dazzle her date.

All the distractions meant staying up later than usual to sew, but by Friday the calico practice dress was finished— and a disaster. When she looked at it on the dummy it seemed so far removed from her vision that Angel wondered how she'd ever thought she had a flair for fashion design.

She forced herself to continue and each hour brought her a step closer to her dream dress. If she could just make the last part work, maybe she'd have a gown worth sending to Paris.

Angel smoothed a hand over the calico skirt and sighed. *If* she could make it work . . . but time was running out. In two weeks she had to send her Teen Couture entry to Paris; the ball gown was its centerpiece and she still hadn't cut the velvet.

Picking up the dark-blue cloth, she rubbed it against her cheek and then threw her arms wide, flinging the fabric out across her bed. It was gorgeous. *Surely* she could make a dress worthy of it.

"And I will—starting now."

She picked up her pattern pieces just as rapid footsteps sounded in the hall. Moments later Lily burst through the door.

"I got it, Angel, I got it!" Lily seized Angel's hands and danced her around the room.

"Not London?"

"Yes!" Lily thrust a letter into Angel's hand. "See for yourself. The London Drama Academy wants me in London on June twentieth." She did a pirouette. "I've dreamed of this for so long, I can hardly believe it's real."

"Some dreams do come true!" said Angel.

Lily stopped dancing. "Yours will, too, Angel, I know it."

"I hope so." She hesitated and then said carefully, "What are you going to tell Philip? And Margot?"

Lily jumped up on the bed. "Don't worry, I've got it all worked out."

"Uh-oh."

"Skeptic." Lily bounced. "Listen, Dad's overseas until the middle of next month so I don't need to tell him anything. We're only in touch via cell phone and even that's mega-unreliable because of where he is, but the point is he won't know if I'm in New York or London. As for Margot . . ." Lily grinned. "She's meant to be taking me and Clarissa to our place at the Hamptons for the summer, but," she bounced again, "I've told Margot that Elizabeth Montague has invited me to stay with her at Martha's Vineyard for those two weeks. Naturally, Margot said yes."

Angel tried not to look impressed at this masterly plan. "It might work . . ."

"Of course it'll work. It's perfect." Lily jumped down. "You know my plans always work."

Angel grimaced. "Maybe . . ."

"Oh, you're just thinking of that time your mother found out we'd—"

"Done something dreadful," said a teasing voice. They

turned to find Simone standing in the doorway.

"Maman." Angel got up. "Are you okay?" She cast a worried glance at Simone's pale face and the deep shadows under her eyes. Only that morning she'd found her mother holding her side. She'd tried to persuade her to go to the doctor, but Simone had refused.

"I'm fine, *chérie*—just my indigestion again." She turned to Lily. "Margot wishes to see you."

Lily looked dismayed. "Why? What does she want?"

Simone shrugged apologetically. "She did not say. Only that you are to go to your father's study immediately."

After Lily had gone reluctantly upstairs, Angel picked up her pin-tray and began carefully pinning the pattern pieces to the velvet. She couldn't help thinking about Lily's plan. It might work—Philip was away, after all—but, although she could understand Lily not caring whether she deceived Margot, Angel was surprised she was willing to lie to her dad.

Philip wasn't the sort of father you needed to lie to and, like Angel's papa, he was a good listener. In that first year, when Papa was so often in the hospital (and before Simone found out and put a stop to it), Lily would sometimes take Angel up to Philip's study and insist she be included in story time.

He was always delighted to see them and Angel loved the way his whole face lit up at the sight of Lily. Philip had a smile that could light up a room, with twinkling blue eyes beneath straight black brows and thick dark hair with only the tiniest bit of grey at his ears. He was tall and lean, with an infectious rumbling laugh that made Angel giggle just hearing it.

As soon as he saw them, he'd stop whatever work he was doing, stretch out his long frame, and draw them across to one of the big squishy leather armchairs by the fire.

Lily would climb onto his lap, snuggle down and demand a story while Angel sat on a cushion on the floor by Philip's knee. She'd lean her head against the arm of the chair and sometimes, if he was engrossed in the story, Philip would run his fingers through her hair. Angel loved that because it reminded her of Papa.

When they were settled Philip would read aloud or tell them a fairytale or—Angel's favorite—make up his own story and they would take turns telling the ending. Angel would stare into the fire and think hard about what the hero might do now that Philip had him locked in a dark dungeon or stranded on some dangerous mountaintop in a storm. She'd imagine a fearless prison guard's daughter smuggling him out through a secret passage, or a poor but beautiful peasant girl who'd braved the raging tempest to bring him to safety.

Lily usually scoffed at these romantic resolutions and whenever it was her turn to make up the ending she'd offer some dramatic yet practical conclusion like the hero making a speech in court and proving his innocence or skiing down the mountainside and saving the village in the valley below.

But whatever the story or its ending, it was magical just being there.

Philip and Lily's relationship had always been special and Angel had thought they had an unbreakable bond.

Until last Christmas.

Lily had gone up to Philip's study to see if he'd take her ice-skating at Rockefeller Center, and when she'd come down it was as if a door had closed somewhere inside her and not even Angel had been able to break it down.

Angel sighed, put down her pins and eyed the velvet thoughtfully. She'd expected Lily back by now. It was getting late—maybe she should put off cutting the velvet until tomorrow. It'd be a slow process because the fabric marked easily and she had to ensure the nap faced the same way on each piece. Still, if she stayed up, Lily might return and tell her what Margot had wanted.

Angel picked up her scissors. The sooner she got cutting, the sooner she could start sewing.

As she smoothed out the velvet, she wondered what Margot could be talking to Lily about for so long. Maybe Philip had called from South America or Lily had forgotten a Junior League meeting again and Margot had insisted on taking her. Or *maybe* Margot had decided to have a heart-to-heart with her . . .

"Don't be ridiculous," said Angel aloud. "Lily wouldn't have stayed five minutes."

She pushed the thought away. If she were going to cut the velvet, she needed to focus.

By midnight she was done and the velvet lay in pieces on her bed. This was her ball gown—all she needed to do was sew it together.

Angel smiled. It was such an easy thought—but sewing the gown together and making it look exactly like her design was going to take every minute of the time left before she had to send her entry to Paris.

She put on her pajamas and got into bed. She lay awake for a while, thinking about Lily and the Teen Couture, and only realized she'd fallen asleep when a hand on her arm woke her.

"Lily? Is that you?"

"Who else?" Lily switched on the bedside lamp.

"Are you okay? You never came back. What did Margot want?"

"To ruin my life."

Angel froze. "Margot's found out about London?"

"Worse. She's had a letter from my grandmother."

Chapter Seven

Angel stared. "A letter?' she said at last.

Lily nodded.

"From your grandmother?"

"Yes."

"The one in Paris?"

"I've only got one grandmother," said Lily.

"Yes, but she never gets in touch," said Angel. "And why would your grandmother write to Margot?"

"She didn't. She wrote to my dad—her first letter in over ten years." Lily scowled. "Naturally Margot opened it."

"Naturally," agreed Angel. "What did it say?"

"Margot says it's an invitation, but I know it's an order." Lily put on a posh accent: "The Comtesse de Tourney requests the pleasure of my company in Paris for this year's summer season."

"But that's fantastic!" cried Angel. "Lucky you."

"I'm glad you think so, because I'm not going."

Angel gasped. "But—I don't understand. It's Paris—why wouldn't you want to go to Paris?"

"Well, for starters because it's the exact same two weeks as the London Academy."

"Oh," said Angel, suddenly unsure of what to say. She knew how much the London Academy meant to Lily, but this was an invitation to Paris. *Paris!* And Lily hadn't seen her grandmother since she was five. "That can't be your only reason," she said.

Lily hesitated and then said slowly, "It isn't that I don't want to see my grandmother. It's just that . . . I don't want to see her *now*."

"Why not?"

Angel was surprised to see Lily's face tinge with color.

"What's wrong with now?" persisted Angel.

This time the pause was even longer. At last Lily said, "It's Dad, he . . ."

"What?" asked Angel.

Lily shook her head.

"Is this about what happened last Christmas?"

Lily nodded.

"You had a fight?"

Lily nodded again.

"About?"

Emotion flitted across Lily's face, then she sighed and the secret she'd been holding in since Christmas burst out.

"He said he was thinking of getting married again. He said I needed a mother because—because *he* couldn't give me everything I needed. And then when I argued with him it all just got worse and worse—like everything I said came out the wrong way and then when I'd run out of words he told me he really liked Margot and that he was so pleased I'd overcome my resentment and how great it was that I liked her because she liked me and how she had all this empathy and understanding 'cause she had a teenage daughter of her own—as if that made her the perfect candidate and . . . and then he said it would be such a relief to him if there was someone in the house I could talk to about *things*!" Lily looked miserably at her friend. "Oh, Angel, if you'd heard him you'd know exactly—" She broke off.

Angel nodded. She could only imagine how hurt Lily must've been. She and her dad were so close and Philip had always tried to make up for her not having a mother. And it helped that Simone was downstairs because when Philip was away Lily could talk to her.

For Philip to suggest that he needed to get married again just to provide her with a mother was nuts. Angel sighed. Sometimes adults were weird.

She looked at Lily. "But I still don't get what this has to do with you going to visit your grandmother in Paris?"

"That's because I haven't told you the rest," replied Lily.

"Go on."

Lily dropped onto the bed. "I told Margot that Dad and the Comtesse don't speak and he wouldn't want me going to Paris to see her."

"What did she say?"

"She laughed that annoying laugh and said that was all in the past and the best way to help my dad was to accept my grandmother's invitation."

Angel frowned. "I don't think Philip would agree."

"That's the trouble, he *has* agreed."

"How can he? Margot only just got the letter and he's not in phone contact."

Lily's face puckered. "Apparently he had a few minutes at an airport and called Margot."

Angel stared at Lily in dismay. "Did you have a missed call on your phone?"

"No."

"Oh."

Angel digested this in silence. Philip had had an opportunity to call home and he'd chosen to ring Margot instead of Lily. That meant things were serious. Maybe Lily was right and her dad really was planning to marry Margot Kane.

Angel looked up. "So, you don't want to go to Paris right now, because . . .?"

"Because I'm not doing *anything* to help Margot get what she wants and what she wants is for Dad and my grandmother to reconcile because the Comtesse knows all 'the best people and goes to the best parties—even the Versailles Ball.'" Lily mimicked Margot's voice perfectly.

Angel gave her a shove. "Don't do that, it's scary."

"Sorry." Lily hugged her knees. "Anyway, to hell with Margot. There's no way I'm helping her marry my dad and I'm *definitely* not missing out on the Academy just so she can schmooze up to the Comtesse de Tourney." She looked directly at Angel. "So those two weeks I'll be in London."

"But how can you be in London when your dad and Margot want you in Paris?" asked Angel. "I mean, even if your dad were happy for you to go to drama school—which he's not—it's obvious he wouldn't want you choosing that over visiting your grandmother."

"I don't care! I am *not* having Margot as a stepmother, so I'm *not* going to Paris. And I'm definitely *not* missing out on the London Academy."

Angel blinked at the ferocity of Lily's reply. "There's always next year," she said.

"No way." Lily stood up. "I've made up my mind: I'm going to London."

"But you can't be in London *and* Paris at the same time. How can you?"

"Come here."

Lily pulled Angel to her feet. Snapping on the light, she drew her to the mirror.

"Look," said Lily.

Angel looked at Lily's face, heart-shaped and animated, her eyes alight with mischief and then at her own puzzled reflection.

"See?" said Lily, pointing to the mirror.

"What?" asked Angel, mystified.

"We could be sisters."

The penny dropped. "No way! Don't even think about it."

"But why not?" Lily looked surprised. "We'd have an

awesome time—you in Paris, me in London. Think of it, Angel—two whole weeks in the city of your dreams and no one would ever know."

"Oh yeah? What about your grandmother?"

"No. That's why it's so brilliant. She hasn't seen me since I was five—not even a photo—she'd never know you weren't me."

"Other people would know."

"Nuh-uh." Lily looked triumphant. "I haven't been back to France—no one in Paris knows me."

"But what about your dad? And Margot? What's to stop her turning up and exposing me?" demanded Angel.

"No chance," said Lily. "When Dad phones he never knows where I am—so London, Paris, New York—it doesn't matter. As for Margot," she wrinkled her nose, "she'll be way too busy sucking up to the in-crowd out in the Hamptons."

"But—"

"If you go to Paris in my place, the Comtesse will take you to all the best couture houses. Jacqueline Montague says she knows all the top designers, including Antoine Vidal. Think about it, Angel—you could meet him."

Angel hesitated. Imagine meeting Antoine Vidal! And seeing the great couturiers: Chanel, Dior, Versace, Givenchy, Karl Lagerfeld, Balenciaga, Oscar de la Renta, and Vidal. She might get to see his fall collection, after all.

She imagined talking to him about his latest designs and the Teen Couture, his grey eyes smiling . . .

Then another vision flashed into Angel's mind: of lying flat on her face on the floor of the Waldorf Ballroom while Antoine Vidal stared down at her. Angel shivered. That was reality, not this crazy plan of Lily's.

She lifted her chin. "I'm sorry, Lily. I can't."

Lily seemed to deliberately misunderstand. "Yes, you can—it'll be easy. Think about it—you know everything about me—you even speak French better than me." Lily's eyes sparkled. "There isn't anyone who could be me better than you."

"Except that I'm not you," replied Angel firmly. "And I never could be you, no matter how hard I tried."

"Sure you could," urged Lily.

Angel paused. How was it that the most difficult things seemed so simple to Lily? She always had some plan or idea that she was sure would solve everything. But this was different. This was taking things to a whole new level and if it went wrong—Angel couldn't risk hurting her mother. Not when Simone had already lost so much. And what would Papa have said to such a crazy plan?

"I can't," said Angel firmly.

"But why?" cried Lily. "I thought you'd love to go to Paris."

"Well, duh, of course I would. Just not like this."

"But I've told you why I can't go to Paris, and I *need* to go to London."

"Well, maybe you can't always have what you want."

"But *why*?" demanded Lily. "Why won't you do it? It would mean so much to me—to both of us."

"It's too big a risk."

"There *is* no risk. I told you—no one will even know!"

"And what happens at the end of the two weeks?" demanded Angel. "Sooner or later, you'll have to see your grandmother and then what? I'm pretty certain she'll notice that you're not me and then we'll be in real trouble."

"Not if I go to Paris at the end of the two weeks and explain. Even if the Comtesse *is* mad—she'll be mad at *me*, not you. And by then you'll be safely back in New York."

Angel frowned. Did Lily really not get it? Did she *truly* not understand what she was asking? "You make it sound so easy," she said. "But I know there'd be consequences. Maman might even lose her job."

"As if I'd ever let that happen," cried Lily. But even as

she said it, Angel saw the flash of doubt in her face and knew she was thinking of Margot.

A chill ran down her spine at the thought of what Margot might do once Lily's ploy was discovered. From Lily's account of the Margot behind the mask, it would be just like her to exact revenge in some sweet, insidious way.

But Lily seemed oblivious to the risks. "Trust me, Angel. I *know* my plan will work. I've got it all worked out."

Angel felt an unfamiliar anger. "I'm sure you have," she snapped. "And I'll bet it's a great plan for *you* because I'll be the one taking all the risks."

"How can you say that?"

"Because it's true," said Angel, and before she could stop herself she spoke the thought that had been simmering in the back of her mind for weeks: "You're spoiled, Lily, and so used to getting everything you want that sometimes you don't think about others."

Lily looked hurt, but Angel didn't care. "I won't do it, Lily. For once in your life, you can't have what you want."

Lily stood in silence, as a tear slid down her cheek. Angel knew she'd upset her, but she wasn't going to apologize. Not yet, anyway.

Eventually Lily spoke. "But Angel," she said, holding out her hand, pinky finger extended. "Friends?"

Angel shook her head as she opened the door. "Goodnight, Lily."

Chapter Eight

It was two days before Angel saw Lily again. She missed her, but she was immersed in her sewing and happy to spend the hours alone in her room working on her ball gown. Sundays were when she missed Papa most. Those were the days she and Simone had always visited him and Angel often yearned for their quiet conversations and his way of making her feel like she could do anything. She'd always take her latest sketches to show him and he would carefully examine each one and listen to her ideas and encourage her to pursue her dreams.

Now, when Angel sewed she thought of Papa and those quiet afternoons and each stitch would feel like a tiny reminder of his belief in her.

***

Late on Sunday night there was a knock on Angel's door.

She opened it to find Lily kneeling in the doorway.

"Peace offerings," said Lily, holding up a fat paper bag.

"Get up," said Angel, trying to look stern.

"Not until you've forgiven me."

Angel put down her needle. "Forgiven you for what?"

Lily hung her head. "I was hateful and I'm sorry." She peeked up at Angel through her lashes.

"Do you mean it?" demanded Angel.

Lily smiled. "Definitely. You were right, I am a bit spoiled sometimes and not *all* my plans work out."

"I'm sorry, too. I didn't mean all those things I said."

"I know. That's why I brought you these." Lily stood up and held out the paper bag.

"You know my weakness," said Angel, taking a chocolate.

"Well, I had to do something to make up. You *are* my best friend." Lily hesitated and then said, "Which is why I have to warn you that I haven't given up on my plan."

Angel choked on the chocolate. Lily banged her on the back. "You know, you really shouldn't get so worked up."

Angel glared at her with streaming eyes.

From the moment they'd met, Lily had pushed, cajoled and persuaded Angel into joining her in countless crazy schemes. Admittedly, some of them had been fun—but not this one. This was an insane idea that meant only one thing—trouble.

"Don't look at me like that," begged Lily. "You just need to think about two weeks in Paris seeing fashion shows and going to the Louvre."

"Which sounds great, so long as you leave out the bit about me pretending to be you," said Angel, picking up her needle. "You can talk all you want, but you'll never convince me to go to Paris in your place."

Lily just smiled.

***

For the next week she came down to Angel's room every evening, outlined her plan and explained how awesome it would be for them both. Angel sewed and listened, but wouldn't change her mind.

On Wednesday night she went to see *Our Town* and was awestruck by Lily's performance. She lit up the stage and Angel almost felt guilty for denying her the chance to go to the London Drama Academy.

Almost.

The school year finished and Angel retreated to her room to sew. She sewed all day and into the night and only went to bed when her eyes grew too tired. She wouldn't risk a single stitch being anything less than her best.

Ten days later her ball gown was almost complete. She'd finished tambour beading the delicate stylized angel on the bodice and all she had left to sew were the last bits of silver gauze.

***

Angel glanced at her watch and walked faster. She'd run out of silver thread and been forced to rush downtown to buy more. She did a quick mental calculation. Another few hours sewing ought to do it. The courier was coming in the morning and he'd guaranteed to get her entry to Vidal's before the Friday deadline.

Angel gave a little skip of excitement.

Tomorrow her designs would be winging their way to Paris. She tried to imagine them hanging on a rack at Vidal's and wondered whether Clarissa's entry would be there too. If they both made the finals she'd get to see the black-and-silver cocktail dress as well as Clarissa's ball gown. Angel's heart beat faster at the thought and she quickened her step.

"Angel! Wait up."

Angel turned to see Lily dodge a large white delivery van as she ran across the road to join her.

"Look, Lily, it's Harrington's again," said Angel, nodding towards the van. "Do you think Margot's ordered more clothes?"

Lily didn't reply.

"You okay?" asked Angel.

"Oh, Angel." Lily's mouth quivered. "It's not too late. I leave for Paris on Saturday so you can still take my place, *please*, Angel!"

Angel's heart sank. She'd thought Lily had accepted her decision not to embark on her mad plan. Obviously she was wrong. Struggling to know what to say, Angel was momentarily diverted by the sight of the Harrington's man carrying several large boxes into the house.

At last she said, "I'm sorry, Lily. I know it's hard to give up the London Academy, but I can't do it." Lily's shoulders slumped and Angel's heart went out to her. "I can't go to Paris for you, but maybe there's something we haven't thought of—some other way to beat Margot. Let's talk about it at home."

As they entered the foyer, they found Simone carrying two of several large white boxes towards the stairs.

"I'll do that, Maman," said Angel.

"Let me take those, Simone," said Lily.

"Thank you," panted Simone.

Angel frowned. "Are you feeling all right?"

Simone smiled tiredly. "Just my wretched indigestion again."

"Oh, Maman—" began Angel, but Simone interrupted.

"It is all right, *chérie*. I have a cup of peppermint tea waiting for me in the kitchen."

"Go have your tea," said Lily. "We'll put these in Margot's room."

"Clarissa's room," corrected Simone. "These are for Clarissa."

"Okay."

Picking up the remaining boxes, they ran upstairs to Clarissa's room and dropped the boxes on her bed. Angel ran her fingers lightly across the *Handmade by Harrington's* logo on the lid and wished she could look inside.

"I wonder what the evil diva has ordered from Harrington's this time," said Lily, as Angel headed for the door.

Angel considered the boxes, "Maybe she's had some of

her designs made up for Miki Merua. Didn't you say she'd shown him some of her sketches and he'd asked her to bring in some samples?"

"Yes, but I didn't believe her."

"Well, maybe she was telling the truth for once."

"Let's find out," said Lily mischievously, grabbing the nearest box.

"I don't think you should do that," began Angel, but Lily had already pulled off the lid and was parting the swathes of pink tissue paper.

A moment later she held up a green-and-white silk dress. "Gorgeous—" Lily stopped as Angel uttered a strangled cry and leapt forward. She grabbed the dress, flipped it around and sank onto the bed.

"What is it? What's wrong?"

"It's *mine!*" croaked Angel. "*My* design, in a Harrington's box."

"No way! How can that be?" demanded Lily. "You've never . . ."

Suddenly Angel grabbed the nearest box and tore off the lid. Lily stared as tissue paper flew through the air. Moments later Angel held up a striking red cocktail sheath.

Before Lily could speak, Angel was ripping a third box apart. She pulled a navy-blue suit with fine white trim from its nest of paper, threw it on the bed, and wrenched the lid off the next box. Thrusting both hands into the papery depths, she lifted up a hot-pink frilled bathing suit.

White and trembling, Angel turned to the last box.

It was by far the largest of the five and the lid was tight. Angel tugged at it, her nails raking the edges, until it gave way. She parted the tissue paper and lifted out the contents.

Lily gasped. Angel was holding up a stunning midnight-blue velvet ball gown with filigreed silver straps and a small silver angel delicately embroidered on the bodice. Tenderly caressing the velvet was a layered half-skirt of sparkling silver gauze pieces which floated to the floor.

Angel clasped the gown to her breast and sank slowly onto the bed amidst a sea of pink tissue paper.

"My designs," she whispered. "They're all my designs."

Lily stared helplessly at the agony on Angel's face. "I don't understand," she faltered. "Are you saying that Clarissa has had Harrington's make your designs?"

Angel nodded.

"How dare she!" cried Lily. "I knew she was bad, but I didn't know she was a thief."

"She's worse than that," said Angel, and the color rose in her cheeks. "Think about it. Why would Clarissa have Harrington's make my designs?"

"Because they're the best?"

"Because they make everything by *hand*."

Lily stared as the light slowly dawned. "She couldn't— She wouldn't—"

"Enter my designs in the Teen Couture?" finished Angel angrily. "It's exactly what Clarissa would do if she'd messed up her own entry. That Japanese silk wouldn't take resewing."

"But she'd never get away with it," declared Lily.

Angel considered. Surely that was true. After all, her own entry was within hours of being ready and if two identical entries arrived in Paris, Clarissa would be found out. Unless she could sabotage Angel's entry somehow. It sounded ridiculous, but suppose . . .

"Suppose Clarissa could delay my Teen Couture entry so that only hers got to Paris before the competition closed—the House of Vidal would only ever see *her* entry."

"But you'd know."

Angel shook her head. "Any entry received after five o'clock this Friday isn't even opened and nothing's sent back unless you've paid the shipping cost. Clarissa could've guessed I wouldn't do that."

"She's evil!" whispered Lily.

Angel glowered. "And a thief and a cheat! But she's also

clever, because if I heard nothing I'd just assume I hadn't made the cut."

"But didn't Clarissa have to send original sketches with her entry? I thought your designs were still in your portfolio?"

Angel nodded slowly and said, "Clarissa must have sneaked downstairs, photographed my final sketches and put them back. Once she had copies she could easily draw what looked like original drawings."

"Could she?" asked Lily incredulously.

Angel thought of the sketches she'd seen in Clarissa's room. "There's nothing very original in her drawings, but she's a brilliant copyist. In fact, she could probably set up as a very successful forger," she added bitterly. Angel suddenly remembered the sketchbook she'd found under Clarissa's bed. The flash of red that had seemed so strangely familiar must have been a drawing of Angel's cocktail sheath. No wonder Clarissa had leapt at her.

"I can't get my head around it," said Lily. "You really think Clarissa's ambitious enough to enter the Teen Couture with your designs?"

Angel nodded.

"It's incredible," said Lily, shaking her head.

"The only thing I don't get," said Angel, "is how the heck did Clarissa know I was entering the Teen Couture?"

Lily paled. "OMG, it was me," she groaned. "It was Dad's birthday dinner—Clarissa kept going on about Miki Merua admiring her designs. Apparently he'd told her she should enter the Teen Couture. He said he'd give her a full-time place in his studio if she made the finals." Lily scowled. "Then she said that if I was lucky, she'd consider designing my prom dress. So I told her not to bother because my best friend was a brilliant fashion designer and if anyone was going to win the Teen Couture, it'd be her."

"Oh, Lily," whispered Angel.

"I am *so* sorry."

"It doesn't matter." The light of battle gleamed in Angel's eyes. "Because Clarissa's not going to get away with it."

"Absolutely," agreed Lily, frisbeeing a Harrington's lid across the room.

"I'm taking these." Angel reached for the clothes scattered on the bed.

"What the *hell* is this?"

Startled, both girls looked up to find Clarissa standing in the doorway, her face contorted with rage. "How dare you let this—this *nobody* touch my things, Lily!" she shrieked.

"*Your* things!" cried Angel and Lily in unison.

"You've gone too far this time, Angelique! I'm calling Mother." And before they could stop her, Clarissa was gone.

Angel ran after her. She caught Clarissa at the top of the stairs and spun her around. "I know what you're planning, Clarissa, but you won't get away with it. Those are *my* designs and I—" Angel's head snapped round.

Her mother was calling her name, "Angel!" There was a note of panic in Simone's voice that struck terror in her.

Looking over the balustrade, Angel's heart stopped beating. Her mother was leaning against the banister, clutching her side, barely able to stand. Pushing past Clarissa, Angel raced down the stairs and reached the bottom just as Simone collapsed.

Chapter Nine

The rest of the day passed in a blur. After a nightmare ride in the ambulance, during which Simone's moans of pain almost convinced Angel her mother was going to die, Angel was directed to a sterile waiting room to wait for news. Lily found her there soon after and spent the next few hours trying to convince Angel that Simone would be all right.

Eventually a nurse came. "Your mother is resting comfortably," she told Angel. "She's got some abdominal trouble and will need surgery but a doctor will come and speak to you about that."

"Can I see her?"

"She's heavily sedated, she won't know you're there."

"*Please*, I—"

"My friend needs to see her mother," said Lily firmly.

The nurse frowned.

"After that I'll take her home," promised Lily.

***

Back home, Lily coerced Angel into eating a bowl of soup and made her watch two of their favorite movies before helping her into bed.

She offered to stay with her, but Angel insisted she was fine and wanted only to sleep. But after Lily had gone she lay awake staring into the darkness and wondering if her mother would be okay.

All she could think of was Maman lying pale and still in the hospital bed. It had reminded her of Papa in the days before he'd finally slipped away. Angel felt terrified at the thought of losing Maman as well. The surgeon had come to speak to her in the hospital and had said that they would need to operate. Her mother had pancreatitis and Lily had tried to call her father, but she couldn't get through, and eventually the two of them left the hospital.

It was long past midnight before Angel finally fell asleep, so she woke late the next day. She rushed to the kitchen to ring the hospital and found that Lily had already spoken to the nurse. They hadn't told her much—only that Simone was out of surgery and resting comfortably. Angel burst into tears.

She wanted to go straight to the hospital, but Lily was firm. "You need breakfast. There's no point going to see your mom half-starved. Besides, the nurse said to visit after three."

Angel hugged her.

Simone was sleeping when Angel arrived at the hospital. To Lily's disgust, Margot had insisted on taking her shopping for something she could wear to Paris, so she hadn't been able to come.

Angel couldn't help feeling relieved. She'd been terrified of breaking down again and hadn't wanted to share her worst fears with anyone.

It was a shock to find her mother looking so pale and fragile. As she sat beside the bed Angel had to fight hard not to cry.

"I love you, Maman," she whispered, and wondered what she would do if her mother died.

She forced the thought from her mind and tried to think of something else.

She suddenly remembered the Teen Couture. Her entry should have gone to Paris this morning, but the courier must have come and gone away empty-handed. She'd been so worried about Maman she hadn't even thought about it.

Was it really only yesterday she'd been so full of hope, imagining her designs at Vidal's? How quickly everything had changed. It seemed like eons since Maman had collapsed, but Angel could still hear her cries of pain as they'd loaded her into the ambulance.

She mustn't think about it. She wouldn't.

Angel pulled the magazines she'd brought for Simone from her bag and settled down to read.

***

It was nearly six when Simone stirred, opened her eyes and whispered, "*Chérie? C'est toi?*"

Angel smiled down at her. "Yes, it's me, Maman. You've had an operation, but you're going to be fine."

Simone frowned. "I can't stay here." She tried to sit up and gasped, pulling at the oxygen tubes and her drip.

Angel gently pushed her back down. "It's okay, Maman, you're in the hospital. Just rest."

Simone stared up at her and Angel saw the same fear in her face that had haunted her in the weeks after the surgeon had told them that, despite all their hopes, Papa's final operation had not succeeded and he would need full-time care.

Angel's stomach churned. "What is it, Maman?"

Simone plucked at the sheet. "I heard them talking. They are sending me to a rehabilitation home, but I know our medical insurance won't cover it." She clutched Angel's hand. "We can't afford it, *chérie*. Your father . . . Most of our money—"

"Went to his care," cut in Angel softly. "I know, Maman, but it'll be okay. If the insurance company won't help, I can ask Philip."

"No!"

The tortured cry made Angel flinch.

"Promise me, you will not accept charity from Philip," whispered Simone. She moved restlessly in the bed. "I have never—I will *never* take charity from him and you must not either!"

"No, I won't—of course not." Angel managed a tiny smile. "Don't worry. First thing tomorrow I'll talk to the insurance people. It'll be okay—I promise. Just focus on getting well. Please, Maman."

Simone seemed suddenly aware of the worry in Angel's face. She stroked her cheek and said softly, "I am being foolish, *chérie*. Do not listen to my crazy talk, it is only the drugs for the pain that make me speak so. *Certainement*, all will be well."

The nurse came in. "The doctor's here. He wants to talk to you." Angel followed her into the hall.

Outside, the doctor was talking to a smartly dressed woman. Angel blinked. It was Margot.

The doctor turned. "Here she is," he said heartily, "the lucky young lady whose mother got to the hospital in the nick of time." Noticing Angel's pale face, he added, "But all's well. Your mother has acute pancreatitis and biliary colic. She had several large gall stones so I've had to remove her gall bladder. We are treating her pancreatitis," he patted Angel's shoulder in a fatherly fashion, "and I'm confident that with the right care your mother will make a full recovery."

He gestured to Margot. "I've been chatting with Ms. Kane and we have a plan."

Angel stared. Margot was smiling at her. Not a nasty, malicious smirk, but a gracious, caring smile.

Margot stepped forward. "My dear," she said gently, "your mother has had a serious operation and what she needs now is rest and the finest care." She took Angel's hand. "Doctor Somers and I agree that a rehabilitation home in Florida would be ideal."

"Florida!" exclaimed Angel. "No, I—"

"Sunnydale is one of the finest facilities in the country," said Dr. Somers. "With an outstanding patient recovery record."

"Good food, rest and sunshine are what your mother needs now," added Margot.

Dr. Somers nodded. "Ms. Kane has generously agreed to fly your mother down on Saturday with a private nurse and pay all the expenses." He patted Angel's hand. "Your mother's very lucky to have such a kind and generous employer." He looked at Margot. "You'll leave it to me to make all the arrangements?"

"Certainly, Dr. Somers, and you'll send me the bill?"

He nodded and she smiled graciously. "Then I'll take this young lady home now, it's been a long day."

As shaken as she was by Margot's change of personality, Angel could not agree to this. "I'm not tired and Maman—"

"Needs to sleep," said the doctor. "You can come back on Saturday to say goodbye. Tell your mother that Ms. Kane is looking after you *and* the bills and she'll have nothing to worry about."

He smiled at them as Margot put her arm around Angel's shoulders, her face a picture of tender concern as she walked her down the corridor.

Angel was trying to think of how to express her gratitude when they reached the exit door. As they passed through, Margot whipped her arm from Angel's shoulders.

"Right," she snapped. "Follow me."

Minutes later Angel found herself in the back of the Rolls. The kindly Margot of the hospital corridor had vanished and the woman Lily insisted was the real Margot sat beside her, calmly lighting a cigarette.

"Clarissa tells me there was some sort of mix-up with her designs," she said, sending a thin stream of smoke towards Angel. "My daughter is so excited at having sent off her Teen Couture entry to Paris. She's made the most beautiful blue velvet ball gown."

"*She* didn't make it," declared Angel.

Margot inhaled and regarded Angel through narrowed eyes. "Clarissa has her heart set on a career in fashion design. Becoming a finalist in the Teen Couture will ensure she succeeds."

"Those are *my* designs," said Angel.

Margot's eyes glinted and she leaned forward. "Dr. Somers told me it was touch and go with your mother. She nearly died. Without the proper treatment she may never recover fully. You are lucky that I am able to send her to Sunnydale."

Angel shifted uncomfortably. She *was* incredibly grateful to Margot. She was helping save Maman's life and how could she ever repay her for that?

"You're very kind—"

"It would be *so* unfortunate if anything should happen to upset the arrangements I've made for Simone's recovery." Margot inhaled deeply. "Clarissa has worked *so* hard on her Teen Couture entry. She was very upset when that Japanese silk proved to be sub-standard and I *won't* have her upset again. I'd find that *very* distracting. I might even forget to pay my bills, and that," she stubbed out her cigarette, "could be fatal."

She smiled. *Like a snake about to eat its prey*, thought Angel.

"But I'm sure I'll have no trouble remembering so long as I'm convinced that Clarissa's Teen Couture entry will have its chance in Paris without interference."

Angel stared at her. What could she say? Her mother had almost died—she might still die without proper care. She thought of Papa and how much she missed him. If she lost Simone, Angel would be all alone . . .

She pushed the vision of Clarissa wearing her midnight-blue velvet ball gown from her mind. What did the Teen Couture matter, when Maman's life hung in the balance?

The car pulled up outside the townhouse and Margot laid a hand on Angel's knee. "There's no need for you to say anything to anyone about our . . . *arrangement*," she said silkily. "I'm so glad we've had this little chat, it makes everything *so* much clearer."

The door closed and Angel was left alone in the dark.

Chapter Ten

A ngel didn't know how long she sat there, her mind seething with images of her mother in the hospital, of Papa—so frail and gentle and loving—and of Margot smiling triumphantly.

Those that have the power make the rules. Her mother's words echoed in her head. Papa had never believed it, but now Angel knew it must be true. In a few hours Clarissa's forged sketches and the Harrington's-made copies of Angel's designs would arrive at Vidal's and there was nothing she could do about it.

If she contacted Vidal's, Margot would know and Maman's recovery would be jeopardized. She wouldn't let that happen.

Angel felt the tears gathering and bit her lip hard; this was no time for self-pity.

A sudden tap on the car window made her jump.

Roberts opened the door. "Sorry, Angel, I didn't mean to startle you."

"That's okay, I'm holding you up."

Roberts walked her to the door. "Sorry to hear about Simone—will she be okay?"

"I think so," replied Angel, slipping inside.

It felt strange to be all alone downstairs and when she turned on the kitchen light, the sight of her mother's apron on the bench was too much.

She gathered it up, went into Simone's bedroom and burst into tears.

Eventually Angel stopped crying and sat up. On her mother's bedside table were the two pictures Lily had taken last Thanksgiving when Simone had taught them how to make chocolate soufflé. Maman had been triumphant when Angel's had emerged from the oven perfectly risen, and Lily had snapped them grinning at each other.

She'd also captured the look on their faces a moment later when the soufflé had collapsed.

Angel carried the photos to her room.

Her ball gown was where she'd left it, with the needle still waiting for its silver thread. She stood there for a moment looking at it, then squared her shoulders and turned resolutely away.

Putting the photo frame on the desk, she picked up her Teen Couture entry form. She was about to rip it in two when the photo caught her eye. She gazed at her mother smiling so proudly, considered her ball gown, and then slowly put down the entry form.

***

It was after three a.m. when Angel quietly opened Lily's door. Groping through the darkness, her foot hit something hard.

"Ow!"

Lily turned on the light. "What *are* you doing?"

Angel glared at the four large Louis Vuitton suitcases in the middle of the room.

"I stubbed my toe on what I can only imagine is your entire wardrobe. I thought you were going to Paris for two weeks, not forever."

Lily scowled. "Margot insisted the maid pack everything in plenty of time. Left to me, I'd just shove a few clothes in my duffel bag tomorrow morning." She patted the bed. "Come here."

Angel sat. Lily massaged the offended toe.

"Are you okay? How's Simone? Clarissa told me about Florida. Not that I'm speaking to the evil diva since she stole your designs. You know the courier picked up her Teen Couture entry while we were at the hospital yesterday? Clarissa was so smug, I nearly—"

Angel interrupted. "Do you still want me to take your place in Paris?"

Lily stopped massaging.

"Well, do you?"

Lily squealed.

"Shhh! You'll wake Margot."

"Do you mean it?" whispered Lily.

"Margot's told me that so long as I let Clarissa enter my designs in the Teen Couture she'll pay for Maman's recovery."

"That blackmailing bitch! She's not going to get away—"

"With it," finished Angel. "No, she isn't, and nor is Clarissa, which is why I need to go to Paris."

"So you can pretend to be me and tell Vidal in person?"

Angel shook her head. "No one at Vidal's can know Clarissa has cheated until Maman is completely well. I need Margot to pay for her to go to Florida, but if she gets even a hint that I'm in Paris she won't do it. I can't risk that."

"But if you're not going to expose Clarissa, why go to Paris?" asked Lily.

"Because there's *no* way I'm letting Clarissa enter the Teen Couture with my designs," declared Angel. "Papa always used to say that sometimes in life you have to roll with the punches, but sometimes you have to stand up and fight."

"And you're going to fight?"

Angel nodded. "If I can get into Vidal's, then I can swap my designs for Clarissa's. By the time anyone finds out, Maman will be better and there'll be nothing Margot or Clarissa can do. And if I win the Teen Couture prize money, Maman will be cared for and nothing Margot can say or do will prevent it."

"And getting into Vidal's should be easy, because Jacqueline Montague said that Antoine Vidal is my grandmother's favorite designer," said Lily enthusiastically.

"Just so long as the Comtesse thinks I'm you."

"Of course she will. All you have to remember is your name is Lily."

"My name is Lily," repeated Angel. "I'm Lily de Tourney."

"That's it." Lily grinned. "Tomorrow, you'll go to Paris and I'll go to London. You'll swap your designs, I'll earn my place at the London Academy and in two weeks you'll fly home. Once you're back in New York and we're sure Simone is better, I'll fly to Paris and tell the Comtesse the whole story."

"And you're sure you want to take the rap?"

"Definitely." Lily did a jig. "It'll totally be worth it. I'll book my flights online tonight."

"So how do we explain my disappearance?"

"Summer camp," she said firmly. "You're going next month anyway, so we'll just tell Simone and Margot that you're leaving early. That way, Margot won't be suspicious and your mom won't worry about you while she's recovering."

"Okay."

"Which just leaves our passports," said Lily.

"Maman got me a new one to go to Grandpère's funeral, only we never went."

"Where is it?"

"In my room."

Lily pulled her passport from her bag. "Come on."

Downstairs, Angel found her passport. She held her breath as Lily compared the photos.

"It's okay. They were taken a year apart, but we've both got blue eyes and dumb expressions. My hair's lighter than yours, but we can put some blonde highlights in yours tomorrow. We'll need to work on our eyebrows, but, really, who's gonna care about a couple of high school students?"

"Security," said Angel suddenly.

"Only a problem if they've got biometrics at the Paris airport, but I asked Elizabeth Montague and she said not until next year."

"Well, they've got 'em at JFK, so what'll we do there?"

Lily thought for a moment. "Going out we can swap them after we've passed through security and coming home we can send our passports to each other before you leave Paris."

Angel nodded. "And visas?"

"Not necessary for visits under ninety days."

"Great," said Angel. "So all I need now is for you to tell me everything you can remember about Paris and your grandmother."

***

Angel spent Friday afternoon at the hospital. Simone seemed a little better but she was preoccupied and Angel suspected she was worrying about the hospital bills. For a moment she thought of telling her about Margot's generosity and then she remembered what Margot had said about keeping their "arrangement" secret. Instead, Angel took a deep breath and recited the speech she and Lily had rehearsed over lunch.

It was a convincing account of her imagined conversation with the medical insurance company. Angel hated to lie, but it was worth it to see the fear fade from her mother's face as she explained that her policy had a new provision for rehabilitation that would cover most of the cost of her stay in Florida.

From there, it was just a short step to telling Simone

about summer camp and how awesome it would be to spend two extra weeks there.

"You'll come and see me tomorrow, before I leave?" asked Simone anxiously, as Angel kissed her goodbye.

"I'll be here at nine, Maman, all ready for your last-minute instructions about how not to get lost in the woods at camp."

Simone smiled faintly. "And you will be all right?"

"So long as I know you're getting better," said Angel, hugging her again.

"Jean-Pierre has promised to drive me up to Camp Wilderness as soon as I am back from Florida, so you can see how well I am."

"Can't wait," said Angel.

Chapter Eleven

The international terminal at JFK was crowded. Angel scanned the hall, but couldn't see any sign of Lily or the four Louis Vuitton suitcases she'd promised to repack with Angel's clothes and Teen Couture outfits.

Angel smiled at the thought of Lily having to run up and down the stairs swapping their clothes while Margot and Clarissa were at the hair salon. They'd agreed that Lily would leave her clothes in the closets in the butler's old room in case Clarissa went snooping around before she and Margot left for the Hamptons.

Angel gripped Lily's duffel bag and wondered if she should call her. She'd meant to touch base after she'd left the hospital but all she'd been able to think about was Maman.

It had been hard saying goodbye, despite the agency nurse's assurances that Sunnydale was exactly what Simone needed. "She'll be feeling much better in a week and quite fit in a fortnight. You'll be surprised. You can ring her tonight and see how she is because she'll want to know you're all right. After that you may ring her once a day," she'd held up a warning finger, "but not for too long."

Angel had made a mental note to ring Sunnydale from the airport.

She moved towards the Air France counter and saw Lily standing at the first-class check-in. Angel frowned—was Lily wearing Prada? She moved nearer. Yes, it was definitely a cream Prada two-piece—gorgeous, but totally out of character for Lily, who always wore jeans and a sweatshirt when she travelled.

Angel was about to call out when the words died in her throat. Standing next to Lily, looking superb in a burnt-orange Tommy Hilfiger shirt and black trousers, was Margot.

Angel looked around wildly for somewhere to hide. She saw Lily catch sight of her and Margot turning to see what she was looking at. She ducked down behind the crowd waiting in the economy class line and almost tripped over a honeymoon couple with confetti in their hair.

"Hey, watch it," cried the man.

"Sorry." Crouching low, Angel made a beeline for the bathroom. Risking a quick glance over her shoulder she saw Lily grab Margot's arm and point to the luggage.

Angel burst into the bathroom and made for the last stall. She closed the door and waited.

It seemed like hours before she heard Lily's piercing whisper.

"Angel."

"Here."

"It's okay, she's gone."

Angel opened the door. "Are you sure?"

"Yes, she's dining with friends, so she had to go."

"Thank goodness." Angel slumped down onto the toilet seat. "What was she doing here? I thought she was sending you with Roberts in the Rolls."

"She was." Lily looked embarrassed. "It was my fault. I got distracted and I'd only just started unpacking the first suitcase when she came home and saw what I was doing. She went all icy and polite in that scary way—you know—when you sit there like a total doofus and can't think of what to say."

Angel nodded: she knew exactly.

"She asked if I thought I could do a better job of packing

than the maid." Lily looked guiltily at Angel. "But the worst part was that I couldn't swap any of our clothes and now the suitcases are checked in and that means—"

"I'll have only your clothes to wear in Paris," cried Angel. "But I'm three inches taller than you and a different size and shape!"

"I know, but I did manage to bring you these." Lily handed Angel a plastic carrier bag. "It's a pair of your jeans and a T-shirt. I grabbed them out of the dirty laundry."

"What!" Angel was incensed.

"I couldn't go down to your room, Angel. Margot stayed with me practically the whole time. She even made me wear this disgusting outfit *and* make-up. It was the worst." She grimaced. "And there's something else."

"Oh, no."

"It may not be so bad," said Lily. "It's just that with Margot there I couldn't pack your Teen Couture outfits either. I'm sorry, Angel. I know I messed up."

Angel sighed. "I don't suppose it'll matter. I wasn't sure about swapping the clothes anyway. The most important thing was always to swap the designs and the entry form because they'll have Clarissa's name on them, and I've got my designs here." She patted her backpack.

"Okay then," Lily grabbed Angel's hand, "Ready?"

Angel swallowed hard, "I think so."

"It's crazy and totally out there, but we can do this," said Lily firmly.

"We have to," replied Angel, lifting her chin.

"Okay, let's go and check you in for my flight to London."

***

Two hours later Angel was sitting in the gate-lounge waiting to board her flight to Paris and wondering how she'd ever let Lily talk her into such a crazy scheme.

Except she hadn't—it was all her own doing. Maybe it wasn't too late to change her mind. Angel glanced at her watch. Nope, Lily had already boarded her flight to London.

Angel suppressed the whirling butterflies in her stomach. She was going to Paris to take a stand. That's what Papa would have told her to do—Papa who had fought right to the end and who had never stopped believing in her. For sure, he'd have told Angel to stop Clarissa Kane from cheating.

Still, Angel wished she had a more concrete plan. Getting into Vidal's was one thing, but finding a way to swap her designs was another. The butterflies whirled again. Maybe she should think this through.

"GOOD EVENING. AIR FRANCE FLIGHT AF139 TO PARIS IS NOW READY FOR BOARDING. COULD PASSENGERS PLEASE HAVE THEIR BOARDING PASSES READY . . ."

Angel didn't hear the rest. She leapt up, heart pounding as she fumbled for her boarding pass and joined the queue. When she reached the front the flight attendant looked at her in astonishment.

"But Mademoiselle de Tourney, there is no need for you to queue. Just go through." She pointed. "The first door on the left, whenever you're ready."

Angel kicked herself mentally as she entered the plane. She should've remembered she was travelling first-class.

"I'm not me, I'm her," she muttered as the flight attendant led her to an enormous leather seat. I'm Lily de Tourney, Lily, Lily, *Lily*. And I'd better remember that!

If only it were that simple.

Chapter Twelve

"**M**ademoiselle? Mademoiselle de Tourney."

Angel was dreaming: Lily was cutting a book with a huge pair of scissors and Angel was desperately trying to make out the title when a piece of midnight-blue velvet floated down and covered it. She was pushing it away when she saw Philip reach out and say something about Simone.

"Mademoiselle de Tourney."

Angel woke to find the flight attendant gently shaking her arm.

"Sorry?"

The attendant gestured to the window. "We are approaching Paris. If you look, you will see."

Angel was suddenly wide awake. She pressed her forehead against the window and there, bathed in the late-afternoon sunlight, was the most beautiful city in the world.

Paris!

Below her the city gleamed like a jewel and Angel could see the wide boulevards radiating out from a center circle like a giant wheel. She felt her skin tingle with anticipation. She'd dreamed of coming to Paris for so long, it was hard to believe she was actually here. If only . . .

Angel stopped. There was no point thinking about the if-onlys. She'd agreed to be Lily and now she was in Paris. It was awesome.

A cloud of butterflies rose up in her stomach. She pushed them away, pressed her nose against the window and tried to see the Eiffel Tower.

Angel waited nervously at passport control. The immigration official had examined Lily's passport, then looked at Angel, before signaling to a colleague. The two men conferred in whispers while Angel's stomach tied itself in knots.

She wondered what the penalty was for travelling on a false passport and whether French jails allowed you to phone America.

The second officer stepped forward, picked up Angel's backpack, and said in English, "Please follow me."

It was over before it had begun. Her legs felt wobbly as she followed him and Angel wondered if she might faint. Jet lag, she told herself, trying not to panic.

She followed the officer along a corridor, down a flight of stairs and past several rooms. Angel was wondering which one was for interrogation, when he pushed open a security door and led her into the arrivals hall.

Looking around, he beckoned to a silver-haired man in a chauffeur's uniform standing beside a trolley loaded with four Louis Vuitton suitcases.

The officer gave Angel her backpack and passport.

"The Comtesse de Tourney regrets that she is unable to meet you. She asked that we assist you. Welcome to Paris, Mademoiselle de Tourney."

Angel's knees almost buckled with relief. The chauffeur touched his cap and beamed at her. "Welcome, Mademoiselle Lily," he said in French. "It is good to have you home again. It's been a long time."

Angel gaped at him. The staff! She and Lily had forgotten about the staff; this man must have known Lily when she was little. And now … Angel tried to think of something to say.

"The car is this way." When she did not respond, he said in English, "This way." He took the trolley and headed for the exit.

Angel followed.

She didn't notice the young man looking at her. Nor did she see him pocket his cell phone and stride after her.

"Lily!" The clipped English tones sounded across the arrivals hall. Oblivious to her new name, Angel kept walking.

"Lily! Lily de Tourney."

Angel stopped dead. Surely there couldn't be someone else who knew Lily? She spun round and found herself looking up into a pair of sparkling brown eyes beneath a tangle of curly chestnut hair.

She held her breath.

"Lily de Tourney, after all these years." Noticing her blank look, he said, "It's me—Nick Halliday. As soon as I saw Henri," he nodded to the chauffeur, "I knew it had to be you."

She stared at him, speechless, while inwardly cursing Lily for her assurances that no one in Paris knew her.

He didn't seem to mind her silence, but stood there looking at her, his eyes wandering over her face and body as if trying to match the girl before him with the girl he'd once known. Angel shifted uncomfortably and Nick whistled. Not a wolf-whistle exactly, more a long, low whistle of—surprise? Appreciation? Lust?

Angel felt her hackles rise.

Before she could speak Nick took her hands, held them wide and said, "You've grown up."

She pulled her hands free. What did he think he was doing, grabbing her like that? And that whistle!

He seemed amused by her irritation. "Long flight?" he asked, grinning.

"Very."

"You'll be tired then." He looked at her uncombed hair and crumpled shirt. "And probably dying for a shower."

Angel flushed. Was he serious? He'd only met her two

minutes ago and he was acting like he'd known her forever. Who was this guy?

She searched her brain, trying to remember anything Lily might have said about a gorgeous, annoying Englishman named Nick. Not *that* gorgeous, she chided herself, scanning him for some clue to his connection to Lily.

Nick Halliday was about eighteen or nineteen, six-foot-two, and had the tanned, well-muscled body of a sportsman. And naturally he's rich, thought Angel. I'd recognize that oh-so-casual, I'm-just-one-of-the-boys, private-school look anywhere. Anyone could wear a white Ralph Lauren polo shirt, but Nick's pants were tailor-made and his accent definitely said upper-class English.

He reminded her of the seniors from the boys' school back home, and a warning bell sounded in her head. She frowned. That was it—Nick Halliday looked like another stuck-up, egotistical, all-the-girls-love-me kind of guy.

"I haven't seen you since that summer we spent together in Paris," said Nick. "And you never even called me," he added wistfully.

Angel frowned. What was he talking about? Lily hadn't been to Paris since she was five.

Nick grinned and she suddenly got the joke. He was talking about Lily's last summer in Paris—he hadn't seen her since she was little. Angel breathed again. If she trod carefully she'd get through this minefield unscathed and never see him again.

She felt a tiny pang of disappointment and shook herself mentally. As if! The last thing she needed right now was to get friendly with some snobby rich guy. She was in Paris for one reason only—to get into Vidal's and swap her designs for Clarissa's—*nothing* more!

She looked up at Nick again and this time took in the full glory of his smile.

He would have a gorgeous smile, she thought. No doubt

his parents had spent a fortune on orthodontists—maybe even a plastic surgeon—his cheekbones certainly looked impossibly chiseled.

"The last time I saw you," said Nick, "you were wearing your grandmother's tiara and demanding I play kings and queens with you."

Angel relaxed. Of course Nick Halliday wasn't interested in her—he didn't even know *she* existed—he thought she was Lily. Angel suddenly realized what her deception meant. She was no longer Angel Moncoeur— whose experience with boys could be written on a Post-it note—she was Lily de Tourney: outgoing, confident and completely at ease with the opposite sex.

All she had to do was *be* Lily. It was that simple. She felt strangely liberated.

She grinned. "I still miss that tiara."

"I seem to remember you wanted to send me to the guillotine, but I—"

"Nick!" An imperious French voice sounded behind Angel. She looked round to see a girl coming towards them. She was about eighteen, tall and model-thin, with a sleek black bob, dark eyes and the poutiest lips Angel had ever seen.

She took Nick's arm and looked Angel over. Apparently seeing nothing to perturb her, she said in French, "Nick, darling, the flight."

He answered her in English, gesturing to Angel. "I found an old friend, Yvette. Lily, this is Yvette Saint-Gilbert. Yvette, Lily de Tourney."

Yvette seemed slightly more interested. "Ah, the American granddaughter of the Comtesse de Tourney." She held out her hand. Angel shook it and tried to think of a sparkling reply. Nothing occurred to her.

It was harder being Lily than she'd thought.

Yvette turned to Nick. "We'll be late."

Nick looked at Angel apologetically. "I have to go."

"Right. Yes. Me too."

He touched her hand, his fingers were warm against her skin. "See you."

Not if I can help it, thought Angel.

Yvette tugged his arm. "Nick, the time."

"You'd better go," said Angel. "Nice meeting you, Yvette."

"*Et vous.*" Yvette turned away, pulling Nick with her.

As Angel moved away to where Henri stood waiting by the exit doors, she couldn't resist glancing back.

Nick's arm was across Yvette's shoulders, his head close to hers. She was definitely his girlfriend. A perfect match. Both good-looking, well-dressed and probably headed for some exotic destination popular with the rich and famous.

Just then Nick looked round, saw her watching and waved.

Blushing, Angel turned and hurried after Henri.

Minutes later she was sitting in the back of a magnificent silver Bentley being driven towards Paris.

***

It was after six when the car passed the Bois de Boulogne and entered a quiet tree-lined street. Henri drove in through elegant iron gates and up a curving gravel driveway. Through the trees Angel could see a two-story, grey stone villa covered in vines.

The Bentley stopped outside the front door.

Angel's heart thumped as she got out of the car and studied the bronze doorknocker. Should she use it or wait for the chauffeur? Before she could decide, the door opened and an elderly butler appeared.

"*Bienvenue, Mademoiselle Lily. Entrez, entrez.*" He waved Angel inside.

She stepped into a circular foyer with a colored-marble

floor and a high, domed ceiling that rose to the full height of the house. Across the foyer a doorway was framed by a heavy gold curtain and to Angel's right a wide, white marble staircase curved upwards to the floor above. On her left, a beautiful flower garden grew behind a low stone wall with vine-clad pillars rising up to support the ceiling cornice.

It took Angel a moment to realize she was looking at a painting—a French trompe-l'oeil picture designed to trick the eye. The garden, wall, vines and pillars were all painted. On either side of the garden was a pair of white double doors, paneled and trimmed in gilt.

Angel was still staring at the amazing painting when the butler stepped forward and said rapidly in French, "Henri will bring your baggage and Marie . . ." He coughed and a maid stepped through the curtained doorway. "Marie will show you to your room."

Angel dragged her gaze from the painted garden and tried to think of what Lily would say to a butler. Nothing sprang to mind.

The butler regarded her doubtfully for a moment, before bowing and saying in English, "Forgive me, Mademoiselle Lily, I had assumed you spoke French. But of course it is many years since you were in Paris."

Angel blinked, but before she could assure him she spoke fluent French, he said, "Marie will take you up to your room." He leaned forward and whispered conspiratorially, "It is your old *chambre*. Madame thought you would like it best."

Angel nodded mutely.

He smiled at her. "You will wish to change your clothes. When you are ready, come downstairs. Madame is expecting you in the drawing room." He pointed at the doors to the right of the trompe-l'oeil painting and left her.

Marie led Angel up the wide, curving staircase. On the first landing hung a stunning silk tapestry exquisitely embroidered with clusters of gold and purple irises. Beneath it stood a magnificent mother-of-pearl inlaid Chinese cabinet.

On the next landing a beautiful blue-and-white Chinese *cloisonné* vase sat atop an alabaster pedestal. Angel paused. The vase looked almost identical to one she'd often admired at the Metropolitan Museum back home in New York. The design was different but the shape and colors were the same—a real Ming vase on the landing!

Angel felt the butterflies stir in her stomach again. She ran up the last few stairs and followed Marie down a corridor lined with paintings in elaborate gilt frames. They were mostly of aristocratic-looking men and women; many in the powdered wigs and elegant clothing of the seventeenth century. Angel would have liked to stop for a closer look, but Marie was waiting by an open door.

"Your room, Mademoiselle Lily," she said in English.

Angel stepped inside and froze. Nothing downstairs or in the de Tourney's New York townhouse had prepared her for this.

Evening light filled the room, illuminating the soft tones of an antique Persian rug and the blue-greens of the silken wallpaper. A huge four-poster bed, hung with matching draperies, stood in the center of the room. It was covered with the most beautiful bedspread Angel had ever seen: gold and crimson birds of paradise flew through a dense satin forest of blue and green trees, the colors so deep and rich that the birds almost looked real.

At the foot of the bed stood an enormous cedar chest and opposite was a marble fireplace. The grate was filled with pinecones and Angel could smell their faint scent. On either side of the marble mantelpiece was a huge armoire painted with scenes of the French countryside. A mahogany dressing table with a matching chair stood in an alcove beside the window and above it an enormous mirror reflected the beautiful room.

But it was the frescoes on the ceiling that took her breath away. A chariot drawn by four winged horses carried Helios across the heavens and all around him the pantheon of Greek gods looked down from sunlit clouds.

Angel could only stare in open-mouthed wonder.

"Your baggage, Mademoiselle Lily."

Angel came back to earth with a thump. Henri was standing in the doorway, Lily's suitcases behind him. She stepped aside as he brought the luggage into the room.

"I will unpack," said Marie, opening the first suitcase. "You will want something fresh to wear."

"No!" said Angel abruptly. "You're very kind, but I'd prefer to do it myself."

Ignoring her shocked face, Angel shepherded Marie out the door and closed it behind her. Leaning back against it, she gazed around the room and found herself trembling. She crossed to the dressing table, dropped into the chair and looked at herself in the mirror—at her hair, unbrushed since the plane and at her travel-worn shirt and pants. Then she looked up at the ceiling again.

"What was I thinking?" whispered Angel. It was all very well to take a stand, but this house was so far out of her league that she couldn't even begin to comprehend it. Everything in it breathed history and elegance and old money.

But it was more than that.

The room was a perfect harmony of space and light, color and furnishings. It belonged to someone with a keen eye for detail—someone who'd probably see straight through a deception.

"I can't do this." Angel stood up. "Forget Clarissa and the Teen Couture," she told her reflection. "Forget Paris and this whole stupid plan. You've got to go downstairs and tell the Comtesse the truth."

Chapter Thirteen

Angel walked slowly across the foyer, trying to think of how to explain herself to the Comtesse de Tourney. She stopped outside the drawing room, took a deep breath and grasped the door handle. Just then someone opened the door from the inside and Angel, still holding the door handle, was pulled into the room.

Inside, the babble of conversation faded as about thirty designer-clad guests, all about her age, turned to stare at her. Then, almost as one, they turned away and looked over to where an impeccably dressed woman stood by the fireplace. The butler let go of the door handle and said, "Mademoiselle Lily de Tourney."

The conversation slowly swelled as Angel moved towards the aristocratic figure. The room was long and beautiful, with tall French windows opening onto a terrace down one side. Several older couples stood outside enjoying the warm summer evening while groups Angel's own age sat together on the velvet-covered chairs and sofas that stood in the alcoves between the windows.

Around her people laughed and talked, but all Angel could think of was what she was going to say to Lily's grandmother. Even from twenty feet away she could see that the Comtesse was not someone to mess with.

Elena de Tourney wasn't tall, but she didn't need height to command attention. It wasn't the elegant chignon of silver hair or the graceful face with its pointed chin and high cheekbones, or even the Chanel suit, which gave her presence. She had that indefinable something—confidence, poise, power—Angel couldn't say exactly, but she could feel it.

About five feet from the Comtesse she stopped. "I—I had to see you."

"And you could not wait even to change your clothes. I am flattered." The Comtesse's voice was soft and lightly accented, her English perfect. Her piercing blue eyes traveled over Angel's face, hair and clothes, but if she was displeased by her disheveled appearance she gave no sign.

Around them conversation ebbed and flowed, but Angel knew that everyone was watching to see what the Comtesse de Tourney would say to her scruffy American granddaughter. She tried desperately to think of the right words to explain that she wasn't the grandchild the Comtesse had waited more than ten years to see. She was just a New York housekeeper's daughter pretending to be her.

Perhaps if they went somewhere private she could explain. Angel opened her mouth to ask, but the Comtesse spoke first.

"Marcel tells me that you do not speak French. A pity. I had thought that your father would have ensured . . ." For an instant the Comtesse looked flustered, then she gave a delicate cough and said, "Still, it does not matter. You will find that many of our young people speak English." She gestured towards her guests. "And perhaps while you are here some French will return to you." She smiled. "I am sorry I was not at the airport to meet you, but your plane was delayed and I had to be here to greet my guests."

"Yes, I—" Angel began.

"I had hoped you would be at my side when they arrived, but it can't be helped." She considered Angel for a moment, before adding softly, "Naturally, I am delighted to find you so eager to see me, but," she eyed the groups of well-dressed teenagers, "I believe I can wait a little longer to become re-acquainted with my dear granddaughter."

She looked pointedly at Angel's crumpled shirt and pants, leaned forward and whispered, "You see, my dear Lily, this is Paris and we do not wear casual clothes to dinner."

Angel flushed. She knew she looked awful and that every one of the designer-clad guests thought so too, but she didn't care. Not when she needed to tell the Comtesse the truth. She lifted her chin. "I'm sorry, Madame, but I must speak with you."

"And you shall," said the Comtesse kindly, "as soon as you have changed."

She beckoned to the butler. "Marcel, please ensure Marie helps Mademoiselle Lily dress for dinner." She held up a finger to silence Angel's protest. "We will wait for you."

Upstairs, Angel found Marie hanging Lily's clothes in the *armoire*. The maid looked apologetic. "I'm sorry, Mademoiselle Lily, but Marcel insisted."

"It's okay, Marie. I understand."

"I will help you dress."

"No, I can manage." Ignoring the maid's protests, Angel pushed her gently from the room and opened the closet with a sigh.

Confessing was going to be harder than she'd thought.

***

Twenty minutes later she re-entered the drawing room. As she'd expected there was another lull in the conversation as the guests took in her appearance.

Angel tossed back her hair and squared her shoulders. She knew she looked awful because how else could she look in a dress that was the wrong shade of blue, the wrong size, shape, length and cut? Lily's clothes were not her style at all.

Angel scanned the room and found the Comtesse surrounded by a group of chattering girls. As she moved towards them Angel couldn't help wondering why her drawing room was full of high-school students. Maybe they were part of some charity? Though they didn't look like orphans—not in those clothes. Maybe foreign-exchange students? Though everyone was speaking French. Perhaps a youth group?

A waitress appeared in front of her holding a tray of canapés. Angel hesitated; she hadn't eaten for hours and was starving. The savouries looked delicious—perhaps a mouthful of food might give her courage.

Heaven knows I need it, she thought, looking across at the Comtesse. How was she going to get her alone so she could confess?

She picked up a wafer-thin slice of toast covered in a thick layer of pâté and popped it into her mouth. It was so delicious she grabbed two more before the waitress moved away.

Angel had just swallowed one when a burst of laughter from a nearby group of girls caught her attention. A striking redhead, wearing a breathtaking mint-green and white Elie Saab dress with three-quarter sleeves and a high neck, commanded the group's attention and it was obvious that, like the Comtesse and her staff, she and the others had concluded that Angel spoke no French.

Angel pretended not to hear as the redhead said, "Can she *really* be the Comtesse's granddaughter when she has no style or eye for color? Of course, she *is* American, which must be why she has no taste."

Several of the group laughed and a brown-haired girl said with a snigger, "Perhaps it's hillbilly chic?"

"Yes, she probably bought it at Walmart," added the redhead, smirking.

Angel sighed. Apparently the evil diva type wasn't confined to America. Well, she wouldn't give them the satisfaction of letting them know she'd understood. Let them think she was an uncultured American who couldn't speak a word of French. What did she care?

But, despite her determination to remain aloof, it made Angel seethe. Only a stupid French girl would be so arrogant, she thought crossly, conveniently forgetting her own heritage. How dare they look down their snooty French noses at America!

Angel stopped herself. Forget them, she thought. Eat your pâté, get a grip on yourself and go and tell the Comtesse you're an imposter.

She swung round and collided with the person behind her. Caught off-balance, Angel grabbed at the body in front of her. Her hands connected with a hard, masculine chest and she felt the squish of pâté against superfine wool. Pushing away, she stared in dismay at the mess of rich brown paste coating one perfectly cut charcoal-grey lapel.

"Oh!" gasped Angel, gazing at the stain. "I am *so* sorry." She dabbed at the lapel with her napkin.

A male hand, well-shaped and tanned, closed over her fingers. "Probably best if I do it."

Angel looked up and inhaled sharply.

Smiling down at her was the boy from the airport. She pulled her hand free from his grasp just as a voice behind her said, "Thank you, Nicky. Perhaps you would be so kind as to escort my granddaughter into dinner."

Chapter Fourteen

A ngel stared at Nick. What was he doing here? Wasn't he in the Bahamas with what's-her-name? Apparently not.

"Take Nicky's arm, Lily. He won't bite," said the Comtesse. "Everyone is waiting to follow you into dinner."

Angel looked around to see Elena de Tourney's guests standing in pairs, the girls' hands resting lightly on the boys' arms. She blushed—this wasn't how it was supposed to go—how could she go into dinner when she hadn't told the Comtesse the truth?

But, short of blurting out her true identity to a room full of strangers, it seemed she had no choice. Angel sighed and put her hand on Nick Halliday's arm.

As they entered the dining room, its splendor made Angel want to turn and run. But before she could move, the guests were dispersing around the table and Nick was pulling out a chair for her.

She sank onto the velvet seat and tried to take in the paintings, the mirrors and the chandeliers. There were works of art everywhere, but it was the table that took her breath away.

It was mahogany and the largest she'd ever seen, with twenty gilt-edged chairs down each side and an imposing carver chair at each end. Each place was set with four cut-crystal wine glasses, gleaming silverware and a fine bone-china dinner plate with royal-blue edging and a gold crest on the rim. At Angel's elbow lay a white damask napkin in a silver ring. Peeping from the napkin's folds was a crimson rosebud. Down the table tall, white candles flickered from a dozen silver candelabra and between them stood porcelain bowls filled with violets, freesias and old-fashioned roses. Angel breathed in their heady scent and tried to stay calm.

Just then someone nudged her. Looking round, she discovered Nick still standing by her chair. *What now?* she thought. Why was he still standing there gawking at her?

It took her a moment to realize that Nick wasn't the only one standing, and another moment to realize she was the only person seated; around the table the guests stood waiting by their chairs.

Angel's cheeks grew hot. They were waiting for their hostess to sit. She scrambled to her feet, silently cursing herself for forgetting something she'd been taught from childhood.

"*Bienvenue*—welcome everyone." The Comtesse's voice rang down the table. "Welcome to the first dinner of the summer season." There was a smattering of applause. "This year's season is particularly special because my granddaughter has come to Paris for it." She raised her glass to Angel. "Welcome home, Lily."

Around the table forty voices echoed hers as Angel's cheeks burned.

"And now, let us eat." The Comtesse sat down.

A babble of talk broke out as everyone was seated. Nick took his place beside Angel. She almost groaned aloud. It was bad enough being introduced to everyone as Lily de Tourney, but spending the evening chatting with Lily's old playmate only made it worse. She wished she'd told the Comtesse the truth before they sat down, because there was no way she was confessing in the middle of the dinner party—she'd have to wait till later.

A waiter placed an elegant fluted bowl in front of her.

Angel stared down at delicate lobster flesh nestled atop a bed of steaming yellow rice. A tantalizing smell invaded her nostrils.

The food looked divine. Angel was pretty sure she wouldn't be eating lobster risotto once she'd confessed, so she might as well enjoy it. She put a forkful into her mouth and her tastebuds practically squealed with delight.

"It's wonderful."

"Always," said Nick. "The Comtesse's dinner parties are legendary."

Despite herself, Angel was interested. "Have you been to many?"

"A few. This is my third summer season and there's always a dinner here."

"The summer season," repeated Angel. "What is it, exactly?"

He looked at her in surprise. "You don't know about the summer season? But isn't that why you're here?"

"Kind of."

"Well, you'll love the summer season," grinned Nick, "because we all know how to party and we've got two whole weeks hanging out together."

Angel stared at him. "That's it? That's all this is? Rich kids partying together?"

"Not ex—" Nick began, but she cut him off.

"So the summer season's just some fancy-schmantzy get-together for rich kids so they can, what?" She thought of Margot and her lip curled. "Meet the right people, attend the right parties and get together with other rich kids?"

There was a pause.

Nick let out a breath. "Whew! I gather you don't like rich people very much. Would that include you and your dad, by any chance? Or are you just too good and pure to ever have anything to do with something as dirty and unpleasant as money?"

Angel blinked. Was she crazy? What was she doing

going off at him like that? She didn't even know where that rant had come from.

Worse, she'd forgotten to be Lily. She couldn't imagine what he thought of Lily de Tourney venting about *rich* people. He must think she was weird.

A waiter discreetly removed their plates. When he'd gone, Angel looked at Nick. "Jet lag! I'm sorry, it's jet lag. I haven't slept for eighteen hours—it must've affected my brain."

"That's a relief," replied Nick. "For a minute I was worried you'd taken a vow of poverty and were set on becoming a nun or something."

"Oh no," she retorted. "I could never be a nun: those habits they wear are so last century."

He laughed and Angel's hostility faded.

He might be rich and interested in nothing but pleasure, but at least Nick Halliday had a sense of humor. She kind of liked the way he'd dealt with her outburst. He hadn't been angry or unpleasant—just honest.

The waiter put the next course in front of them.

"Oh, wow," said Nick enthusiastically.

"What is it?" asked Angel, staring at her plate. As a waitress she'd seen lots of gourmet food, but she'd never seen this dish.

"It's guinea fowl. Don't look so scared. You'll like it, everyone does."

"I'm not scared," she shot back. "I'm dying to eat it. I've barely eaten a thing today."

"You did have some pâté," Nick reminded her.

"Actually, I think you got most of that," she replied, looking at the dark stain on his lapel. "I should pay for the dry cleaning."

He shook his head and began eating.

Angel followed suit. Nick was right: the food was unlike anything she'd eaten before.

"What do you mean you haven't eaten all day?" asked

Nick suddenly. "Didn't they feed you on the plane?"

"They tried, but I was too nervous to eat."

"Nervous? Why?"

"Oh, you know," said Angel, trying to speak lightly, "coming back to Paris after so long." It wasn't a total lie—they'd flown from Paris when they'd taken Papa to New York.

"Are you glad to be back?" asked Nick.

"I guess. I don't remember much."

"You *were* only five."

He means Lily, she realized and she didn't want to talk about Lily—better to get Nick talking about himself. She said brightly, "And you were . . .?"

"Eight. And thinking I was so grown-up." He shook his head ruefully. "You still ran rings around me, though."

"I did?"

"Sure did. I remember that summer vividly and I remember *you* as a bewitching little girl—full of fun and very feisty." He touched her hand. "Nothing's changed."

Angel blushed. What did he think he was doing? Was he actually thinking he could charm her with anecdotes of some ancient childhood friendship? And what about Yvette? Had he already forgotten his gorgeous girlfriend? That was the trouble with rich guys; they were used to having it all. Angel pulled her hand away and cradled her glass.

"I'm not that girl anymore," she said stiffly.

"No?"

"No. I'm someone *quite* different."

"Not so different that you can't enjoy being back in Paris, I hope," smiled Nick.

"That depends . . ."

"On?"

"Lots of things," replied Angel. Keeping Nick at a distance for one; it'd only complicate an already complicated situation if he decided he wanted to reignite his friendship with the girl he thought was Lily.

Angel swallowed the last morsel of food and stared down at her empty plate. She suppressed a sigh. She'd never imagined deception could be this exhausting.

"*Fortuna favet fortibus*," said Nick.

She looked up. "Pardon me?"

He tapped the crest on the rim of her plate and Angel noticed three tiny gold words beneath it.

"*Fortuna favet fortibus*," he repeated. "It's Latin for 'Fortune favors the bold.' It's the de Tourney family motto."

It was news to Angel, but when she thought of Lily it seemed the perfect slogan.

"It's one of the things the Comtesse tries to instill in us during the summer season." He ran his forefinger over the crest. "Not only that, but other things as well." He frowned. "What I said before—I wasn't serious—the summer season isn't all parties—not in the way you think." Angel followed Nick's gaze down the table to where the Comtesse was listening attentively to her neighbor.

"Your grandmother is an amazing woman. She can seem hard at times and she's ruthlessly principled, but she's also incredibly generous and kind. She just doesn't show her emotions easily."

A family trait, thought Angel.

"She's pleased you're here, you know," added Nick, looking at her.

"Really?" said Angel.

"You mustn't expect her to be gushing. She's from a generation that believes in restraint." He hesitated. "She hoped you'd come. She really wanted to see you."

"But she hasn't contacted Li—*me* for over ten years. Why now?" Angel suddenly wanted to know what had split the de Tourney family in half all those years ago.

"I think she's always wanted to see you, but your father wouldn't allow it."

Angel stared down the table to where the Comtesse had her dinner companions' complete attention. "I can't imagine *her* taking orders from anyone."

"No, she's pretty formidable," agreed Nick. "But she's a wonderful godmother."

Angel looked at him in surprise. "She's your godmother?"

"Yes. We lost touch with your side of the family after your dad left Paris but my parents and the Comtesse have been friends for years."

"So what happened between her and my dad? Did she disinherit him or something?"

"I don't think so. All I know is that your dad and the Comtesse had a big bust-up the summer you turned five. Philip took you to New York and has never been back. As far as I know, they don't even speak."

"That's so sad."

Angel tried to imagine not speaking to her mother for ten years and a wave of guilt swept over her. How long was it since she'd called Sunnydale? She'd rung from JFK, but that was hours ago. What time was it in Florida? Had she missed her scheduled call?

She felt the panic rise as she thought of her mother, so far away. It'd been a near thing, the doctor had said, and Angel hadn't made contact since yesterday. What if she had a relapse—or worse? The thought hammered at her brain and she barely heard Nick's next words.

"I sometimes wonder if that isn't why your grandmother began the summer season. I think she always hoped that one day you'd come to Paris."

He stopped as Angel leapt to her feet. She had to call Sunnydale.

Chapter Fifteen

Angel's sudden movement caught the Comtesse's attention. "Are you all right, Lily?" she asked.

"Yes—that is—I was going to call home . . ." Her voice trailed away as she realized everyone was staring at her.

"Perhaps it can wait until after dessert," said the Comtesse quietly.

Angel sat down.

Dessert came in a delicate teacup and she forced herself to taste it. Nick explained it was Soufflé Pompadour—an orange soufflé baked inside a whole orange. It was delicious, but all Angel could think about was Maman and how soon she could ring her.

Perhaps Nick sensed her anxiety because, for the remainder of the meal, he talked lightheartedly about everything but family.

To her surprise, Angel found it easy to talk to Nick. Once she'd cleared the minefield of questions about school and New York she was able to ask him about life in England. She found out he was going to Oxford in the fall, liked most sports, and that his passion was polo.

They chatted right through the cheese and coffee course but no amount of cheerful banter could allay Angel's anxiety and by ten-thirty she was growing increasingly restless. At last, the Comtesse rose from her chair and conversation faded into expectant silence.

"Tonight's dinner marks the first event of this year's

summer season," she said. "For the next two weeks you young people will have the chance to get to know one another at dances, parties and cultural events. And we older people," she smiled at her friends, "will have the privilege of chaperoning you."

A ripple of laughter went round the table.

She continued. "As you know, most of our events are charity fundraisers providing opportunities for you to help those less fortunate. Naturally, I expect to see you all doing your best to make this our most successful season yet."

"Tomorrow we attend the fashion show. Afterwards the girls may select a gown for the Versailles Ball." There was a burst of excited chatter and the Comtesse held up her hand. "You must all be there before midday, so don't stay out too late tonight."

Everyone laughed and she smiled and sat down. The guests began moving about the room and the buzz of conversation grew louder. It was clear that the formal part of the evening was over; Angel decided she could slip away at last. She rose from her chair and felt Nick's hand on her arm.

"Don't go."

"I have to call home," said Angel. "And I'm super tired."

"Will I see you at the fashion show tomorrow?"

"I don't know, maybe." She met his gaze. His eyes were so dark they were almost black. "I'm not sure what I'm doing tomorrow." *And that's the most truthful thing I've said all day*, she thought, before asking curiously, "Are *you* going to the fashion parade?"

"Absolutely! All the guys go." He grinned. "How else would we know what to wear to the ball?"

"So you'll be wearing a dress?" asked Angel, unable to resist the obvious comeback.

"Definitely . . . not!" he quipped.

"That's a relief," said Angel. "I'll sleep better thinking of you in trousers."

Nick looked triumphant, "Sweet dreams then. It's good to know you'll be thinking of me."

***

Back in her room, Angel put down her mobile with a sigh of relief. Maman was okay. At first she'd been worried because Simone's voice had sounded thin and weak, but the nurse had come on the phone and assured Angel it was normal.

"She's had a big operation, but give her a week or two and she'll be a new woman," she'd said briskly. "Worry-free time, that's what she needs. No stress. If she knows you're all right, we can do the rest."

So Angel had told Simone all about the fabulous time she was having at summer camp. She hated to lie, but it was worth it to hear the relief in Maman's voice.

Angel flopped back on the bed and looked up at the ceiling. Two cherubs holding a lyre laughed down at her. "It's okay for you," she said. "You only have to fly round all day making music and looking cute." She pulled her pillow over her head. "Take a stand," I said. "'Fight the fight.' What *was* I thinking?"

Her phone squealed and she flipped it open.

Lily's voice rang out. "Angel! It's me! Are you okay? How's Paris? Have you met my grandmother? What's she like? Does she think you're me? Have you been to Vidal's yet? Is it wonderful?"

Angel held the phone away from her ear. When Lily finally paused for breath she replied crossly, "No, it isn't wonderful! Your grandmother is terrifying, the house is full of overdressed girls, your old playmate Nick Halliday is here and you forgot about the staff who all remember you and are *so* thrilled you're back!" She sighed. "Except you're not back. It's just me pretending and—I can't do this, Lily."

"Of *course* you can do it!" insisted Lily. "You *are* doing it. Has anyone been suspicious? Asked difficult questions?"

"Not yet," admitted Angel.

"And they won't," declared Lily. "I vaguely remember Dad talking about the Hallidays, but Nick shouldn't be a problem. I shouldn't think he'd even remember me."

"Actually, you seem to have made quite an impression," replied Angel, recalling the sparkle in Nick's eyes as he'd talked about that long-ago summer.

"So you need to avoid him, but that shouldn't be too difficult."

"I don't know, Lily. I think this is going to be harder than we thought. Our plan made sense in New York, but now I'm here I'm not so sure."

"I promise it'll work! Anyway, we're committed and *nothing's* taking me away from the Academy!" There was a note in Lily's voice Angel had never heard before. "Oh, Angel, it's so brilliant here! It's only been a day and already it's amazing. And guess what? The production's going to be *Our Town*—isn't that incredible? I've auditioned for Emily. I know I won't get it, but I'll find out tomorrow."

"I'm happy for you, Lily, I am, but I can't go through with it."

"And what about Clarissa?" demanded Lily. "She *stole* your designs, Angel! *Your* designs! They're sitting at Vidal's with *her* name on them. Is that what you want—for Clarissa to win the Teen Couture with your hard work?"

"Of course not!" replied Angel hotly. "It's just that I think we should tell the Comtesse the truth. If I explain—"

"You'll ruin everything!" cried Lily. "For the both of us! Think of what Clarissa's done—and Simone—what about her? *Please*, Angel, don't tell."

There was a knock at the door. Angel heard Lily say,

"Margot will—" before she closed her phone and shoved it under her pillow.

The Comtesse entered. "Ah, Lily, you are awake."

"Yes." Angel sat up. "I'm glad you came, I need to tell—"

She stopped as the Comtesse flung open the armoire doors and examined the clothes inside.

"Just as I thought. Marie!"

The maid entered the room. "*Oui, Madame?*"

"Everything."

"*Oui, Madame.*" Marie gathered an armful of clothes and carried them away. Angel heard a murmur of voices in the hall before Marie returned for more.

"My clothes, Madame, you can't—"

"You may have them back when you return to America."

America. Angel took a breath. This was it, now or never. "I wanted to talk to you about that."

"My dear, don't let's talk about your leaving when you've only just arrived." The Comtesse smiled. "You are in Paris for the summer season. You are home again." She held out her hands. "And I am delighted to have you, but," she gestured to the closet, "you cannot wear those clothes. Tomorrow we will start afresh: a whole new wardrobe."

Angel stared.

"Did you think I would let my granddaughter wear anything but the best?" asked the Comtesse. "Tomorrow morning we go to Vidal's."

"Antoine Vidal's?" gasped Angel.

"Certainly. We will soon see if he can make anything of you."

Once again the Comtesse seemed unsure of her words. "It is many years since we last met but I wish . . . Now you are here I hope we may make up for lost time." She touched Angel's cheek. "You are my only grandchild and I should like to—"

Angel's phone shrilled from under her pillow. She grabbed it, fumbling for the off button, but the moment was gone.

"I expect it is someone from home." Lily's grandmother looked suddenly constrained. "Call them back and then I suggest you go to sleep. It has been a long day for you. We can talk tomorrow." She touched Angel's cheek again. "We will leave for Vidal's at eleven."

As the door closed, Angel grabbed her phone and punched Lily's number. She picked up instantly.

"You can stop stressing," said Angel. "She's taking me to Vidal's in the morning."

Chapter Sixteen

A ngel woke before ten and was amazed to find she'd slept soundly.

Maybe it was because after talking to Lily she'd decided to stop worrying and just get on with their plan. She was here now and there was no taking that back. It definitely helped that the first step towards swapping her designs had been made so easy. Angel could hardly believe that in a couple of hours she'd actually be inside the House of Vidal.

She jumped out of bed, opened the closet and gazed at the empty space where Lily's clothes had been. She was about to put on yesterday's outfit when there was a knock at the door and Marie came in, carrying a jade linen dress.

"*Excusez-moi*, Mademoiselle Lily, but Madame thought you might like to wear this to Monsieur Vidal's salon."

"Thank you, the Comtesse is very kind."

"She also asks that you meet her downstairs at eleven."

"Okay."

"And when you are ready, *le petit déjeuner*—the breakfast—is downstairs."

"Is the Comtesse waiting for me?"

"Oh no, Mademoiselle Lily. Madame always takes her breakfast in bed."

***

Breakfast was delicious with fresh strawberries, crisp

golden croissants and thick, creamy *chocolat*. The food was freshly prepared and Angel ate slowly, savoring each mouthful.

The breakfast room lay beyond the drawing room and had the same tall French windows opening onto the terrace. Outside Angel could see formal garden beds laid amongst the trees and a gardener trimming a topiary hedge. Neat gravel paths met at a circular fountain in the middle of the lawn and an ornate iron arch curved over the stone steps leading down from the terrace to the garden. Purple wisteria and crimson roses clambered over the arch together, their scent wafting across the breakfast table.

Angel gazed out at the blue sky and sunshine and found it hard to feel anything but hopeful.

The linen dress felt fresh and cool and she remembered what the Comtesse had said about a whole new wardrobe. It was an alluring concept. She glanced at her watch and her pulse quickened.

She was going to Vidal's.

***

The Bentley stopped outside a stately cream-colored building on the Avenue Montaigne. Henri opened the car door and the Comtesse gracefully stepped out. Angel stared at the awning above the windows. Across it, in flowing gold script, were the words: *Antoine Vidal Couturier.*

"Come along, Lily," said the Comtesse briskly. "Let us not keep everyone waiting."

Inside, the decor was all ivory and gold. Great vases of pink-and-white lilies stood on columns along one wall and an elegant marble-topped table served as a desk for a smartly dressed receptionist.

The only sign of the couturier's art was a magnificent black silk evening gown in a glass case. Angel stared in awe; wasn't that the dress Vidal had designed for Princess

Diana? The dress that had catapulted him into superstardom.

She moved closer. She'd only ever seen pictures of it and now here she was in front of one of his greatest creations.

The receptionist rose. "*Bienvenue* Madame de Tourney, welcome, Mademoiselle. Monsieur Vidal is expecting you."

She led them through a door, down a hallway and into a large studio. Angel caught her breath. In the middle of the room, surrounded by models in various stages of undress, was Antoine Vidal.

Beside him several assistants stood ready to take his instructions. Angel saw him beckon to a sultry-looking model in a fitted dress of mauve chiffon and silk. Vidal examined the bodice, the fabric and the zip, then spoke to one of his assistants who instantly whipped out a tape measure and ran it over the dress.

When Vidal saw the Comtesse, his face lit up. "Elena."

Angel's heart thumped as he came towards them. He greeted the Comtesse and turned to her. "So this is your American granddaughter." He took her hand, and frowned. "But surely we have met before?"

Angel's heart skipped a beat. She saw herself lying amongst the broken crockery in the Waldorf Ballroom with Vidal looking down at her. She held her breath. Would he recognize her?

He gazed at her. "Perhaps you have been to one of my shows?"

"I—I'm afraid not, Monsieur."

Suddenly Vidal smiled and clapped his hands. "Ah!" he cried. "It is undoubtedly the resemblance to your *très belle grandmère* that I am seeing. That will be it! Welcome to Vidal's, Mademoiselle Lily."

The Comtesse coughed delicately. "As you see, Antoine, my granddaughter is in need of something to wear."

"Ah." Vidal eyed Angel appraisingly, walked slowly around her, then stepped back and put his hand on his chin.

Angel resisted the urge to pinch herself. Was she dreaming or was Antoine Vidal actually thinking about clothes for *her*? Suddenly, Angel didn't care that she was an imposter. Antoine Vidal was thinking about her! *Antoine Vidal!* Her hero, her inspiration, her idol! She wanted to scream with excitement. Instead, she bit her lip and waited.

Vidal looked at the Comtesse, "You are here for the showing, *n'est-ce pas*?"

She nodded.

"Then we shall see what Mademoiselle Lily likes from the collection before we decide."

The Comtesse looked at him doubtfully and Angel felt sure she was about to explain the imprudence of allowing someone who had worn last night's dress to choose her own wardrobe. But all she said was, "As you wish, Antoine."

They followed Vidal into a large showroom with a catwalk down the center. Around it, rows of chairs were rapidly filling with guests. Among the crowd Angel saw the boys and girls from last night's dinner. They sat in groups, laughing, talking and so at ease that Angel felt a pang of envy. She was wondering where to sit when the Comtesse touched her arm.

"You will like to sit with the other young people." She regarded Angel thoughtfully. "Afterwards we will see if your apparent resemblance to me extends to your taste in clothes." She took Vidal's arm and moved towards a front-row seat.

Angel dreaded the thought of having to approach the girls from last night's dinner. What if they were all like the spiteful redhead? She could see her in the middle of a group—gorgeously attired in a vivid cherry-red jacket and trousers that Angel instantly recognized as Atelier Versace.

Out of the corner of her eye she saw Nick wave and

indicate the empty chair beside him.

Sitting next to Nick was *not* a good idea. He thought she was Lily, the Comtesse's granddaughter, his childhood friend—someone rich and well-connected—consequently Nick was the person most likely to ask difficult questions or trip her up in the lie. Angel pretended not to see. Lily was right—she needed to avoid him. She walked quickly towards the empty chairs in the back row and sat down.

She felt a mixture of disappointment and relief when moments later the lights dimmed. It would've been fun to watch her first real Paris fashion parade with a friend—someone she could talk to afterwards about the clothes. Of course, she'd love every minute of the show, but it would be nice to share it with someone.

The lights came up on the catwalk and Angel leaned forward eagerly just as a girl appeared in the aisle.

"Excuse me," she whispered. "Can I sit there?" She indicated the empty chair beside Angel.

"Sure." Angel leaned back to let her go by.

"Thanks a bunch," said the girl and Angel caught the twang of an American accent. She had time to take in a cloud of curly black hair and a plump, curvaceous figure, before the lights dimmed and music signalled the start of the show.

For the next two hours Angel sat mesmerized as Vidal's models paraded up and down the catwalk. Each garment seemed to have been designed with youth and beauty in mind. Nothing was too severe or formal or stiff. Angel could only watch in awe as each new garment outdid the one before.

She'd just decided that nothing could ever exceed the rapture of Vidal's evening wear, when the ball gowns appeared. Angel sat there, drinking in the details, as one exquisite dress followed another. It was like being filled with an emotion she'd always known existed, but had never experienced until now.

This must be what it feels like to have a dream come true, she thought, as she watched a Titian-haired model in a heavily embroidered indigo and copper gown turn and slowly walk down the catwalk.

And then, it was ending. The star model paraded the wedding gown that traditionally closed fashion shows and Vidal made his bow to fervent applause. The lights came up and Angel leaned back in her chair with a contented sigh just as the girl beside her groaned.

"What's the matter?" asked Angel.

Her neighbor raised a pair of mournful brown eyes and held up a notebook. "I made notes to help me remember which dresses to look at after the show, but I was writing in the dark and now I can't read it!"

She thrust the book at Angel who could just make out the words: "beads, sleeves, lace" and something that looked like "silver" but could easily have been "golden."

"Can I help?"

"I don't think so," replied the girl candidly.

"I'm sorry," said Angel. "I didn't mean—"

"That's okay. I just don't have a talent for this sort of thing. Although you'd think it would run in the family . . ."

"Right," said Angel, confused.

"Mum was Astride Roget," explained the girl. "She was Vidal's favorite house model and this is where my dad first saw her. He says it was like being struck by lightning: Mum came down the catwalk and that was it. We used to live in Paris—until she died. Now we live in Texas, but Dad likes to come back every year and think about her." She sighed. "Most years it's great, but this year . . . I don't know."

"What's wrong with this year?" asked Angel.

"Dad and I always come to the fashion shows, but I prefer horses so he never minds that I'm not interested in dresses. But this year he's set on me going to the Versailles Ball, which means I have to pick out a ball gown."

"How exciting—" Angel stopped. Her acquaintance looked anything but excited. "Isn't it?"

The girl shook her head. "It might be if I wasn't five-foot-three and fat with awful curly hair."

"You're not fat," said Angel. "You're curvy. And your hair's gorgeous. With the right dress—"

"There *is* no right dress!" cried the girl. "That's the whole problem. You saw those models. How could I ever wear one of those gowns?" She looked so much like a sad puppy that Angel almost wanted to pat her.

"Well," said Angel slowly, "this is Vidal's. I mean, he's one of the great designers."

"Sure, so long as you're six-foot-five and skinny."

"No," replied Angel. "That's the point. Vidal's clients come in all shapes and sizes. He can make anyone look good—" She stopped, flustered at how it had sounded. "That is, I didn't mean . . ."

The girl laughed. "It's okay. I know what you mean." She held out her hand, "I'm Kitty."

"I'm A—" Angel caught herself just in time. "A guest of the Comtesse de Tourney. I'm her . . . her granddaughter, Lily."

"Oh, wow. I heard you were coming over for the summer season. So you'll be picking out a dress for the Versailles Ball, too."

"Maybe." Angel tried to imagine wearing a Vidal gown; it was beyond her wildest dreams.

"So we could look at them together?" asked Kitty.

"What?"

"We could look at the dresses together, if you wanted, I mean . . ." Kitty looked at Angel uncertainly.

Angel smiled. "I'd love to."

"Really?"

"Totally."

Kitty grabbed her hand. "Come on," she said, and dragged Angel from the room.

Kitty led her into a long corridor. On either side, through heavy glass doors, Angel could see people working on Vidal's creations. Here were the workrooms and design studios she'd always longed to see.

She slowed down for a closer look but Kitty was tugging on her hand, pulling her towards a door at the end of the hall.

It opened and a man emerged pulling a rack hung with garment bags, each tied with a large colored label. Behind him a woman carried a pile of colored folders.

Angel and Kitty stood aside to let them pass and watched as the man dragged the rack into one of the studios. The woman followed, shutting the door firmly behind her.

"That'll be the last of the Teen Couture entries," said Kitty.

Angel's heart nearly leapt out of her chest.

"No way!" she gasped. "Can we see?" She ran back to the door and peered through the glass.

"Nuh-uh," Kitty said beside her. "Only Vidal and his personal assistants are allowed in there. Those two will be getting ready for the cull."

"What do you mean—the cull?" asked Angel, transfixed.

"The assistants go through the entries and eliminate anything that isn't good enough or doesn't meet the rules. Usually about half of what's entered is culled."

"Half?" echoed Angel.

"Sometimes more than half."

"Whoa, that's tough," whispered Angel, wondering if her designs would be among those eliminated. Half-fascinated, half-fearful, she asked, "What happens then?"

Kitty shrugged. "They do the cull Thursday and Friday and judging begins on Monday. Monsieur Vidal and his assistants go over each entry with a fine-tooth comb. They examine the cut and stitching, look at the designs and check them against the finished garments. By Wednesday of next week they'll have notified the six finalists in time for the big announcement at the Versailles Ball." She tugged Angel's hand. "Let's go. Better to get there before the others."

But Angel was mesmerized. The woman had handed the man a purple folder to check against the matching purple label on the garment bag. He nodded, unzipped the bag and put the folder inside. As he withdrew his hand a flurry of silken fabric billowed from the opening.

Angel gasped. *Green and white silk!* She'd recognize it anywhere—Clarissa's copy of her dress.

Without thinking, she grasped the door handle and turned it. The woman looked up and frowned, then crossed to the door, locked it and pulled down the blind.

"Come on," said Kitty.

Reluctantly, Angel turned and followed her down the hall.

Chapter Seventeen

K itty led Angel into a large workroom with racks that held the garments from the show. In the center of the room Vidal and the Comtesse stood talking to the models.

"Ah, Lily. And Kitty." The Comtesse turned to greet them.

To Angel's surprise, Kitty ran eagerly across the room and in perfect French said, "Hello Madame," before turning to Vidal. "Congratulations Monsieur Vidal, the ball gowns were superb."

He smiled down at her. "*Merci, tu es très gentille,* Kitty." He looked around. "But where is your papa?"

Kitty laughed, looked at Angel, and said in English, "You know Dad never stays after a show. But it's okay because I found a new friend."

She pulled Angel beside her. "We watched the show together."

"And did you see anything you liked?" asked the Comtesse, looking at Angel.

"Everything," breathed Angel rapturously.

The Comtesse raised her eyebrows. "And did you think that everything would suit you?"

"Oh no, I mean, that is, I thought—" Angel stopped and smiled shyly at Vidal. "It was all wonderful and I'd love to own every bit of it. But," she considered, "if I *had* to choose, I'd pick nine outfits."

"Only nine?" The Comtesse looked amused.

Angel flushed and bit her lip. She'd forgotten to be Lily! She'd been so excited at seeing the show and meeting Antoine Vidal that she'd spoken as herself. It seemed amazing they couldn't see the guilt on her face and it was fortunate they couldn't read her mind because if they knew about her plan to swap her designs—Angel didn't even want to think about it.

"And Lily is going to help me choose a dress to wear to the ball," explained Kitty gleefully.

"Really?" said the Comtesse. There was no mistaking the skepticism in her voice. "And what would you recommend, Lily?"

Angel looked at her uncertainly. The Comtesse was pointing to the long silver rack hung with Vidal's beautiful ball gowns.

"Oh, no," she stuttered. "I couldn't."

"Why don't you show us?" the Comtesse insisted.

As if in a dream, Angel moved towards the rack.

About three feet away she stopped and looked doubtfully at the fragile organzas, the delicate laces, the intricately beaded panels, hand-embroidered bodices and exquisite silks, satins and velvets.

"It's all right," said Vidal. "You can lift them down by their hangers. Put them here." He pointed to an empty rack beside him.

Angel considered the dresses. She remembered each one, as if they'd been burned into her brain. Gathering her courage, she walked over to the rack and lifted down an amaranth-red silk dress.

Carrying it over to Kitty she tried to think of the sorts of sophisticated phrases she might use to explain her choice to a world famous couturier, but her mind was blank. She could see the doubtful amusement on Vidal's and the Comtesse's faces, while Kitty just smiled expectantly.

Taking courage from Kitty's smile, Angel held the dress against her new friend and said quickly, "This color suits

Kitty's hair and complexion, the cut draws the eye lengthwise and it's not too full in the skirt."

Vidal and the Comtesse exchanged glances.

"Go on," said the Comtesse.

Ignoring her over-rapid pulse, Angel hung up the dress, returned to the main rack and took down a beaded silver gown. Returning to Kitty she tried to speak more slowly.

"This is a great style and color for Kitty, but there's a little too much beading for her height and the skirt is stiffer than I'd like for her."

Angel hung the dress and walked slowly along the main rack until she reached an ice-blue satin gown. She lifted it down and held it against Kitty.

"This is what I'd choose for you. It's the perfect cut for your figure and the fabric moves beautifully. The cinched-in waist will be flattering and the color is gorgeous. Although," Angel hesitated. "Perhaps a shade darker?"

Vidal stared at her, but before anyone could speak, the door burst open and the summer season group poured into the room.

In a moment Angel found herself on the edge of a cluster of girls all vying for Vidal's and the Comtesse's attention. And the boys were just as vocal, pointing out the dresses they admired and arguing about which gown was best.

Kitty called several girls over to show them the three dresses Angel had selected, before joining the group around the Comtesse. Angel stood back as the girls drew the Comtesse across to the rack of ball gowns and plied her with questions.

Vidal had been commandeered by the redhead and her cronies and Angel watched them pointing to the dresses and talking eagerly to him in French.

She considered the noisy, swirling mass of people for a moment and then slipped quietly away.

Walking quickly down the hall she reached the Teen

Couture room. She tried the door but it was locked. There had to be a way in. Angel peered into the room next door. It was a large, empty workroom. She went in and closed the door behind her.

Angel thought of the films where the hero gets from room to room by crawling through the ceiling ducts. She looked up. There were vents, just like in the movies, and in the corner was one of those hatch things. Angel had a sudden vision of herself dressed in black, her face darkened, slithering commando-style through the ducts.

It was a ridiculous picture.

She picked her way between the workbenches to the wall separating her from the Teen Couture room. Numerous rolls of cloth had been placed against the wall and, incredibly, half-hidden behind them was a door.

Angel ran over and was moving the first roll when she heard voices in the hall. Quickly, she darted across the room and pressed herself into the space behind the door. To her relief, the voices grew softer, a door closed and there was silence.

Perspiration trickled down her back. What was she going to do? She didn't have a proper plan. Opening the door, she peeked out. No one was in sight. She stepped into the hall, ran back to the Teen Couture room and tried the door handle just in case. It was still locked.

Angel pressed her forehead against the glass and sighed. This wasn't going to be easy.

Someone tapped her on the shoulder and Angel shrieked. She spun round. Nick Halliday smiled down at her.

"Looking for something?"

Angel tried to breathe. "You gave me such a fright!"

"There speaks a guilty conscience." He nodded at the locked room. "Trying to work out the winner? You could always ask me."

She gazed at him doubtfully. "Do you know?"

"That depends." He leaned closer.

Angel found herself at eye level with the point where Nick's shirt opened to reveal a triangle of chest. She could see his skin, smooth and tanned, and smell the tantalizing scent of his aftershave. Her heart drummed and she was aware that it was no longer fright that made it beat so fast.

She tried to focus. "Depends on what?" she asked carelessly.

"On whether you'll let me be your escort."

"My escort?" she asked, bewildered.

"For the summer season. It's your first. Who better than me to help you through it?"

"What about Yvette?"

"Who?"

Typical, thought Angel. *Why do guys always pretend they've forgotten all about their girlfriend?*

"Yvette Saint-Gilbert," said Angel silkily. "You know, at the airport, your girlfriend."

"Oh, she's not my girlfriend," replied Nick easily. "She's a friend. We're in the same class at school and she's dating one of my chums." His eyes twinkled. "I don't have a girlfriend at the moment, but it's nice to know you're interested."

"I'm not!" Angel glared at him and pushed away the vision of sitting beside Nick at a fashion show or walking hand in hand with him along the Seine. *He thinks you're Lily*, she reminded herself firmly—*granddaughter of a comtesse—someone from his own world*. Angel was an imposter and she couldn't let Nick escort an imposter around Paris. It wouldn't be fair. She stepped away. "Thanks for the offer, but I'll be fine on my own."

Nick looked at her in mock horror. "Paris on your own—that's practically blasphemy. In fact, I wouldn't be surprised if there were a law against it."

Angel couldn't help smiling.

Nick took her hand. "Let me show you the city of light. I

know places in Paris the tourists never go."

She gently withdrew her hand. "Thanks, but I'd rather fly solo."

"Think of the fun we'd have," he said. "It'd be like old times, only without the tiara."

Angel shook her head. She was turning him down for his sake as well as her own. She couldn't risk getting close to Nick Halliday.

"There you are, Lily," the Comtesse's voice floated down the corridor. "You disappeared and we need to . . . Ah, Nicky."

She stopped in front of him and held out her hand. He took it and bowed. The old-fashioned gesture brought an affectionate twinkle to her eye.

Nick straightened and the Comtesse shook a reproving finger at him, "I trust you are not leading my granddaughter into mischief, Nicky?"

"Darling Godmother, how can you think such a thing?" He glanced at Angel. "I'm merely trying to convince Lily to let me be her escort for the summer season. Please tell her I'd be the ideal partner, Godmother. I know you can persuade her."

The Comtesse looked at him and then Angel, who was astonished to see her mouth lift into a wicked little smile.

"An excellent idea, Nicky," said the Comtesse, holding up her hand to silence Angel's protests. "My dear, you will enjoy seeing Paris with Nicky. He knows the city well and he will, how do you say it in America? Guarantee your inclusion in the group."

Angel gazed at her. It was an impossible situation but only she knew that. The fact was that she needed them to think she was Lily and, so far, they did. She looked from the Comtesse to Nick and made a decision. For good or ill, for the next two weeks, she'd be Lily—only she'd be the *Angel* version of Lily. She'd play out the masquerade just as she'd promised, but she wouldn't try to *be* Lily anymore, she'd just be herself and if Nick wanted to reminisce about the past, she'd just have to find a way to distract him . . .

"All right," she said.

"*Bon*," said the Comtesse. "That is settled. Nicky will be your escort, Lily. He will show you Paris and guide you through the summer season."

"Starting tonight," said Nick.

"Tonight?" cried Angel.

"Not tonight, Nicky," interjected the Comtesse. "Lily is in urgent need of a new wardrobe. We have a great deal of shopping to do before we go to *Casa Fortuna* tomorrow afternoon. Tomorrow night will be soon enough."

"I'll pick you up at eight then," said Nick.

"Perfect," said the Comtesse. "Now, Lily, we must not keep Antoine waiting any longer. *Au revoir*, Nicky."

She held out her hand. Angel hesitated, then slowly reached out and took it. As they walked back to the salon, she glanced over her shoulder.

Nick was still standing there, watching her go.

Chapter Eighteen

It was evening when the Bentley pulled up outside the villa. Angel had thought she would still feel anxious and exhausted; instead she felt like she'd been given wings and taught how to fly.

When she and the Comtesse had returned to the salon, Vidal had been waiting for them. He'd immediately asked Angel which gown she wished to wear.

She'd stared at him blankly until the Comtesse had said crisply, "Don't be shy, Lily. Monsieur Vidal only wants to know your choice of gown for the Versailles Ball."

"Gown?"

"Certainly," replied the Comtesse. "We must choose your ball gown today in order to allow time for your fittings."

"Fittings?"

Vidal nodded. "But *naturellement*, Mademoiselle Lily. You will need several fittings between now and the ball."

The Comtesse looked at Vidal. "I believe the first is on Wednesday?"

"*Oui.*"

"Do not worry, my dear," said the Comtesse. "The fittings will not interfere with the season. They do not take long and Henri will bring you if I have another engagement."

The Comtesse had completely misread Angel's expression. She wasn't thinking about the summer season, but about her designs. Regular fittings meant she needn't try to get into the locked room today. The cull didn't begin until Thursday and she'd be back here on Wednesday.

So that meant, for now at least, she could push all thought of the Teen Couture from her mind and give Antoine Vidal her complete attention.

To her amazement he'd stayed with them for nearly an hour discussing ball gowns. Angel had quickly discovered that he and the Comtesse had definite opinions about what she should wear to the Versailles Ball. Before long, she'd found herself in the middle of a strange kind of haute couture tug-of-war.

The three of them had been looking at the ball gowns when the Comtesse had lifted down a beautiful amethyst organza dress with a skirt like whipped meringue. She'd held it against Angel, nodded in a pleased kind of way and called out to Vidal, *"Regardes Antoine, c'est parfaite."*

To Angel's astonishment, instead of agreeing it was perfect, Vidal had rolled his eyes, slapped his fist into his palm and cried aloud, *"Non! Non! Certainement pas!"*

He'd then paced along the row of dresses, taken down a stunning chocolate-brown dress made of silk tulle and lace with a high, sheer neckline, and thrust it towards the Comtesse who had sniffed and turned her face away in disgust.

After that it had become a sort of contest as they lifted down dress after dress, holding them against Angel and extolling their virtues only to have the other pronounce it the wrong style, the wrong color or the wrong fabric.

Angel drank in every word.

The Comtesse had been holding a magnificent bronze shantung gown while Vidal argued the case for a delicately beaded pink satin dress with an embroidered train, when Angel had suddenly seen the gleam in his eye and the Comtesse's wicked little smile and realized they were enjoying themselves!

She'd suppressed a sudden urge to laugh. Who'd have

guessed that beneath the Comtesse's cool exterior lay such passion and humor? What had Nick said about his godmother's restraint? Well, she might maintain it with most people, but not with Antoine Vidal.

And he was just as bad.

But the amazing thing was that they were both right.

When Angel thought about the dresses they'd chosen and the things they'd said she realized that she was in the presence of two people with impeccable fashion sense and the visual equivalent of perfect pitch when it came to clothes.

But she still couldn't let them pick her dress for her.

If being Lily de Tourney meant she got to wear an Antoine Vidal ball gown, then Angel was determined to choose it herself.

She turned to them. "Would it be all right, do you think . . ."

They'd both looked at her and she'd managed to ask, "May I show you what I like?"

Vidal had smiled at the Comtesse and said, "Well, Elena, what do you think?"

And the Comtesse had smiled back at him. "An excellent idea, Antoine."

Then they'd hung up the bronze gown and the pink dress and sat down and waited.

Angel had moved slowly along the rack of ball gowns, before turning to Vidal and the Comtesse. "Although every gown is beautiful, I know only a few would look good on me because ultimately it's all about line, cut and color." She saw them glance at each other and added seriously, "You can't be a slave to fashions. You have to find your own style."

Vidal nodded.

"I want a gown I will always remember and I think this is it."

She lifted down a dress with a full skirt of deep crimson duchesse satin. The long-sleeved bodice was made from clinging black wool crepe and designed to wrap sinuously around the torso, leaving the shoulders exposed. The black fabric met the crimson satin at the waist where it was encircled by a heavy black satin sash. Two long black satin ribbons fell like shards of ebony against the ruby sheen of the skirt.

The dress was a masterpiece of simplicity in design and stunning in its effect.

Angel held the dress in front of her and stood looking shyly out over the bodice at them.

For a moment there was silence and then Vidal leapt to his feet and cried, *"Mais oui, c'est ça!* You are right, *ma petite.* Your taste is excellent." He turned to the Comtesse. "Is it not so, Elena? I think perhaps Mademoiselle Lily has her grandmother's eye for a dress, after all."

"You may be right, Antoine," replied the Comtesse. "Certainly she seems able to choose a ball gown."

Vidal glanced at his watch. "I must leave you to attend another client—the daughter of a Spanish prince." To Angel's surprise, he lifted her hand and kissed it. "Sadly, she does not have your taste in gowns," he said, then turned to the Comtesse. "I have no doubt, Elena, that if you allow her to do so, your granddaughter will successfully choose her own clothes."

As soon as he'd gone, a *vendeuse*—a saleswoman—had appeared. After the Comtesse had asked Angel about the outfits she'd liked from the collection, the woman had hurried away to get them. When she returned, the Comtesse examined them and ordered them all to be made in Angel's size.

Then a fitter and a seamstress had carefully measured her, before conferring over whether the hem of her ball gown should be allowed to brush the floor. Angel had never felt so wonderful. She was going to the Versailles Ball.

When they'd finished at Vidal's the Comtesse had whisked Angel off to a nearby café for a late lunch.

At first, she'd felt shy being alone with Lily's grandmother and worried that she'd want to hear all about Philip and Lily's life in New York. But the Comtesse had seemed content to talk mostly about fashion and they'd spent a whole hour discussing the finer details of cut, style and design.

By the time they'd finished eating they'd moved their conversation to designers. Angel had been thrilled to discover that the Comtesse had actually known Alexander McQueen—Angel's favorite designer after Vidal—and adored his controversial approach to fashion and his love of spectacle. The Comtesse had been to all his shows and clearly admired his clothes.

"His death was one of the great tragedies," she told Angel. "For he was a true genius and I doubt I shall see his like again."

After lunch they'd gone shopping at *Galeries Lafayette* (which Angel decided was the French equivalent of Saks Fifth Avenue) and bought what the Comtesse insisted on calling "the basics."

By the time they returned to the car, Angel had lost track of all the shirts, pants, skirts, lingerie, hats and shoes that Henri had loaded into the trunk. She wondered how he'd managed to fit it all in.

They'd driven home in comfortable silence—Angel too elated to talk and the Comtesse apparently content to gaze out the window.

It was only when they'd been driven through the wrought-iron gates of the villa that the Comtesse spoke. "It has been a long day, but I hope you have enjoyed it."

"I have!" replied Angel. "It's a dream come true." She stopped, suddenly unsure if Lily would react so enthusiastically. Perhaps rich people didn't get excited about buying a whole new wardrobe. Angel was relieved to see the Comtesse smile.

"I'm glad," replied the Comtesse. "Tomorrow we will

purchase some suitable *prêt-à-porter*. There are several boutiques where I hope we may find some dresses you can wear immediately." She frowned. "I think you will not mind buying some 'off-the-rack' as you say in America."

"Oh no, Madame," replied Angel earnestly. "But I don't need any more clothes. You've already bought me too much."

"Too much?" The Comtesse looked at her in astonishment. "I do not think so. While you are in Paris it is imperative that you dress appropriately. The summer season demands a certain style and naturally you will wish to look good at every event. And tomorrow night Nicky will be escorting you to dinner."

The thought of dinner with Nick brought a blush to Angel's cheeks.

The Comtesse smiled. "You will not mind going out to dinner with Nicky if you have something nice to wear, Lily."

Before Angel could reply, the car had stopped and Henri was helping the Comtesse out.

As they entered the house Marcel hurried forward. "The President's office called, Madame," he said. "*Monsieur le Président* apologizes for the late notice but begs the pleasure of your company at the Petit Palais this evening. It seems the Russians have decided to attend after all, so you will understand why he requires your presence."

The Comtesse sighed and turned to Angel. "Lily, my dear, will you mind dining alone tonight?"

"No, Madame. Actually, I'd be happy to eat in the kitchen." The look on the Comtesse's face told her that this was going too far. "Or a tray in my room?"

To her relief, the Comtesse smiled. "Yes, I think a tray in your room would be acceptable. Marcel."

"*Oui*, Madame?"

"Tell chef to prepare a tray for Mademoiselle Lily. She will eat her dinner in bed."

"In bed?" exclaimed Angel.

"Why not? I have breakfast in bed, so why should you not have dinner in bed?" asked the Comtesse. "Are you not *fatiguée*?"

Angel nodded. "I am a bit tired."

"That is not surprising. But a good day, I think?"

"Oh, yes, Madame!" Angel's voice was filled with enthusiasm. "A magical day! The best day of my life! Meeting Monsieur Vidal, seeing his collection, choosing a ball gown, shopping—I will remember it always." She met the older woman's gaze and added shyly, "I don't know how to thank you, Madame."

"I need no thanks," replied the Comtesse. "But, if you could call me Grandmama—that would be perfectly acceptable."

Chapter Nineteen

The Comtesse's request echoed in Angel's ears all the way up to her bedroom.

"She wants me to call her Grandmama," she whispered, running up the stairs. "Lily never thought of that."

That was the trouble with deception—people could imagine how it would be, but the vision never matched reality. It was only when you were inside the lie that you found out just how difficult and complicated it was.

Angel sighed as she passed the portraits of Lily's ancestors. What had Nick told her about the de Tourney family motto? Fortune Favors the Bold? Well, she wasn't a de Tourney but she'd been both bold *and* lucky in her lie so far.

She entered her bedroom and found her phone. She'd left it behind in case Lily rang. It would've been disastrous to get a call from the person she was meant to be.

So many lies, thought Angel, collapsing onto the bed. And now I have to tell my mother a whole bunch more.

She dialled the number for Sunnydale.

It was a relief to hear Maman's voice. Simone sounded a little stronger and she assured Angel that she was being treated like royalty. Angel told her how great camp was, assured her she was eating well and promised to call again tomorrow.

She closed her phone, pulled on her new silk pajamas and climbed into bed just as Marie knocked and entered with a large wooden tray. "Your dinner, Mademoiselle Lily." She put the tray across Angel's lap.

"*Merci*, Marie."

Maybe it was because Maman sounded better or maybe it was the novelty, but Angel enjoyed her first-ever meal in bed. The chef had sent up a delicious roast chicken dinner with a chocolate torte and fresh raspberries for dessert.

After Marie had taken the tray away Angel lay back in the great bed, looked up at the painted ceiling, and thought about the day.

"I should be feeling *so* bad and super guilty," she told a pair of cherubs, "but I don't. Pretending to be Lily meant I got to go to Vidal's." She shut her eyes and remembered that incredible parade of ball gowns, each one as colorful and real as if they were in front of her.

Sure, she was a fraud, but at this moment she found it hard to care. Her mother was getting better and Angel had just had *the* best day of her life! She'd actually *met* Antoine Vidal and talked to him about fashion.

Angel smiled. "And he liked the ball gown I chose," she announced to a faun looking down at her from his painted corner. "He told me I had better taste than a Spanish princess." She reached up towards Helios in his chariot. "And Antoine Vidal kissed my hand."

But it wasn't just Vidal who had made the day so perfect. For the first time in her life Angel had met someone who felt as passionately about fashion as she did. When it came to clothes the Comtesse was definitely a kindred spirit. At first Angel had felt horribly guilty that Lily's grandmother was buying her so many new clothes, but the Comtesse's obvious pleasure in finding just the right things for her to wear had swamped her protests.

She could hardly believe she had a whole new wardrobe *and* the most divine dress to wear to the Versailles Ball.

Margot had told Lily it was the most sought-after event on a girl's social calendar and Angel Moncoeur, housekeeper's daughter, was going. If Clarissa Kane knew that, she'd be sick with envy.

But Clarissa must never know, thought Angel, sitting up with a jerk.

What was she thinking? This was no fairytale. This was a brief, magical interlude in an otherwise ordinary life. She'd let herself enjoy it because that was what she'd decided yesterday at Vidal's.

But she *had* to remember that the masquerade would only succeed if she didn't fall into the trap of thinking of herself as some kind of modern-day Cinderella. At the end of this story there'd be no fairy godmother, no prince, and no happy ending. When the Versailles Ball was over she'd leave her new clothes in the closet, say goodbye to the Comtesse, and go home.

Home to New York and back to her old life where all of this splendor would be nothing more than a beautiful memory.

Angel lay down again. At least she could try to enjoy the time she had now. What had Nick said? The summer season meant parties and other fun stuff. That shouldn't be too hard to take. She'd already been to Vidal's—imagine what they might do over the next ten days.

She had a sudden vision of herself at the ball dancing with Nick.

No, not him. Someone else. She was sure to meet some of the other boys during the summer season; maybe one of them would ask her to dance.

She pushed Nick from her mind and thought about the ball. It was where Antoine Vidal would announce the winner of the Teen Couture.

If only Angel's entry stood a chance.

Clarissa's entry, she reminded herself sharply. At least, that's what it says on the entry form. And if Clarissa makes the finals then she'll be at the Versailles Ball and so will Margot.

And then I will be in trouble, thought Angel, horrified at the idea of Clarissa at the ball. She could see her now, swirling round the floor in Angel's midnight-blue velvet ball gown with the silver . . . Her stomach flipped. Whatever happened, Clarissa must not attend the Versailles Ball!

Angel balled her hands into fists. Margot and Clarissa would not win—not if she could help it—and that meant getting hold of Clarissa's forged entry as soon as possible.

She smoothed the sheet across her chest and tried to think calmly. What had Kitty said? The cull would be finished by Friday and Vidal would begin judging on Monday. Angel had a fitting at Vidal's on Wednesday. She'd have to get into the Teen Couture room then.

It was a pity Lily hadn't managed to pack her Teen Couture garments, but it couldn't be helped. The most important thing was to swap the entry form and designs. She'd need to get into the empty workroom, find a way past the bolts of cloth and open the connecting door. That way she could get into the Teen Couture room without anyone knowing.

"Get in, swap them, and get out," she told the ceiling. From now on that had to be the sole focus of her stay in Paris.

But not until Wednesday. *I've still got one day*, she thought, snuggling down under the covers. *Tomorrow I'm going shopping with the Comtesse, who understands the importance of cut and line when buying clothes.*

It must be nice to be rich, she decided, trying not to yawn.

Her eyelids were drooping and she kept seeing herself dressed all in black and dropping from a cable into the Teen Couture room. Just like Tom Cruise in *Mission Impossible*, she thought sleepily.

"Silly," murmured Angel. "You should never wear all black."

A moment later she was asleep.

***

The next morning passed like some kind of delicious dream. Angel and the Comtesse left the house just before nine and returned at lunchtime a little weary, but pleased with their shopping.

They'd brought home half a dozen gorgeous dresses; each of them bought off-the-rack, just as the Comtesse had said. From Oscar de la Renta's, Vivienne Westwood's and Elie Saab's *prêt-à-porter* collections. The clothes were unspeakably lovely and several times Angel had to pinch herself to make sure she was awake.

Now she and the Comtesse had returned to the villa for lunch. The great mahogany table had been reduced to more reasonable proportions and the Comtesse sat at its head eating delicately, with Angel on her right.

"We must leave straight after lunch, Lily," said the Comtesse as the main course was cleared. "We are due at Monsieur Martinez's by two." She studied Angel's silk shirt and Altuzarra pants. "You will wish to change. I think perhaps the red vintage Versace dress."

From the way the Comtesse said his name, Angel got the impression that Monsieur Martinez was someone she was meant to know about.

"And your shoes." The Comtesse looked at Angel's feet. "The patent leather pumps we bought yesterday will match well. This is an important afternoon, Lily. You will wish to look good. *Bon chic, bon genre*: that is the rule."

Right style, right sort, thought Angel, translating in her head. Well, right style was no problem after all their shopping, but as for being the right sort . . .

"I expect your father has told you that before?"

"What?" Angel was startled. For a moment she thought the Comtesse meant Papa and then she remembered. "Yes, he has."

"Good." The Comtesse said, then added hesitantly, "Philip is well?"

"Yes."

"And busy?"

"Very busy."

"But he makes time for you, I hope?" asked the Comtesse, frowning.

"Absolutely!" replied Angel, relieved she could speak honestly about Lily's dad. "Philip, I mean, Dad's away a lot, but when he's home we spend heaps of time together. Weekends at the Hamptons, the beach, the country club." She paused, trying to think. "Oh, and Meadowbrook. I always watch Dad play polo there—we love polo."

"I am glad," said the Comtesse in a stilted voice. "Your father always played polo here, before . . ." She fingered the gold chain around her neck. "Do you know, I think I will take a short rest before we leave."

Angel looked at her in concern. Was the Comtesse a little pale or was it just her imagination? She thought of Maman and how she'd ignored her pain and ended up needing emergency surgery.

Angel put her hand gently on the Comtesse's arm. "Are you all right, Madame?"

The Comtesse straightened. *"Bien sûr*—I'm fine. Just not as young as I once was." She patted Angel's hand. "A short rest will help."

"Yes, Madame."

The Comtesse smiled. "And I think it would help if you remembered my request."

"Madame?" replied Angel, puzzled. Then she remembered. She hesitated for a moment and then said softly, "Yes, Grandmama."

Chapter Twenty

It was almost two when they arrived at a large house beside *Parc Monceau*. As they got out of the car the front door opened and a dapper-looking man with glossy black hair and a neat moustache came out to greet them. He wore an exquisitely tailored suit with a silver bow tie and a tiny red rosebud in his buttonhole.

"Elena." He spoke with a marked accent. Not French, Angel thought. Perhaps Spanish. "You are just in time," he smiled.

The Comtesse made the introductions. "Lily, this is Señor Martinez, the famous Spanish master who will be teaching you. Felix, my granddaughter, Lily."

He clapped his hands, "Delightful! Welcome to *Casa Fortuna*, my home away from home."

Angel managed a smile. Being introduced as Lily made her uncomfortable and she was dying to ask what Señor Martinez taught, but before she could speak he had swept them inside and down a wide entry hall lined with sculptures. There was no time to admire the white marble figures before they were ushered into a huge empty room with a polished parquetry floor. A row of high-backed gilt chairs lined one wall and above them an enormous mirror reflected the room's glittering chandeliers and gold-inlaid panelling with such clarity that Angel was dazzled.

"We are here!" pronounced Señor Martinez, throwing his hands wide.

"So shall we begin?" asked the Comtesse.

"At once," replied the Spaniard. "Ready?" he asked Angel.

"Ready?"

"To dance." And to Angel's astonishment, he executed a series of rapid steps, spun a perfect pirouette and stopped with his hands outflung.

The Comtesse clapped and said, "Felix was five times world champion you know. He is the most sought-after dance teacher in Europe."

"Not Europe, Elena," corrected Señor Martinez, "the world! And now I have the honor of teaching your granddaughter, the charming Mademoiselle Lily." He clicked his heels together and smiled at Angel, who tried to smile back.

"Don't look so worried, my dear," said the Comtesse. "Felix will give your dancing a polish before the Versailles Ball. A lesson here, a lesson there—you will enjoy them."

Angel eyed her doubtfully. She'd known there'd be dancing at the Versailles Ball—it was a ball, after all—but she'd thought she'd get by with the basics. And it wasn't that she didn't know how to dance—she knew how to waltz and last year she and Taylor and Katie had done Latin and ballroom as an after-school extra; she just wouldn't have said she was an expert.

"I am sure Mademoiselle Lily will learn quickly," pronounced Señor Martinez. He beckoned to the butler standing discreetly by the door. "Bring a chair for Madame la Comtesse. I will call the others."

"The others?" asked Angel.

But Señor Martinez was already gliding to the far end of the room where he threw open a pair of tall doors artfully concealed in the panelling.

A burst of warm air billowed into the room and Angel found herself looking into an enormous conservatory. Palm trees rose up to a domed glass ceiling and tropical plants filled the room. People wandered among the greenery and

Angel saw Kitty sitting on a rustic seat talking to a handsome blond boy, while beside a large potted fern the redheaded girl stood chatting to Nick.

Angel's heart seemed to rise and sink in the same moment as she realized it was the summer season group, and she would not be dancing alone.

Señor Martinez clapped his hands. "Come along everyone, time to begin."

Laughing and talking, they poured into the ballroom. Angel stood aside as they spread out across the parquetry floor. Everyone seemed to know exactly what to do and Angel was trying to figure out where to go when Kitty grabbed her.

"Lily!" She threw her arms around Angel. "I couldn't find you yesterday and I wanted to thank you."

"Thank me?"

"For helping me choose a dress. Dad was *so* excited—he said it reminded him of Mum."

"Which one did you choose?" asked Angel, pleased to see Kitty so happy.

"The ice-blue satin—you said it was the best."

"It's true. You'll look gorgeous in it."

Kitty linked her arm through Angel's. "And Monsieur Vidal ordered it to be made a shade darker—just like you said."

Angel halted. "You're kidding!"

"Nuh-uh," Kitty replied nonchalantly, as if Antoine Vidal regularly listened to suggestions from sixteen-year-olds. "They've already begun making it and I've got a fitting tomorrow."

"Me too," said Angel dreamily.

"Awesome! What time? We could meet."

Angel groaned inwardly. What was she thinking? She couldn't meet Kitty at Vidal's tomorrow—she had to get in, swap the designs and get out.

"If you'd rather not . . ." Kitty looked hurt.

"No, I'd love to meet you. It's just that . . . I was thinking about the dancing." Angel looked at the group who were rapidly forming two large circles with boys on the outside and girls on the inside. "I'm a bit nervous."

"So was I, my first time," said Kitty. "But don't worry, if anyone can make you light on your feet, it's Fred."

"Who?"

"Him." Kitty pointed to Señor Martinez.

"Isn't his name Felix?"

"Yes, but his students have always called him Fred after Fred Astaire."

"Oh."

"We'd better take our places. You're over there." She pointed. "I'll see you after class."

Kitty peeled away, leaving Angel to find her place. All the girls were in position, each with a boy opposite them. It wasn't until she reached the last remaining space in the girls' circle that Angel realized she was the only one without a partner.

Kitty smiled encouragingly, while beside her, Angel saw the redheaded girl lean forward and whisper to the girl on the other side of her. She looked at Angel and muttered a reply. They both laughed.

Angel lifted her chin. Let them laugh, she thought. She wasn't going to let some American-hating French diva upset her—even if the girl was wearing the most divine plaid skirt and jacket. It looked like Dior, but Angel wasn't going to give her the satisfaction of appearing to admire it.

Instead, she smiled, threw back her hair, squared her shoulders and tried to look unfazed by the prospect of dancing solo.

She'd just managed to convince herself that dancing alone was her preference when a voice behind her said, "You see girls and boys, *this* is the perfect posture." Angel was startled to feel Señor Martinez's hands on her shoulders. "The chin is up, the neck is long, the shoulders are back and yet all is calm as we wait for the music."

He stepped forward, took Angel's right hand and put his other hand on her waist, then nodded to the butler.

As "The Blue Danube" filled the room, Angel discovered the difference between waltzing with a ninth-grader and waltzing with a world champion. His dancing was sublime and his lead so perfect that Angel thought her feet had grown wings.

He guided her around the dance floor and then led her back to her place when the music stopped. Angel felt exhilarated. She'd never danced so well.

Señor Martinez bowed. "Bravo, Mademoiselle Lily," he said, before moving to face the girl next to her. All the boys moved to the right and Angel found herself opposite a new partner.

It was the boy she'd seen sitting with Kitty in the conservatory. He looked about eighteen, with shaggy blond hair and a broad smile. He bowed and said in painstaking English, "Hello, I am Giles."

"Hello Giles," replied Angel. A moment later she was in his arms being waltzed around the room.

The afternoon flew by as Angel passed from one partner to the next. She tried to remember their names: Giles with the delightful grin, handsome Sebastian, Jean with the green eyes, Rémy who had two left feet but was charming, Chris who spoke five languages and Pierre who had been dancing since he was six.

To her amazement, Angel found it easy to talk to the boys while they danced. She'd thought she'd be too nervous, worrying about her steps and whether they'd be like the boys back home. But it wasn't like that. These boys seemed keen to talk and to hear about New York and Paris, her gown for the Versailles Ball and her plans after the summer season was over.

Angel sidestepped the last question, but she told them about New York and how she loved Paris. Then she asked them about their families and what sports they played. The conversation flowed easily back and forth. It was as if the intimacy of the dance pulled down barriers, while the formality of the steps made such close contact feel safe.

As she moved around the room in each boy's embrace, Angel found herself relaxing. It didn't seem to matter if she stumbled or missed a step, or that both Jean and Rémy stood on her toes, or that Pierre tipped her back in the foxtrot and made everyone laugh. This time it seemed to Angel as though the group's laughter was friendly.

And Señor Martinez made it so easy. With each new dance he took a new partner and as he danced he called out instructions: "Lift your chin, Monique," "Giles, raise the arm," "Slower on the turn, Leon," and, "Do not crush your partner, Pierre. It is true that you must lead and she must follow, but you are not abducting her."

Everyone had laughed at this—even Pierre, who was by far the best dancer in the group. Angel was just thankful that so far their teacher hadn't singled her out for comment.

She watched him now, dancing with the redhead, who was—Angel had to admit—a lovely dancer. He'd dance with Angel again next and she was looking forward to it. As the music came to an end she thanked her partner, straightened her back and waited for him to take his place opposite her.

But it wasn't Señor Martinez who stepped into the space. It was Nick.

Before she could speak, he stepped forward and took her in his arms. And as the music began he said, "Terrific! The tango."

"But I . . . I've barely learned the tango," gasped Angel, wondering if it was Nick that made her feel giddy or the dance.

"Don't worry, just follow my lead."

"But—"

"Relax, just feel the rhythm and let me take you," Nick

whispered, moving in time to the music.

And, without thinking, Angel did as he asked.

Dancing with Nick was amazing—even better than it had been with Fred. Angel knew Nick could not possibly be a better dancer than Fred, but somehow he *felt* better.

As they moved round the room, it was as though Angel was melded to Nick's body. He led her in the tango, quickly, then slowly, then quickly again. Quick, quick, slow: her steps keeping up with the sudden turns and long languorous strides of the tango. The ballroom tango was different from the Argentinian one, but for Angel it was every bit as laden with fire.

She could feel Nick's body, warm and hard against her own, and smell his cologne and the faint tang of masculine sweat as he held her close, never allowing more than an inch or two to separate them.

Angel's heart drummed in her chest, her skin tingled and her breath came fast and shallow. It's the dance—the exertion, she told herself, but she knew it was a lie.

The music reached its crescendo, Nick spun her round one last time and with a flourish of violins, the dance ended.

Neither of them moved. All around them couples were hurrying back to their places in the circle but Angel and Nick just stood there staring at each other. Nick's breath was coming in quick pants and Angel couldn't seem to find her voice.

Nick stepped back. He looked slightly dazed, like he wasn't sure what had just happened.

"I think that was the last dance," he said eventually.

"Oh," said Angel, trying to feel relieved.

"The class has finished," he added.

"Yes," said Angel, trying to take her eyes off his.

"Maybe we can do it again tonight?"

"Tonight?" Angel struggled to think beyond the moment.

"We could dance again tonight. After dinner."

"Sure."

"Only if you want to?"

"Yes . . . if you do . . . I mean . . . sure." Angel took a breath, "We'd better get back to our places."

She turned away, heading for the safety of the group. She didn't know if it would stop the tide of heat rising up inside her, but it was better than staying close to Nick.

She'd never felt this way. It must have been the dance, she told herself firmly, trying to ignore that moment when Nick had looked into her eyes and she'd felt complete.

Angel moved faster. She had to find the Comtesse and go. Once she was back at the house she could ring Lily. Hopefully she'd know what to do.

Because the only thing Angel knew was that she had to do something, *anything*, except fall in love with Nick Halliday.

Chapter Twenty-One

Lily's didn't answer her phone. Angel rang and rang and left a zillion urgent messages begging Lily to call, but by evening she'd still heard nothing.

She sat at the dressing table and pondered the situation. It was a mess. The truth was she should never have agreed to have dinner with Nick.

If only she could talk to Lily. Angel tried her again. Nothing.

Finally she rang her mother, but it was more to hear her voice than anything else. Simone still sounded kind of faint so Angel had told her how awesome summer camp was and then got off the phone.

She looked at herself in the mirror. It was funny how telling lies didn't seem to show on your face.

She frowned. If only she'd told Nick she was ill, or still jetlagged, or something! The last thing she needed was to spend the evening alone with a guy who made her insides turn to mush. *Especially* when he thought she was somebody else.

But it was too late now. She'd just have to try to keep things short and simple. Like only having a main meal with no entrée or dessert. And definitely no dancing. She'd be boring and tired. He wouldn't be interested after that.

"Focus on the Teen Couture," Angel told herself firmly. "Don't get too close or say too much to him." She poked her tongue out at her reflection. "Shouldn't be too hard— I'll just remember he's probably like one of those jerks from the boys' school." But even as she said it, her reflection revealed the truth. She knew that Nick wasn't like them at all.

When Marie came up to tell her that he was waiting downstairs, Angel was just putting on her new silver shoes. She stared at herself in the mirror; she was actually wearing Oscar de la Renta! It was a gorgeous dress: pure silk, just short of knee-length and a perfect cornflower blue with silver clasps at the shoulders and a narrow silver belt. Angel felt utterly Parisian in it and she couldn't help doing a twirl just to see how beautifully the skirt billowed around her.

It was extraordinary how good a pretty dress could make you feel, Angel thought, as she ran down the stairs. And how much harder it made remembering her resolve of appearing dull and tired and keeping the evening short.

Nick stood up the moment she entered the drawing room and Angel couldn't help noticing how good he looked in his dark-blue sports jacket, white linen shirt and trousers that just had to be Armani.

"You look lovely. Ready to go?" asked Nick, gazing at her. He turned to the Comtesse with a smile. "I see you managed to find Lily something to wear, Godmother."

The Comtesse laughed. "*Naturellement*, what did you expect?"

"Only the best, as usual, but I think you and Lily have exceeded expectations."

Angel felt the blood rush to her cheeks, but it wasn't Nick's compliment that made her blush. Lily! She *had* to remember that he thought she was Lily. She mustn't allow herself to be beguiled by his compliments, her new dress or a dinner in Paris. And she definitely mustn't think about how pleased the Comtesse looked at seeing them together.

The masquerade was a wretched thing. It was bad enough deceiving Nick, but deceiving the Comtesse was worse.

For a moment she was tempted to confess everything—right there in the middle of the drawing room—and then Nick held out his hand.

"Shall we go?"

Angel nodded. There'd be no confession tonight. For better or worse, she was going to dinner with Nick. It wasn't ideal, but at least she'd see Paris.

The Comtesse rose. "Bring Lily home by midnight, please Nicky. She has a fitting tomorrow morning and the polo in the afternoon. I think you are playing?"

"Yes." Nick grinned at Angel. "You'll love it, Lily, we're playing the—"

"Why don't you tell her all about it over dinner, Nicky," said the Comtesse.

***

Outside, Nick helped Angel into his black Mercedes convertible. "Okay with the top down?" he asked.

"Sure."

Nick got in and a moment later they were driving through Paris at night.

"It's not far," said Nick.

"Mmm," was all Angel could think to say. What *could* you say when you were out (on a date?) with a guy who thought you were someone else?

"How did you like dancing class?" asked Nick.

"More than I thought I would," replied Angel, grateful that on this subject at least she could be honest. "I was totally nervous, but Señor Martinez makes you feel like you can actually dance."

Nick laughed. "That's Fred—my first class with him, I was two left feet and zero rhythm."

"Really?" Angel was surprised. That hadn't been her impression while dancing with Nick. Quite the opposite. She thought of being in his arms and feeling the firmness of his chest as she'd followed his lead. How he'd held her hand in his, tenderly yet firmly, his other hand on her waist, pushing her away, pulling her close, moving as one. It had seemed pretty near perfect.

What was she doing? Don't think about him, she told herself. Just talk!

"Have you had many lessons with Fred?"

"Every summer season for the past three years. I should've learned at school, but I was so clumsy I always found a way to avoid that particular class."

"I can't imagine you being clumsy."

"Couldn't take two steps without falling over my own feet," said Nick laughing. "I was sure you'd remember that—you used to tease me about it enough."

"I'm sorry, that wasn't kind of me," whispered Angel.

"No, but I never minded because you were always nice to me afterwards."

"I was?"

"Sure, in fact I think I used to fall over a lot more when you were around just so you'd be extra nice to me later."

"I sound awful," said Angel, pulling a face.

"No, you were fun."

She was surprised and Nick, seeing the look on her face, laughed and nodded. "You were, you know. You were the one bright spot in that awful summer. I remember it vividly because my parents had brought me to Paris to tell me they were getting a divorce and when summer was over I'd be going to boarding school."

"That's horrible."

"Yes. I spent plenty of time at the Comtesse's, while she was trying to get them to reconcile. You and I were together a lot." He smiled. "You were so bright and funny, you made me feel better."

A wave of guilt washed over Angel. These memories weren't meant for her. She had no idea what to say. She only knew that she couldn't pretend to remember that summer when Lily and Nick had played together and she'd helped him forget his troubles for a while.

She leaned her head back against the soft leather seat, let the night air flow across her face and tried to think of a safe topic. She found herself musing about *Roman Holiday*— her favorite movie in which Audrey Hepburn pretends to be an ordinary girl instead of a princess and has one marvellous day in Rome with Gregory Peck.

I'm pretending, too, thought Angel. *Except that it's the other way round—I'm an ordinary girl pretending to be a princess, I'm lying to Nick Halliday instead of Gregory Peck and I'm in Paris not Rome.*

Angel sat up and looked around. She was definitely in Paris—right in the center of it! Nick had driven into the Étoile—the giant roundabout where twelve roads meet— and right in front of them was a huge marble archway with an enormous French flag waving gently from its centerpoint.

"The Arc de Triomphe," said Nick.

Angel gazed at it in awe.

"There's a great view of Paris from the top. We could go up this weekend, if you'd like."

"That sounds wonderful," replied Angel. She'd love to see Paris—although it was probably better not to see it with Nick.

"Afterwards we could walk down the Champs Elysées to the Louvre." Nick glanced at her. "If you wanted."

"I've always wanted to visit the Louvre," said Angel, wishing she could think of a nice way to turn him down.

"Great," replied Nick, pleased. "There's a painting I'd love you to see."

"*La Joconde?*" Angel asked. "I've always wanted to see that."

"Everyone wants to see the Mona Lisa," replied Nick. "But da Vinci did another painting I like even better."

"He did?" asked Angel.

"It's probably my favorite painting in the whole museum. I'll show you, rather than explain it."

With the Étoile now behind them, Nick turned into a maze of narrow side streets. Angel was wondering when they'd reach the restaurant when he pulled into the curb and switched off the engine.

Swivelling in his seat, he faced her. "If you're willing to battle the tourist hordes I'll take you to see the Mona Lisa, too."

"That's okay," said Angel, wishing he wouldn't look at her quite so intensely. "I'll be fine on my own."

"I thought we decided it was a criminal offense to see Paris alone," said Nick, reaching out and brushing an errant strand of hair from her cheek. His fingers were cool against her skin and Angel felt suddenly warm—warmer than the night air.

"Shouldn't we be going? We don't want to be late." She knew it was abrupt and awkward, but she couldn't sit there a moment longer. Nick was too . . . too . . . She didn't know exactly, only that she shouldn't be alone with him.

Nick jumped from the car. "You needn't be afraid of me, you know," he said as he helped her out.

"I'm not," she shot back. "It's just that I—I don't like being late. It's—it's one of my quirks," she ended lamely.

"Well, I wouldn't want to mess with a quirk," said Nick, grinning. "So let's go."

They walked quickly down the street. As they turned the corner, Angel stopped. In front of her flowed the River Seine and, a few hundred yards away on the far bank, stood the Eiffel Tower. It was a stunning sight: the tall iron column reaching upwards against the evening sky, its graceful curves and soaring arches illuminated by a million fairy lights.

"Nice, isn't it?" said Nick.

"Nice? Oh no, it's much, *much* better than nice."

"You're right, it's spectacular." Taking her hand, Nick led her across the bridge.

Angel looked around. She could see no sign of a restaurant, only a mass of people walking along the bank enjoying the warm evening.

"Looks like it might rain," said Nick, leading her through the crowd. "Lucky we can dance inside."

"Were we going to dance outside?" asked Angel, surprised.

"There's room on the foredeck." He saw her puzzled look. "It's dinner and dancing on a *bateau-mouche*."

It took Angel a second to remember that a *bateau-mouche* was a riverboat; they were having dinner on one of the famous Parisian pleasure-boats that took sightseers up and down the Seine.

And there it was below them: an elegant white craft, with a wide wooden deck at the front and enormous glass windows that met overhead to form a transparent ceiling. Through the windows Angel could see candlelit tables laid out around a dance floor with a mirror ball above it and a DJ putting a record on a turntable.

It looked wonderful.

She and Nick hurried along the dock to join the crowd waiting beside the boat. As they drew near, Angel realized that they wouldn't be dining alone.

Kitty and the rest of the summer season gang were all waiting to board.

Again, Angel felt that strange mixture of disappointment and relief as she realized that "dinner" with Nick was just another event in the summer season calendar.

And, if the steady beat of the music pulsing out across the water was any indication, she was in little danger of intimate conversation. As they reached the others, the gangplank came down and the steward waved them aboard.

Chapter Twenty-Two

A ngel had never been to a party like it. As the boat cruised slowly down the river she and the other guests danced, ate and danced some more. For the first time in her life Angel had no lack of partners. She danced with Nick several times, but also with Rémy, Sebastian and Giles and then with a string of boys whose names she didn't even try to remember.

It was a heady experience. Unlike the boys back home, the summer season boys were charming. They chatted with her, admired her dress and pointed out the different sights along the riverbanks. Between dances she'd run over to the window to watch another beautiful Parisian landmark glide by.

She was looking out at Notre Dame when she felt someone beside her.

Nick gestured towards the floodlit cathedral. "Beautiful, isn't it?"

"Magical."

As the boat drifted slowly past Notre Dame's great rose window, Nick took her hand. Angel's heart skipped a beat. The cathedral slid away behind them and she suddenly thought, I should tell him now.

But Nick spoke first. "Lily, I wanted to ask you something."

He had a look on his face that filled Angel with panic. She *couldn't* let him say anything heartfelt—not when she was lying to him. She felt him pull her towards him and tried desperately to think of something to say.

Just then the music changed and a familiar beat filled the room.

"'Be My Lover!'" cried Angel.

She heard Nick's sharp intake of breath and saw his eyes widen before she realized what she'd said. Her cheeks burned.

"The song!" she gasped. "'Be My Lover' by La Bouche. It's . . . it's great for dancing!" And before Nick could speak, she plunged into the crowd on the dance floor.

It felt like forever before she could look in Nick's direction. When she did, she was relieved to see he'd stayed put. She needed time to recover from that moment of total humiliation. How could she have blurted out the song title like that? Angel cringed just thinking about it.

The truth was she was out of her depth. She had no idea what he'd been about to say to her, she only knew she was in danger of falling into his arms if she stayed near him.

It was torture dancing, but she forced herself to stay on the floor until the song finished.

At last the DJ changed the music, but Angel's heart sank as the first notes of "La Vie en Rose" filled the room and she saw Nick coming towards her. Not a slow dance. She couldn't. Not with Nick.

All around her couples were forming as he made his way through the crowd. He'd almost reached her when the redheaded girl stepped in front of him. Angel saw her hands run up his chest and rest on his shoulders. She suppressed a sudden spark of jealousy as Nick leaned in close to hear what the girl was saying.

So the redhead liked Nick, did she? Good. Why should Angel care, anyway? This was what she'd wanted after all. With any luck he'd dance with her instead.

She watched as Nick took the redhead's hands in his and began moving to the music.

Angel had got her wish.

Jealousy flared within her and she turned away. It was good that Nick liked the redhead but that didn't mean Angel had to stay and watch them together.

She grabbed her handbag and headed outside.

The night air felt cool after the closed atmosphere of the cabin. To her relief there was no one on the foredeck. Angel leaned on the railing and watched the water foam past. When she looked up, the great glass dome of the Grand Palais was almost opposite and above it she could make out a handful of stars shining faintly in the night sky.

Her mind was in turmoil. What was she meant to do with these unwanted feelings? Nick's appearance in her life was so unexpected and the emotions he was arousing in her were so intense she wasn't sure how to handle them.

She thought of the emotions she'd felt when Papa died—they'd been super intense and hard to bear. But this wasn't like that. This was something entirely new.

***

The slow dance ended and Angel heard a chorus of cheers greet the opening bars of "Gangnam Style." She sighed. It would've been fun to join in that silly dance. She imagined Nick and the redhead dancing it together—

Someone touched her shoulder and she jumped.

"It's only me," said Nick. "I didn't mean to frighten you, Lily."

"It's okay, I just didn't hear you coming," said Angel, trying to calm her thumping heart.

"I was going to call out, but you looked so peaceful," replied Nick. "Not surprising in the face of all this loveliness." He gestured towards the view, but his eyes were on Angel's face.

"Let's go inside," she said desperately. "I'd love another dance." She moved towards the cabin only to find herself being gently pulled into Nick's embrace.

"We can dance out here."

"But it's 'Gangnam Style.'"

"It won't last long," said Nick and, as if by magic, the music changed and the first lilting, evocative notes of "La Mer" filled the night air.

It was impossible not to succumb to the music and Angel found herself melting into Nick's arms. Neither of them spoke as they waltzed around the deck and as the last notes faded they stopped dancing and simply stood in each other's arms watching the Paris skyline.

"You know, I never expected this," said Nick softly.

Angel looked up at him. "What?"

"You."

"Me?"

Nick smiled. "I mean, I expected you—Godmother told me you were coming to Paris—I just didn't expect to feel like this about you." He coiled a strand of her hair around his finger. "You were a cute kid, Lily, but I never imagined I'd ever want to be more than friends with you." Angel caught her breath as his arms tightened around her. "I guess I was wrong," he whispered and bent his head towards her.

Angel lifted her face.

Nick was going to kiss her and she was going to let him.

They were an inch apart when a raucous ringtone shattered the silence. In an instant the spell was broken. Angel pulled free of Nick's embrace, wrenched open her bag and grabbed her phone.

"Hello?"

"Angel!" exclaimed Lily urgently. "Where have you been? Are you okay? I've been ringing for hours. *Please*, don't tell me you've been found out, because I can't possibly leave London. I got the part of Emily in *Our Town!*"

Angel had forgotten all about her desperate messages to Lily asking her what to do about Nick. And she couldn't ask for her advice now. Not with Nick standing right there with a look in his eyes that made Angel long to throw her phone into the Seine.

"Angel? Are you there? Have they found out you're not me?"

"No, it's okay. Everything's fine. That's great news about Emily." Angel smiled apologetically at Nick and tried to focus.

"Thank goodness," said Lily. "I was worried. Your messages were so garbled—something about dancing lessons and Nick."

"Yes, but it's okay now."

"Are you sure?" demanded Lily. "You sound funny."

"Honestly, Li—inda, I'm *fine*."

"Linda? Oh, is someone with you?"

"Uh-huh, and I have to go," said Angel, trying to sound casual.

But Lily's uncanny sixth sense for trouble must've alerted her because she said instantly, "Is it Nick? Is he there with you? He is, isn't he?"

"Uh-huh."

"Angel! I thought you'd agreed to avoid him? Do you want him to find out you're not me?"

"No."

"Then you need to stay cool. Keep him at arm's length and don't give in to temptation!"

The words burned into Angel's brain like a brand, but Lily hadn't finished.

"Remember, you're in Paris to stop Clarissa cheating."

"You're right," whispered Angel.

"And nothing must get in your way."

"No."

"You have to stay focused. Ring me later, okay?"

"Okay. Bye Linda." She closed her phone, turned to Nick and was startled to see people emerging onto the deck.

Just then the boat bumped gently against the dock.

Chapter Twenty-Three

Angel lay awake for ages thinking about Nick.

She could hardly believe she'd almost kissed him. But she'd let herself get caught up in the dance and the music and drifting down the river with Paris on either side. It had been pretty romantic—okay, *incredibly* romantic—but she shouldn't have let it (nearly) happen.

He was so different from the guys she knew and it wasn't just that he was charming and confident and easy to talk to—Nick was *honest*. Which made it even harder that he didn't know who she really was.

Angel considered what Nick had said about never expecting to feel this way about her. Did he mean he liked the Angel version of Lily (which meant he liked *her*)? Or was the attraction dependent on her *being* Lily?

She gazed up at her favorite painted faun. "The point is, would he still feel this way if he knew I was *me*?" she asked. It didn't seem likely, especially once he discovered she'd been lying, but even if it were . . .

"He can't know I'm me until this is over," Angel told the faun. "Lily's promised to come to Paris to tell the Comtesse the truth, but by then I'll be back in New York with no chance of ever seeing him again to explain. And he won't want to see me once he finds out I've been pretending to be Lily!"

It was a hopeless situation and Angel knew it.

She rolled over and punched her pillow. Lily was right.

It'd be better if she avoided Nick. But she couldn't seem to avoid thinking about him and the way he'd held her as they danced and how he'd looked at her and the things he'd said. And she especially couldn't stop thinking about what he'd said about liking her.

At least she'd managed to keep her distance after the boat had docked. Everyone had poured onto the deck to disembark, so there'd been no time to talk, and then they'd all ridden the carousel under the Eiffel Tower before heading home. Angel had managed to avoid sitting with Nick by jumping on a grinning carousel horse and riding solo.

She'd been worried about the drive home but luckily Sebastian had begged a ride and talked the whole way about tomorrow's polo match.

When they got back to the villa, Angel had practically leapt from the car so by the time Nick came round to open her door she was already on the doorstep. She thought he might have tried kissing her goodnight, only Marcel had opened the door before he'd had the chance.

She wondered what it felt like to be kissed. She was pretty sure she'd like it if Nick kissed her. Dancing with him had felt amazing and she could still feel his arms around her as they waltzed on the deck to "La Mer."

Angel lay there humming the tune until she fell asleep.

***

Henri drove Angel to her fitting the next morning. The Comtesse had gone out early, but her instructions had been clear: Henri was to have Mademoiselle Lily at Vidal's by eleven and the Polo Club by one.

Angel's heart thumped as she got out of the car.

"About half an hour then, Mademoiselle Lily," said Henri.

"Can we make it longer? *Please*, Henri," Angel begged.

"I'm expecting to visit one of the workrooms while I'm here." *Not a complete lie*, she thought, clutching her bag and feeling her design folder inside.

"*Bien sûr*," agreed Henri, "but we must leave by noon. Madame la Comtesse will not like it if we are late for the polo."

Angel nodded. It was only an hour but it should be enough time to carry out her plan. "Okay, Henri, I'll be back here right at twelve."

The salon was cool and quiet as Angel followed the receptionist. As they passed the workrooms she could see the seamstresses, tailors, cutters and designers working on the designs that ensured Antoine Vidal's reputation as one of the world's greatest couturiers.

She longed to stay and watch, but there was no time.

The receptionist led her into a small room where a woman wearing the signature grey suit of the House of Vidal was waiting.

"Good morning, Mademoiselle de Tourney. I am Jeanne, one of your fitters."

"Hello Jeanne," Angel replied, with her heart kicking against her ribs. *Get a grip!* she chided herself. *This is the easy bit, so enjoy it. Afterwards you can think about getting into the Teen Couture room.*

Another woman entered with Angel's ball gown in her arms. "*Bonjour*, I am Claudine, the head fitter."

"*Bonjour* Claudine," replied Angel, her eyes on the black and crimson gown. She could hardly believe that in a few minutes she'd be wearing it.

"If Mademoiselle could please remove her outer garments and also the brassiere," asked Jeanne.

Her English was slow and heavily accented, and for a moment Angel was tempted to answer her in French. She opened her mouth—and closed it. So far everyone assumed she knew no French. Maybe it was better that way.

Feeling a little shy, Angel stripped down to her briefs

and stepped up onto the wooden platform in the center of the room. The fitters lifted the heavy satin skirt over her head, eased her into the clinging black bodice and tied the sash.

Angel breathed deeply and tried to take in the fact that she was wearing a real Antoine Vidal gown!

She closed her eyes and felt the cool weight of the satin against her thighs and heard the soft swish of the skirt as it moved. Opening her eyes, she drank in the deep crimson of the skirt and caught the faint fragrance of satin, fine wool crepe and something else—a tantalizing scent that smelled to Angel like the perfume of pure artistry.

Oblivious, the fitters bustled about her, smoothing, measuring, pinning and tacking the fabric with precise, purposeful stitches and all the while talking rapidly to each other in French.

Angel stood still, content to watch them work. It was fascinating to see how subtly the gown altered its shape as the material yielded to the fitters' pins. She thought of her own ball gown and the weeks she'd spent slaving to achieve her vision. And she'd almost done it—a few more hours and she would have created a gown that—

"And will the Teen Couture go ahead as planned?" Jeanne's question jerked Angel back to the present.

"Yes," replied Claudine, unaware that Angel could understand every word she said. "Celeste says it is only the cull that has been delayed."

"Is Bertrand very ill?" asked Jeanne.

"Sick enough that his workroom lies empty and the Teen Couture designs remain unopened. And he will not be back before Friday."

Jeanne looked shocked. "But the cull must be finished on Friday."

Claudine turned up the next piece of crimson hemline and pinned it carefully into place. "Monsieur Vidal has said Monday will do."

"Perhaps Celeste will do the cull alone this year?" suggested Jeanne.

"No need, she and Bertrand have agreed to do it this weekend."

"Ah, those two can work." Jeanne pushed the last pin into place and stood up while Claudine ran a hand over the skirt and said in English, "How does it feel, Mademoiselle?"

"Wonderful," breathed Angel.

"And the length?"

Angel looked down. "Perfect."

"*Bon.* Then we are finished for now."

The fitters lifted the gown over Angel's head and Jeanne carried it away as Angel dressed.

"You will come back in two days?" asked Claudine. "On Friday, yes?"

"Yes," replied Angel, feeling the tension rise as she realized the fitting was over and it was time to execute her plan.

As she'd expected, the door to the Teen Couture room was still locked; there was nothing for it but to try and get in from the adjoining workroom.

To her surprise it was as empty as it had been on that first day, with no sign anyone had been there since.

Angel bent down beside the rolls of fabric blocking the connecting door and tried to see a way between them. Pulling a flashlight from her bag, she aimed its beam through the bolts of cloth. If she could only make a tunnel between them she could reach the door without anyone ever knowing she'd been there.

She set to work. It was hard going but she managed to make a narrow pathway beneath the rolls.

She grabbed her bag, crawled carefully between the bolts to the door and pulled down the handle.

Nothing.

The door was locked.

Angel scrabbled in her bag for her penknife and applied it to the metal slit in the middle of the door handle.

It turned and her heart leapt.

She was about to open the door when she heard footsteps.

She instantly shrank back against a large bolt of denim and tried not to breathe.

"Did Bertrand say where he'd left it?" a woman's voice asked crisply in French.

A man answered, "In the filing cabinet." The footsteps moved past and Angel heard a drawer open and the clatter of files.

"Here it is."

"Thank heaven. It's after twelve and Monsieur Vidal wanted it by noon."

The drawer banged shut, Angel heard footsteps, the door close and then the only sound was of her heart pounding in her chest.

Already after twelve! Henri would be waiting. What if he came into Vidal's looking for her?

There was no time to swap the designs now. She'd have to try again on Friday.

Grabbing her bag, she crawled from beneath the fabric bolts and ran to the door. Opening it carefully, she peered out into the corridor. With a sigh of relief, she pulled the door shut and hurried back towards reception. She was almost running when she rounded a corner and collided with someone coming the other way.

"I'm so sorry," gasped Angel. "I didn't see you."

"Lily!" exclaimed Kitty, "I've been looking for you everywhere." She gazed at her, "You okay?"

"Fine," said Angel. "You?"

"Good, especially now I've found you," Kitty hesitated. "Are you sure you're okay, Lily?" she asked gently. "'Cause you don't look so good."

"Honestly, I'm fine, but I was meant to meet Henri at

twelve and I'm late. I'm sorry, Kitty, maybe we can meet up tomorrow?" Angel began moving away.

Kitty caught her arm. "Wait, Lily. I don't think you're going to want to go anywhere looking like that."

"The Comtesse said these pants were fine for the polo."

"You'd better come with me." Kitty led her into the bathroom and over to the mirror.

Angel gasped in horror. Her hair looked like she'd been through a bramble bush; her face was covered in a fine layer of dust and a large grey smudge ran from her right ear to her nose. Her once clean, sleeveless blue blouse was dotted with dust, her trousers were creased and there was a layer of grime across both knees.

Angel looked at Kitty in dismay. "I can't go to the polo looking like this."

"You got that right."

"But what about Henri—if I don't turn up in the next thirty seconds he's going to come looking for me," said Angel desperately.

"You leave Henri to me," said Kitty. "Fact is, my dad asked your grandma if I could catch a ride with you to the polo. You stay here and tidy yourself up and I'll go and sort out Henri."

By the time Kitty came back Angel had managed to tidy her hair and wash her face and hands, but no amount of brushing or rubbing had restored her clothes to anything close to clean.

"Do you think the Comtesse will notice?" she asked Kitty, trying to smooth out the creases in her pants.

"Are you kidding?" replied Kitty. "With her fashion radar, your grandma'll know you don't look right before you're even out of the car."

"It's true," moaned Angel. "What am I going to do?"

"Wear these," replied Kitty, holding out a short-sleeved white shirt with a mandarin collar and a pair of tan-colored linen trousers.

"Where did you get them?" said Angel, undoing her blouse.

"Wardrobe," replied Kitty. "It's one of the advantages of having practically grown up here."

"I don't know how to thank you," said Angel, buttoning the shirt with feverish fingers and pulling on the pants.

"Well, you could tell me how you got so dirty," said Kitty, grinning. "I'm no expert when it comes to fittings, but I never saw anyone come away from one looking like that."

Angel looked nervously at her new friend. "I'd love to tell you, but I can't. It's nothing bad. It's just something I . . ." How could she make Kitty understand without revealing her secret? She looked at her miserably.

"I won't tell anyone," said Kitty.

"I know, it's only . . ." Angel tried to find a way to explain. "If you could trust me . . ."

Kitty hesitated. "You promise it's nothing bad? You're not like a spy for Dior or something?"

"No! It's . . . it's something personal—something I have to fix. I can't explain right now, but it's nothing to do with anyone in Paris. I know it sounds weird, but if you could trust me, that'd be awesome."

Kitty looked at her intently. "Okay," she said eventually. "I'll trust you, but only if you promise that when you've done whatever it is you're doing, you'll tell me everything."

"If it can wait until I get back to New York, then I promise," said Angel.

Kitty's brow furrowed, then she nodded slowly and took Angel's hand. "Come on then, Lily, let's get to the polo. You don't want to miss the first chukka, do you?"

Chapter Twenty-Four

enri got them to the Polo Club by ten past one. As they drove up the long driveway Angel could see stables on one side and a long stretch of immaculately kept grass on the other. A group of riders in brightly colored shirts cantered across the grass then disappeared behind the clubhouse.

It was a beautiful day. Warm, with a clear blue sky and a light breeze to rustle the leaves. Henri parked the Bentley between a bright red Ferrari and a silver Maserati Spyder.

Angel eyed the cars nervously. "You're Lily, remember, Lily de Tourney," she muttered as she followed Kitty through the clubhouse and down the steps.

There were people everywhere. Beneath the elegant white canopies lining the edge of the polo field, black-coated waiters flitted among them offering hors d'oeuvres and champagne. Angel had never seen so many designer clothes in one spot.

"There's Giles," cried Kitty, grabbing Angel's hand and guiding her through the crowd. He and the rest of the gang were sitting with the Comtesse who looked cool and relaxed in a suit of tamarind silk with a matching broad-brimmed hat and a triple strand of milky pearls around her neck.

"Ah, Lily, here you are." The Comtesse glanced at her watch. "Later than I wished, but perhaps that is Henri's fault?"

"No, no, Mada—Grandmama," said Angel quickly. "It

was my fault. I lost track of time. I'm sorry."

"You have changed your clothes," said the Comtesse, frowning. "Did you dislike what we selected this morning?"

Angel blushed. "Oh, no, it was great. But I . . . I . . ." She struggled to think of a plausible reason.

Kitty came to her rescue. "Lily had a slight accident, Madame de Tourney. It was my fault, I spilled my orange juice."

"Orange juice?" demanded the Comtesse. "At *Vidal's*? Surely you know better, Kitty?"

"Oh. Yes. I do . . ." Kitty glanced at Giles, who was regarding her curiously. She colored and added, "I'm sorry, Madame. I thought . . . I meant . . ." Kitty wilted beneath the steely gaze.

"It was my fault, Grandmama," Angel interrupted. She saw Kitty open her mouth and rushed on. "Kitty's taking the blame so you won't be angry with me, but the truth is that I brought the orange juice into Vidal's. I didn't know— and I was rushing to be on time to meet Henri and I spilled the juice down my clothes. Please don't be angry with Kitty—if it wasn't for her finding me something to wear—"

"I expect they would have barred you from the clubhouse," said the Comtesse, her frown fading. "I'm sorry, Kitty. Thank you for helping Lily. I confess I did not realize you were so enterprising."

Kitty blushed. Giles smiled at her and she shot Angel a grateful look.

"I trust you will not bring drinks into Vidal's again, Lily?" said the Comtesse.

"Not ever!" declared Angel.

"*Bon*, then we may now enjoy the polo." The Comtesse's eyes twinkled. "Your late arrival means that you have missed the Club president's speech, but I don't suppose you will mind."

"Not at all," said Angel, grinning.

"Not even a little bit," said Kitty.

"And the match is about to begin." The Comtesse nodded towards the field.

Angel turned and saw a group of horses and riders cantering across the grass. There were eight of them, each wearing close-fitting white trousers and brown knee-high boots. Four of the riders wore red polo shirts and four wore yellow, the team's shirts numbered from one to four. As they drew nearer, Angel saw that each rider carried a whip in his left hand and a long wooden mallet in his right.

They cantered across the field to where two men in black-and-white striped shirts sat astride their horses.

"There are the referees," said Kitty, looking sideways at Giles.

"Would you like to watch from the sidelines with me?" he asked, pronouncing each word carefully.

"Sure," said Kitty, looking pleased.

People were moving towards the barrier and Kitty beckoned for Angel to follow. She looked at the Comtesse, who nodded and said, "Go along, Lily, you will see better from there. Nicky is number two for the red team and I'm sure you will want to cheer him on."

Trying not to blush, Angel hurried after Kitty and Giles.

From the moment the ball hit the ground Angel was mesmerized. It wasn't just the beauty of the polo ponies as they galloped about the field, alive to every touch of their rider's hand, or the riders' skill at hitting the ball while moving at such speed. What entranced her was the incredible sense of danger.

It was thrilling to watch two players charge full tilt at each other, then fight for possession of the ball. The speed, the adrenaline, the passion with which the eight riders played the game left Angel slightly breathless.

And that was before she'd even begun to focus on Nick.

At first she'd hardly been able to watch as he galloped around the field, swinging his mallet and turning his horse in seemingly impossible spaces. The mallet seemed a fearsome weapon to Angel, and more than once she had to stop herself from crying out when an opposition player seemed about to bring his stick down on Nick's head or arm, but each time he emerged unscathed.

Once he broke free of the pack and scored, and Angel had to stop herself from cheering. She felt terrible, especially when Nick looked straight at her after the goal, but she had to do it.

Angel clapped politely, but that was all. Seeing the look of puzzled disappointment on his face, she gritted her teeth and looked away. She hated making him feel like she didn't care, but for his own sake Angel *had* to keep Nick at arm's length no matter how hard it was to see that look on his face.

Several times during the first four chukkas Angel had to mutter Lily's directive under her breath, "Be cool, keep him at arm's length and *don't* give in to temptation."

She kept watching him, though. In fact, she barely took her eyes off him.

She watched him change horses at the end of each chukka and saw how enthusiastically he praised them. She watched him stand triumphantly in his stirrups and swing his mallet when his team scored and she saw him almost fall when his horse stumbled.

The worst moment was after the third chukka when he cantered right past where she and Kitty were standing and touched his helmet to her. Angel smiled faintly, gave him a half-hearted wave and wished she were somewhere else.

It was almost a relief when the whistle blew for half-time and they returned to the Comtesse's table.

"Five goals to four," called Kitty as they drew near, "and the reds are in front. Did you see Nick's goal just before the whistle went?"

"Indeed I did," replied the Comtesse, smiling. "A stunning

hit." She turned to Angel. "I hope you are enjoying the game, my dear."

"Oh yes," replied Angel, her cool and distant demeanor momentarily forgotten. "I'd never imagined it could be so exciting."

The Comtesse looked amused. "Well, that is quite a compliment—especially as your father was always considered a first-rate player. Still, Philip is older now, so perhaps the games you see at home are not so fast as the one today?"

Angel's tongue seemed to cleave to the roof of her mouth. She'd completely forgotten that Lily always watched Philip play polo.

"It—it does seem different," she began.

"That's because Nick's playing," said Kitty, teasingly.

"And very well, too," said the Comtesse, smiling at Angel. "Indeed, I don't think I've ever seen him play so well. He seems inspired."

"The new horses, perhaps?" suggested Giles, oblivious to Angel's embarrassment. "I think I have not before seen the grey or the—*oof!*" He broke off as Kitty dug her elbow into his ribs.

Giles looked at her in bewilderment. "*Qu'est-ce que—?*"

"Let's go and stomp some divots, Giles," said Kitty, jumping up. "Hey, there's Nick."

Everyone turned to see Nick coming across the lawn towards them.

Angel leapt up. "Would you like a drink, Grandmama? I'd like some ice water."

The Comtesse raised her brows. "No thank you, Lily. I'm sure Nicky would like something—"

But Angel was gone.

The drinks tent was hot and the line long, but Angel didn't care, so long as she avoided meeting Nick. With any luck, by the time she returned, half-time would be over and he'd be back on the field.

"You know there's water in the fridge?" came a voice from behind her.

Angel spun around, her heart in her mouth.

Nick was standing there holding out a bottle of chilled water. "I think this is what you want."

Angel put out her hand but instead of giving it to her, Nick ran the bottle slowly over his face and torso. "That's better," he said, holding it out. "Here you go."

"No thanks," Angel murmured, trying not to stare at the way his shirt clung to his body.

What did he think he was doing, rolling the bottle across his torso like that? It was damp with sweat and showed off the contours of his chest perfectly. And those tight white trousers and dark leather boots that made him look so . . . so . . . Angel didn't know what exactly, only that it was having the most peculiar effect on her insides.

"So, what do you think of the game so far?"

"Okay, I guess," replied Angel, managing to sound bored.

"You're kidding?"

"It's a bit dull."

"Dull!" Nick looked at her incredulously. "But didn't you see that first goal? And the ponies and when the other team hit the—"

"What time do you think it'll finish?" Angel interrupted, eyeing her watch so she wouldn't have to look at him.

"Not soon enough, I guess." The hurt in his voice made her wince.

A bell clanged and she looked up to find him staring down at her.

"Will you watch the second half?" he asked. There was something in his face that made Angel want to reach out and touch him, to explain she hadn't meant it, that it was all a mistake, that she loved the polo and the horses and everything.

Instead, she said indifferently, "Oh, sure, why not?"

"In that case, let me see if I can make it less dull for you!" Nick turned on his heel and strode away.

The second half began and almost at once Angel knew she'd made a terrible mistake.

Nick was playing like a man possessed. He was everywhere: galloping about the field, attacking, defending, hooking, hitting, bumping and never once letting up. He changed horses more frequently and his mallet was never still. Once his horse turned too sharply and overbalanced, throwing Nick to the ground, but he was back in the saddle before Angel had time to draw breath.

Towards the end of the seventh chukka the Comtesse joined her on the sidelines in time to see Nick gallop past in pursuit of the ball and they could see the determination on his face.

Seconds later he scored, but this time he didn't even look in Angel's direction.

"Is Nicky all right, Lily?" asked the Comtesse, as the bell rang for the end of the period and the teams prepared for the last chukka.

"I . . . I guess."

"I thought perhaps you'd had an argument?"

"Not exactly an argument," said Angel guiltily, "more a difference of opinion."

"I see. I wondered why Nicky was playing in such a reckless fashion."

Angel gulped. "You don't think he's in danger, do you?"

"No, child, I do not. I think he is an impulsive young man who has not found it as easy as he expected to get what he wants."

"Oh."

The Comtesse patted Angel's hand. "Whatever was said between you, it is his choice to play this way."

"I know, but I'll be glad when the match is over."

"As will I."

They watched Nick swerve abruptly between two

opposition riders and gather the ball onto his stick. Angel's heart thudded as he narrowly avoided a swinging mallet, turned his horse abruptly and raced for the goal.

The Comtesse squeezed her hand. "I think Nicky may be about to score again."

Nick swung his mallet as a yellow-shirted player galloped furiously towards him. Afterwards, Angel couldn't say exactly what had happened, only that one moment Nick was racing towards the goal and the next his horse's forelegs disappeared beneath its body and Nick was catapulted from the saddle.

He hit the goalpost head-first. His body appeared to hover in mid-air for an instant, before he fell to the ground and lay still.

It was only the Comtesse's grip that kept Angel from running onto the field.

"You will wait here, Lily," said the Comtesse firmly. "In his parents' absence, Nicky is my responsibility." Her eyes held Angel's frightened gaze and she added sternly, "Do you understand, Lily? You will stay here with Kitty."

Angel nodded dumbly. She felt too sick to speak. What if Nick were seriously injured? Or worse—what if he were dead? It would be all her fault.

She watched as the Comtesse made her way to where an ambulance had pulled up beside Nick's motionless body. A medic knelt beside him and his colleague brought a stretcher. Angel's nails dug into her skin as she gripped her hands together and prayed.

The seconds ticked away, each one seeming like an eternity as she stood there watching, never once taking her eyes off Nick's still form.

Seeing him lying there brought back that horrific moment when Angel had seen her mother so pale and lifeless at the foot of the stairs and then she thought of Papa, paralyzed for ten years and slowly fading away. She felt nauseous and wondered if she might throw up.

Maybe it was her fault that Simone and Nick had been struck down? She knew that was stupid—that Maman's illness and Nick falling off his horse weren't even related, but it didn't help.

Angel closed her eyes.

A moment later, Kitty cried out, "Did he move? I saw him move. Look!"

Angel opened her eyes. She saw the medic beside him and then Nick slowly raised his hand.

Angel put her hand to her chest and tried to gulp some air.

"Hey, are you okay?" asked Kitty.

"Don't know," gasped Angel.

"You'd better sit down." She and Giles helped Angel to a chair.

"I'm sure Nick'll be fine, Lily," said Kitty. She pushed a glass of champagne into Angel's hand. "Drink this—for the shock."

"Yes," said Giles, as Angel drank. "Do not worry—they will bring him to the hospital for checking."

"Check-up," agreed Kitty, nodding. "And the Comtesse will make sure—" Kitty paused, "Oh!"

Angel followed Kitty's pointing finger and almost sobbed with relief. Nick was sitting up.

Eventually the Comtesse returned. "He is all right," she said. "Bruised and shaken and rather chastened, but no worse than that. There is a small risk of concussion so they will keep him in the hospital overnight just to be sure."

She saw Angel's face and said briskly, "There is no need to look like that, Lily. Nicky did not want to go and if you had heard him arguing with me, you would be as sure as I am that there is nothing to worry about." She smiled faintly. "In fact, he insisted that I give you a message from him."

"What? What is it?"

"He wanted to know if it was still dull?"

Angel flushed to the roots of her hair. The awful things she'd said to him in the drinks tent had made him go out and play like a maniac—and he wanted to know if she'd enjoyed watching him nearly get killed!

She felt a sudden surge of anger. How could he make jokes about it? Nick couldn't know that seeing him lying unconscious on the grass had brought back memories of Papa and that terrible moment a week ago when she'd thought her mother was dead. But it didn't stop her feeling furious at him.

That was the trouble with loving someone; there was always the chance of losing them—like she'd lost Papa and almost lost Maman. Papa's death had brought a deep sadness, but she'd known for a long time it was coming, whereas Maman's sudden collapse had filled her with terror.

Angel wasn't sure she could bear that kind of pain again.

So what was she doing falling for a guy who'd risk his life to prove a point?

Angel's hands balled into fists. Lily was right, she had to forget Nick and focus on the Teen Couture. Nothing. Else. Mattered.

Suddenly Angel wished it were Friday already. Because on Friday she was going back to Vidal's and this time she'd make sure she got into the locked room and swapped the designs.

Chapter Twetny-Five

Thankfully Friday came around all too soon.

Angel's first thought when she woke that morning was of her mother, her second was of the door leading to the Teen Couture room, and her third was of Nick.

Angel had rung Maman three times since the polo match. It had actually been a relief to be interrogated about summer camp because it was wonderful to hear her mother sounding so much better.

Her thoughts of Nick were not so easily resolved.

Yesterday, the summer season group had visited a homeless shelter and it was there that she'd overheard the redhead say that he was still in the hospital. It'd been a shock because only that morning the Comtesse had told her Nick had gone home.

Ignoring the redhead's blatant hostility, Angel had plucked up her courage and asked, "Is Nick in the hospital? I thought he'd gone home. Do you know how he is?"

But before the redhead could answer, her wide-eyed brunette friend had said haughtily, "Of course Marianne knows—she knows all about Nick. She visited him this morning."

"Thank you, Esmé, I can speak for myself." Marianne regarded Angel with cool disdain. "What are you trying to say?"

Ignoring an uncharitable urge to sock Marianne on the nose, Angel said, "The Comtesse told me he'd left the hospital, but you said he's still there."

"Are you calling me a liar?" demanded Marianne.

"No," retorted Angel. "I simply want to know if he's okay. Surely that's not too much to ask?"

"It's lucky for you one of us speaks French *and* English fluently," said Marianne. "Nick's fine."

"So why is he still in the hospital?"

"Because his parents want him to stay there until they arrive from Dubai."

"His parents?" Angel hadn't thought of Nick's parents. Not since he'd told her how they'd announced their divorce and dumped him in boarding school when he was eight.

"Did you think he had none?" scoffed Marianne. "Lord and Lady Langham flew in this afternoon."

"They did?" Angel tried to digest it all. What did Marianne mean, *Lord* and *Lady* Langham? Were Nick's parents part of the British aristocracy? Angel supposed it made sense. After all, Lily's grandmother was a Comtesse, so she probably knew loads of people with titles and families stretching back generations.

But when Angel thought of Nick—of his curly dark hair and the way his eyes sparkled when he teased her and how his mouth looked when he smiled—he didn't look like royalty, he looked like a boy who'd wanted to kiss her.

"Nick wouldn't discuss his family with you," said Marianne loftily.

"He told me his parents were divorced."

"But he didn't tell you they'd remarried."

Angel was silent.

"Not as close to Nick as you'd thought, otherwise he'd have told you about Charles and Georgiana," sneered Marianne. "They're his parents, in case you were wondering."

***

It was after breakfast on Friday that the Comtesse also mentioned them. "I have invited Nick's parents to the ballet tonight. It's *La Bayadère*, one of Georgiana's favorites."

"Great," said Angel, trying to sound sincere.

"Do you know *La Bayadère*, Lily?"

"No."

"You are in for a treat then." The Comtesse sighed. "My dear friend Rudolf Nureyev's last production, you know. He died not long after its Paris premiere—such a beautiful ballet."

"It sounds amazing."

"You have a busy day today, Lily, but I think you will not be too tired for the ballet."

"Sure."

"After your fitting, we have the charity lunch at *Les Invalides*." The Comtesse glanced at Angel's new sea-green dress and said, "From there we go straight to St. Thérèse's so you will need to bring a change of clothes; jeans and a T-shirt will be best."

"I thought St. Thérèse's was a church?" said Angel, surprised.

"St. Thérèse's is a women's refuge and today is our monthly working bee. I doubt you will wish to wear Vivienne Westwood while weeding the garden or repainting the dining room."

"True."

"When you have finished at St. Thérèse's, Henri will bring you home. I have a board meeting but I will be back in time for the ballet," the Comtesse said. "It is a gala evening, so you must wear something special: the rose-pink Dior dress will be perfect and I have just the necklace to go with it." She smiled at Angel. "Come to my room after dinner and I will give it to you."

Her words brought a lump to Angel's throat and on an impulse, she threw her arms around the Comtesse and hugged her. "You are so kind to me," she whispered.

"Nonsense, child," replied the Comtesse briskly, but Angel felt herself being hugged back before she let go.

There was something about the Comtesse's embrace that filled Angel with an unfamiliar emotion. A longing for something out of reach . . .

She found herself wishing that it was she and not Lily who was the granddaughter of this kind, generous, clever woman whose passions matched Angel's own.

"And now that Nicky is well—"

Angel came back to the present. "I'm sorry, what did you say?"

"Now that Nicky is recovered, he will also be at the ballet tonight. Georgiana rang to say how much she and Charles are looking forward to meeting you again—they have not seen you since you were a little girl."

"Can't wait." Angel forced a smile.

The Comtesse nodded. "I knew you would be pleased. We will meet them at the theatre. I have reserved a box."

"Wow," said Angel, struggling to sound enthusiastic. The thought of spending the evening with Nick sent her heart into overdrive. But even worse was the thought of meeting his parents. They were probably thrilled that Nick was interested in Lily, the daughter of their old friend Philip de Tourney and the Comtesse's granddaughter.

Angel almost groaned aloud.

The Comtesse glanced at her watch.

"What time is your fitting, Lily?"

Angel pushed all thoughts of Nick, his parents and the ballet from her mind. She *had* to focus on her plan. "Ten-thirty, Grandmama."

"That is earlier than last time, is it not?"

"Yes, but they're very busy—what with Bertrand away sick and all."

The Comtesse raised her eyebrows. "You seem very well-informed."

Angel colored. "Not really, the fitters were talking and I

happened to be there because . . . well, they were fitting my gown and . . ." her voice trailed away.

". . . and naturally you listened." The Comtesse eyed her appraisingly. "Do you know, Lily, sometimes I think there is rather more to you than meets the eye."

Angel shifted uncomfortably, but said nothing.

"Run up and get your things, then. Henri will bring the car around." The Comtesse thought for a moment. "Perhaps I will come with you. I have an appointment in Montmartre at eleven, but I should like to see you in your ball gown."

"No!" cried Angel. She'd never be able swap her designs if the Comtesse came with her. "Please don't, I'd much rather you didn't . . ." Angel faltered at the hurt look on the Comtesse's face. "I . . . I want my dress to be a surprise! I know you've already seen it, but you haven't seen it on *me*! And when you do, I want it to be perfect—not stuck with pins or sewn all over with tacking thread."

The Comtesse's face cleared. "I see."

"It's my first Versailles Ball," added Angel. "I don't want anyone to see me in my gown till then."

The Comtesse nodded. "So you have your heart set on a grand entrance. Your very own Cinderella moment. All right, I shall wait until the Versailles Ball to see you in your gown."

***

Vidal's was busier than Angel had ever seen it and the receptionist seemed unusually flustered. The telephone rang endlessly and a steady stream of people ran in and out giving instructions or demanding information. Angel waited until she heard someone call the receptionist by name, before she approached the desk.

"*Bonjour Hélène*," Angel said brightly. "It is busy this morning, *n'est-ce pas?*"

"Oh, yes, mademoiselle," the receptionist replied with a sigh.

"Well, I won't bother you," said Angel. "I have a fitting at eleven, but I can find my own way."

"Oh no, Monsieur Vidal would not like it if I did not escort you."

"Nonsense," said Angel, hoping she sounded a little like the Comtesse. "I'm sure Monsieur Vidal won't mind, not when you're so busy." She looked pointedly at the ringing telephone.

"I'm not sure . . ."

"It'll be fine," Angel reassured. "I know my way."

"Perhaps it's all right . . ." The receptionist eyed the delivery man coming through the door, laden with boxes. "It is true we are very busy. Monsieur Vidal has made several last-minute changes to the collection."

"I understand," Angel interrupted. "It's a lot of extra work."

"*Oui*, but fortunately, Bertrand—our head designer—returns today."

"I heard he's been ill."

Hélène nodded. "It is a great relief he returns, for many things await his attention."

Without thinking, Angel said, "So he'll begin the cull today?"

"I do not know," Hélène answered, suspicion on her face. "You are interested in the Teen Couture?"

"Not especially," replied Angel, kicking herself mentally. "Only, my *grandmère*—the Comtesse de Tourney—was talking about it, and she said the winner would be announced at the Versailles Ball. That's next Saturday and I was thinking maybe the Teen Couture wouldn't be judged in time."

The receptionist's face cleared. "Ah, but *naturellement*, The Comtesse would be concerned. But you may tell her there will be no delay, for Bertrand and Celeste will begin the cull at noon today."

"I'm sure she'll be relieved to hear it," Angel said as she turned away.

It took all of her self-control not to break into a run. She had to swap the designs *now* because once the cull began it'd be too late. She hurried down the hall towards the empty studio. As she approached the door, Angel held her breath. Would it be empty as before?

She passed the Teen Couture room and opened the studio door.

It was empty.

Quick as lightning, Angel was across the room to where the rolls of fabric still stood exactly as she'd left them. Flinging off her dress, she dragged jeans and a T-shirt from her bag and pulled them on.

Grabbing her flashlight and penknife, she pulled her bag onto her shoulder, dropped to her knees and crawled into the space beneath the bolts. Reaching the door, Angel wedged her foot against the roll of blue denim and tried the handle. She gave the door a gentle push and, with one hand bracing the fabric roll, slid through and pulled the door behind her.

Finally, she was in.

In the center of the room stood a dozen large clothing racks, each hung with ten or twelve garment bags.

Angel felt the panic rise. She had less than fifteen minutes to find the right bag, swap the entries and get back in time for her fitting.

What *color* label had been on Clarissa's?

She hurried over to the nearest rack and examined the tags. They were all pastel colors: pale pink, lemon, lilac and ice green. Nothing rang any bells. The labels on the next rack were all different shades of blue and beside it the labels ranged from orange to a deep blood-red.

Angel tried to think. Closing her eyes, she let her mind go back to when she'd seen her day dress spilling from the suit bag. She could see the woman checking the label and . . .

Purple. Clarissa's entry was tagged with a purple label.

Angel scanned the racks. There it was—three racks over between a violet and a brown tag.

Pushing her way between the racks she stopped in front of the bulging garment bag. The name CLARISSA KANE was written on the label in large black letters.

Angel's heart skipped a beat.

Clarissa Kane. In the past few days she and Margot seemed to have faded into the background. Angel had been so busy being Lily that she'd almost forgotten them. But seeing Clarissa's name was a powerful reminder of why she'd come to Paris.

She remembered how Margot had looked that night in the back of the Rolls—like a hideous, gloating snake. And how triumphantly Clarissa had told Lily that her Teen Couture entry had gone to Paris.

Her Teen Couture entry! Not for long. Not now that Angel was here, just inches away from swapping Clarissa's forgeries for her own designs.

She reached up and pulled down the zip. Free of its confines, the green-and-white silk day dress fluttered from the opening. Pushing past it, Angel groped for the purple folder she'd seen that first afternoon at Vidal's.

With trembling fingers she pulled it out and flipped it open. There was the entry form and the sheaf of designs that showed in all their detail her five Teen Couture garments.

As she'd expected, every single forgery had been signed with Clarissa's name. Resisting the urge to tear them into pieces, Angel laid the drawings on the floor and took her design folder from her bag. Easing the pages from their sleeves, she laid them beside Clarissa's copies and stared at the picture on top of each pile.

They were each a sketch of her red cocktail sheath but, other than the signatures, it was almost impossible to tell them apart. If she looked closely, Angel could see variations in the pencil strokes and she thought her coloring was slightly richer, but to anyone else either drawing could have been judged original.

She quickly leafed through the pile of designs, but they were all the same: Clarissa's copies were perfect. Only when she came to the sketch of her midnight-blue velvet ball gown did Angel see any difference.

"Because Clarissa never saw my final drawing," whispered Angel.

She shoved Clarissa's entry form into her bag, and picked up the pile of forgeries. She was about to push them into her bag when her fingers brushed something on the back of the bottom sketch. It felt stiff and unfamiliar. Angel turned the drawing over with a sense of foreboding.

She stared down at the back of the sketch and her heart sank. In the bottom right-hand corner was a heavy white sticker with a House of Vidal logo stamped on it and underneath, handwritten in flowing script, was a name.

Just two words, but they struck Angel through the heart like a knife.

CLARISSA KANE.

She feverishly turned over the next drawing and the next, but they were all the same. Every one of the forgeries was labelled with Clarissa's name.

Angel gazed at her sketches and knew she was beaten: she could never duplicate the logo or the handwriting that identified Clarissa Kane as the designer. But even worse was the realization that the labels indicated a system—that even before the judging had begun, somewhere on a database or in a file Clarissa had been recorded as the creator of Angel's designs.

It was in that moment that Angel realized what she should have known all along. Her plan had been flawed from the beginning because the House of Vidal wasn't some two-bit store; it was a sophisticated business that would ensure all Teen Couture competitors could be matched to their designs.

Angel felt the tears gather. She reached out and caressed the silken day dress. Coming to Paris had been a terrible mistake. She should have found some other way to beat Clarissa.

And now it was too late, because everyone thought she was Lily and if she explained who she really was, they'd all hate her—especially Nick and the Comtesse.

As she sat there, staring down at her sketches in her right hand and at Clarissa's copies in her left, it seemed to Angel that she'd never known such despair. All her efforts had been for nothing. Clarissa had won.

A tear ran down her cheek, just missing Clarissa's sketches. For a moment Angel was tempted to rip them to shreds and throw the pieces into the garment bag.

But what was the point? Her Teen Couture dream was over and she might as well accept it. For Lily's sake she'd get through the next week as best she could, then go home to New York and try to get on with her life.

She pushed her designs into their folder and was about to put Clarissa's forgeries back into the suit bag when something made her stop. Angel hesitated for a split second then shoved the whole lot of them into her bag. She flung the empty folder into the garment bag, pulled up the zip and fled.

Chapter Twenty-Six

A ngel never knew how she got through her fitting. She stood on the platform in a daze while Jeanne and Claudine talked endlessly in French about Bertrand and the cull until Angel thought she might scream.

She didn't want to think about the Teen Couture or the countless hours spent creating her designs or the fact that Clarissa had stolen them without a qualm. Every time she thought of Clarissa, Angel felt ill and shaky—and when she thought of Clarissa's forgeries stuffed into her bag the nausea threatened to overwhelm her.

Why had she taken them?

The question pounded in her brain.

It wasn't as if she'd thought about it. It had been a split-second decision because she'd stupidly imagined that by taking the designs she might somehow still be able to show Clarissa Kane up for the ruthless cheat she was. Instead, all she'd done was alert Bertrand, Celeste and, ultimately, Vidal, to the fact that an entrant's designs were missing.

And when they looked up their database, the designer's name wouldn't read Angel Moncoeur, but Clarissa Kane, who'd never spent a single second designing the Teen Couture entry which bore her name.

Angel felt sick at the thought.

She continued to feel ill right through the charity lunch at *Les Invalides*. She tried to think of other things, to chat and laugh and listen to the speeches, but it was no use. She hardly ate, instead drinking glass after glass of water to try and cool her heated skin and ease the throbbing in her head, but nothing helped.

She watched the other girls eating and talking and laughing together and wondered what they'd say if they knew that a few hours earlier she'd broken into a workroom at the House of Vidal and taken the designs from one of the Teen Couture entries.

They'd say she was a thief. And she couldn't say she wasn't without revealing that she was an imposter. A thief or an imposter: that's how they'd see her.

And what about the Comtesse? Angel practically flinched every time Lily's grandmother smiled at her and when she came over to speak to her after the speeches, Angel wanted to burst into tears.

"Are you all right, Lily?" asked the Comtesse, touching Angel's cheek. "You look a little flushed."

The kind words were like a knife to Angel's heart and the caress like a red-hot brand, but she managed to smile and say, "I'm fine, Grandmama, only not very hungry."

"Too much excitement, I expect," replied the Comtesse. "Was the gown as you'd hoped?"

"Yes, it's beautiful."

"I cannot wait to see you in it." She smiled at Angel and then at Kitty sitting beside her. "And I look forward to seeing your gown, too, Kitty. Is it as you had imagined?"

"Oh, no, Madame, it's better," exclaimed Kitty. "It's so beautiful you can hardly believe it's real." She touched Angel's hand. "And it's all thanks to Lily. I wasn't looking forward to the Versailles Ball until she helped me to choose my ball gown and now I can't wait."

The Comtesse nodded. "I'm glad. I want this year's ball to be very special." She patted Angel's shoulder. "For it is at this year's Versailles Ball that my granddaughter will make her Paris debut."

***

As the afternoon wore away, Angel felt worse and worse. When they got to St. Thérèse's she threw herself into the work, but no amount of weeding or painting walls could take her mind off those moments in the Teen Couture room when she'd taken Clarissa's forgeries.

She tried to tell herself not to get so worked up about it. After all, she'd come to Paris for the express purpose of swapping Clarissa's drawings. So why, when she'd done it, did she feel so terrible? She hadn't felt sick pretending to be Lily and surely deceiving the Comtesse and Monsieur Vidal and Nick and Kitty and the others was far, *far* worse than trying to stop a cheat like Clarissa Kane?

But Angel couldn't seem to stop the tide of nausea that rose up inside her or the hot and cold sensations that made her feel sick and giddy. She couldn't understand her response—it was illogical and stupid, but no amount of reasoning made her feel any better.

By four o'clock, she was aching all over. Her stomach hurt, her head was pounding and she was shaky and weak. Bending down to pick up her paintbrush, she almost fell over.

Kitty looked down from her ladder. "You okay?" she asked, climbing down and dropping her paintbrush into the pot.

"Just a headache." Angel leaned against the wall and closed her eyes.

"Too much sun," pronounced Kitty. "You should've been wearing a hat outside. Do you have anything you could take?"

Angel nodded. "There should be some Aspirin in my bag," she whispered gratefully.

"Sit down while I get it." Kitty crossed to the table where the gang had piled their bags.

"It's this one, isn't it?" Kitty held up Angel's bag.

Angel opened her eyes just in time to see her pulling on the zip.

"No!" she cried. Whatever happened, Kitty mustn't see the designs. Ignoring her trembling legs, she forced herself upright, ran shakily across the room and grabbed the bag from Kitty.

"Sorry, but I remembered I left the tablets in my room." She groaned. "I feel so awful, I guess I'm not thinking straight."

"That's because you're not well," said Kitty, with an odd look. "Let me call the Comtesse."

"No!" Angel caught her arm. "No, don't do that," she said, trying to speak calmly. "She's in a meeting and I don't want to disturb her. Henri can take me home when the working bee's over."

"I think you should go now."

"But we haven't finished." Angel held up her paintbrush.

"You have," said Kitty, taking the brush and putting her hand under Angel's arm. "Don't argue. Anyone can see that you're ill. Come on, I'll help you to the car."

By the time Henri pulled up at the villa, Angel almost felt too ill to move and when Marcel opened the front door he immediately called Marie. Within minutes, Angel was upstairs being helped into bed, her protests ignored.

"You must rest, Mademoiselle Lily," said the maid. "That is the best thing. Madame will soon be here; don't worry."

But that was the whole problem, wasn't it? Angel thought grimly, putting her hand to her mouth as another wave of nausea threatened to overwhelm her. She'd done nothing but worry from the moment she'd realized that Clarissa had won.

Suddenly she remembered her bag. What if Marie or the Comtesse opened it? Ignoring the red-hot hammers pounding in her head, Angel sat up. "My bag," she said, looking wildly about the room. "I need it."

"It is here, Mademoiselle Lily." Marie put the bag

beside her and Angel sank back onto her pillows. "Try to sleep," said the maid, tucking in the sheet. "I am sure Madame would say it was the best thing."

"Indeed I would," said a voice from the doorway.

Angel's eyes flew open. The Comtesse was coming towards her with a look of such concern on her face that Angel closed her eyes again. A moment later she felt a cool hand on her forehead and a voice said, "I have telephoned the doctor. He is on his way."

Angel opened her eyes and said feebly, "I don't need a doctor. I'm not sick, just tired."

The Comtesse put Angel's bag on the floor, sat down on the bed and gently smoothed the hair from Angel's face. It was soothing, and Angel couldn't help feeling glad she was there. If only she could tell her the truth, perhaps she could stop worrying and the surging nausea would go away.

"I have to tell you something," whispered Angel.

"Shhh, try not to talk. Everything is all right. I am here now, Lily."

Lily. She'd forgotten. She mustn't be Angel, she had to be Lily.

A tear rolled down Angel's cheek, followed by another and another. Unable to stop, she wept quietly, all the while aware of the Comtesse's hands tenderly wiping away the tears and her voice, crooning, comforting, telling her not to worry, she'd soon be well.

But Angel wasn't well and when the doctor came and examined her he diagnosed a viral gastroenteritis.

"It is only the twenty-four-hour variety," he told the Comtesse, "but it is everywhere. All over Paris. Many of my patients have caught it."

As if to prove his words, Angel scrambled out of bed and bolted for the bathroom.

When she emerged, she felt washed out and exhausted. The room seemed to dip and sway and she barely registered the fact that the Comtesse had sent Marie away and it was she who helped Angel into a fresh nightgown and tucked her into bed.

The next thing Angel knew was that she was being helped to sit up and a glass of water was being held to her lips.

"Just a sip," said the Comtesse. "And then another with the medicine Dr. Girard has left for you."

Angel swallowed obediently and lay back against her pillows. Her stomach didn't hurt so much, but she felt strange and terribly hot. She looked at the Comtesse sitting in an armchair beside the bed and again felt that overwhelming urge to tell her everything.

She wanted to say how much she hated deceiving her and how much better a granddaughter Lily would be once she'd finished at the London Academy and could come to Paris. She wanted to tell her about the Teen Couture and how much Papa had believed in her . . . He'd been so frail . . .

Angel plucked fretfully at the sheet. She needed to explain about Margot and how Clarissa had stolen her dream and how she and Lily had worked out a plan.

And then it seemed as if Lily was by the bed, only Angel couldn't understand what she was saying.

The images swirled in her brain like a weird kaleidoscope. People's faces came and went, their voices jangling in her head in a cacophony of unfinished sentences. Angel tried to speak but the words kept flying out of reach and she wished she had a butterfly net so she could catch them and make the Comtesse understand. She moved restlessly in the bed. If she could just get the words to stay still, then she could tell the Comtesse about her mother.

That was what she wanted most. To tell the Comtesse about Maman and how hard she worked and how sad and lonely she was since Papa had died. If she could just explain about Maman being ill and how Margot had promised to take care of her so long as Angel gave up her dream of entering the Teen Couture. And Angel had agreed because she loved her mother so much . . .

"Maman," she whispered, and a tear dropped onto the pillow.

"It's all right, Lily," said a voice. "I'm here." Only it wasn't her mother's voice, it was the voice of someone in pain, someone Angel had never heard sound like that before.

She opened her eyes to see who the hurt person was and found the Comtesse still sitting in the chair beside the bed.

She leaned forward and caught hold of Angel's restless hands. There was a catch in her voice as she said quietly, "Your mother cannot come, but your grandmama, who loves you and will take care of you, is here."

"Grandmama?" queried Angel, trying to grope her way through the fog in her brain. "*My* grandmama?"

"Yes, *your* grandmama. And now I want you to sleep and not talk anymore."

"Okay." Angel closed her eyes. Thirty seconds later she was asleep.

***

When she awoke, the room was in darkness save for a small light glowing dimly on the mantelpiece.

For a moment Angel couldn't think where she was. She stared at the light, trying to place it. She gazed upwards, saw her faun grinning down at her from the ceiling, and remembered.

She'd been ill, horribly ill and she'd had all sorts of weird dreams in which she'd been talking to someone— was it Kitty? Or Marie? Or the Comtesse? Angel put her hand to her head, trying to think.

She could recall pushing Clarissa's pictures into her bag and her fitting and the charity lunch at *Les Invalides*, but after that things got kind of blurry. She knew she'd been violently sick and incredibly hot. She must've had a fever, and someone had put her to bed and given her a drink. She had a vague idea that she'd tried to tell them something—something important—something about the Teen Couture.

Angel froze. Had she said anything or had she imagined it? She racked her brain. An image of the Comtesse sitting by the bed swam into Angel's mind; she remembered the touch of her hand and the sound of her voice: soft and kind and anxious. And she heard her own voice trying to explain things and . . . Angel groaned. What exactly *had* she said?

She was still trying to remember when the door opened and the Comtesse came in carrying a tray. "Good, you are awake." She crossed to the bed, put down the tray, and put her hand on Angel's forehead. "Much better. Your fever broke in the night and your temperature has been coming down ever since."

"What time is it?" asked Angel, covertly studying the Comtesse's face for any sign that she'd given herself away.

But there was nothing on the Comtesse's face to indicate anger or outrage. In fact, she looked utterly tranquil as she poured the tea. "It's a little after six in the morning. You have slept better these past two hours." She helped Angel to sit up before handing her an elegant cup and saucer full of clear, greenish liquid.

"Peppermint tea," said the Comtesse, sitting down in the armchair beside the bed, "is ideal after an upset stomach."

Angel nodded but her eyes were on the Comtesse's face and her hair, wound into a hasty knot on top of her head. She'd never seen the Comtesse without make-up or her hair anything but perfectly coifed and—Angel blinked—was the Comtesse wearing a *dressing-gown* over her clothes?

It was such a shock to see her looking almost dishevelled that Angel couldn't help asking, "Are you all right, Grandmama?"

The Comtesse smoothed her hand over her dressing-gown. "It grew cool during the night, but I did not want to leave you so I had Marie bring me my robe." She smiled ruefully. "If you will promise not to tell anyone that you saw your grandmama looking a veritable fright, I think my reputation will survive."

Angel gazed at her in wonder. "Did you truly spend the night here?"

"I did. Much of it in this chair," replied the Comtesse. "Don't look like that, child. I was perfectly comfortable. I even managed some sleep. And it is a relief to see you looking so much better. There was an hour or two during the night when I almost telephoned your father to tell him to take the next available flight to Paris."

Angel nearly dropped her cup. "You didn't call him?"

"No, Lily, I did not. When I thought of ringing him you were too sick to leave and once the worst was over it seemed foolish to worry him unnecessarily." She frowned. "But now that your fever has broken, I do think I ought to let Philip know. He may wish to see for himself that you are all right."

"No!" cried Angel.

"I did not mean to distress you," said the Comtesse. "Naturally, you do not want your father worried unnecessarily, but I think he would like to know you've been ill."

Angel tried to think. She had to stop the Comtesse from ringing Philip.

She sat up. "I'm feeling much better, Grandmama," she said. "That medicine the doctor gave me must've worked because I don't feel sick or anything. I even think I could go out. Aren't we all going to the Louvre today? I'd hate to miss that—I've always wanted to go to the Louvre—and if I'm well enough for that, then there's no point making Philip fly to Paris, is there?" The words tumbled over each other.

The Comtesse pressed her gently back against the pillows.

"Shhh, Lily. It's all right. If you would prefer me not to call your father, then I won't." She sat silently for a moment and then murmured, "It *would* be a pity if my first telephone call to my son in eleven years was to tell him you'd been ill."

"Eleven years," echoed Angel.

The Comtesse nodded and there was an expression in her eyes that made Angel feel as though she'd intruded on something private and very sad.

The blood rushed to her cheeks. "I . . . I'm sorry, I didn't mean to pry. It's just that . . . it's a long time."

"Yes." There was something in the Comtesse's voice that forbade further conversation. After a moment she patted Angel's hand and said, "Now, there's to be no argument. You will spend today in bed."

"But—"

"No buts," said the Comtesse. "I know it is hard to stay in bed while the others are seeing Paris but I promise that you will see the Louvre—just not today." She touched Angel's cheek. "Dr. Girard assures me you only need to rest and that you will soon be well again. So please rest, Lily, because I cannot cope with another night like the last."

Angel's protest died on her lips. How could she refuse after the Comtesse's night-long vigil? She relaxed. It did feel good lying there and a day in bed would do her no harm.

"Do you think you could sleep?" asked the Comtesse, yawning. "I confess to feeling a little *fatiguée* myself."

Angel felt guilt-stricken. "Oh, please go back to bed. I'm sure I'll sleep till teatime."

"If you're certain?" The Comtesse rose from her chair.

"Absolutely! Please, Grandmama, I'll be fine, I promise."

"Very well, I will look in on you after lunch." She bent down and gently kissed Angel's cheek. "Sleep well, *ma chérie*, Lily."

She pulled the door behind her.

Chapter Twenty-Seven

A s soon as the Comtesse had gone, Angel grabbed her bag and emptied it onto the bed.

Her phone was dead. She plugged in her charger, gathered Clarissa's forgeries into a neat pile and considered where best to hide them. After a moment's thought she picked up her design folder, carefully slid her designs into their plastic sleeves and pushed Clarissa's copies in behind them.

Then she lay down and thought about phoning her mother. It'd be after midnight in Florida, so she'd have to wait several hours. And it was still too early to call Lily. At least the Comtesse hadn't called Philip. *That* would've been a disaster—for Lily and Angel, anyway—though it might've been good for the Comtesse to talk to her son after so many years.

What had the Comtesse done, Angel wondered drowsily, to make Philip so angry that he'd cut his mother out of his life? And Lily's life, too.

Angel couldn't imagine.

***

The room was in semi-darkness when she awoke again and it took her a moment to realize her phone was ringing.

She opened it. "Hello?"

"Angel, it's me."

"Lily." Angel was instantly awake. "What time is it?"

"About eight, so it must be nine in Paris."

"In the morning?"

"At night."

"No way! I can't have slept the whole day."

"What are you talking about?"

"I've been sick. But I'm fine now." And she was, thought Angel. That long sleep must've done the trick, because she felt great.

"Are you okay? Did you swap the designs? Tell me everything."

Angel sighed. "It's kind of complicated."

"What happened?"

"I took Clarissa's drawings but couldn't leave my designs because hers had a Vidal label on them and mine didn't. Then I got sick and the doctor came and the Comtesse was amazing—she stayed with me all night and then this morning she said—" Angel stopped. Should she tell Lily that her grandmother had almost called Philip?

"What? What did she say?"

"She was going to ring your dad—to tell him I was sick."

"No!" cried Lily, horrified. "She mustn't! She'll ruin everything. Please tell me you stopped her." The words shot down the phone. "Angel? Tell me what happened— *please.*"

"Okay." Angel lay down again and told Lily as much as she could remember of the previous day's events.

Lily's response was a total surprise. "But you did it, Angel! You sabotaged Clarissa! Without her drawings she can't win!"

Angel hadn't thought of that. "Do you really think so?"

"Definitely! You've done it, Angel. You've beaten her."

"But I couldn't swap my drawings."

"Okay, that's not ideal, but at least you took Clarissa's forgeries so she can't win the Teen Couture with your designs."

"But I can't win either," said Angel.

"Don't worry, I'll think of something. Maybe after I've confessed to Grandmama, I can go and see Monsieur Vidal," said Lily.

"Maybe," said Angel doubtfully.

"The vital thing is that you've stopped Clarissa," declared Lily. "So now all you have to do is enjoy Paris."

"I guess . . ."

"Listen, Angel, in a week you'll be back in New York, so you might as well make the most of Paris while you're there."

"I suppose," said Angel, wishing she had Lily's carefree attitude. "But what do I do about Nick?"

"That depends," said Lily.

"On?"

"On how much he likes you."

"Enough to play like a total nutter at the polo," said Angel. "Though I guess he could've changed his mind since then."

"Not likely."

"Really?" asked Angel.

"Sure. I bet Nick thinks you're great."

"Trouble is, he also thinks my name's Lily de Tourney."

"So swear him to secrecy and tell him the truth."

"No way, he'd hate me!"

"Nah, I don't think he would, not if he really likes you," said Lily. "A *really* nice guy would forgive a little deception if he *truly* cared about you."

"It's not a *little* deception—"Angel stopped. Why did Lily suddenly sound so guilty? She sat up. "Exactly which *really* nice guy are we talking about?"

"Nick, of course."

Angel could practically hear Lily squirming.

"Who is he, Lily?"

"No one!"

"Tell me his name."

"It's no one."

"Lily!"

"Okay, okay. His name's Brett Eastman. We're in the play together." Lily sounded slightly breathless. "He plays George Gibb, the boy my character's in love with. He's amazing, Angel—he's got this incredible stage presence and a voice that makes you—"

"You told him about us, didn't you?" interrupted Angel.

"Yes, but he's totally trustworthy."

"How do you know?" demanded Angel.

"Because he's saved me twice when Margot's rung from New York to check up on me. The second time I was in the middle of rehearsal so I told her I was having a fitting. Brett took the phone and pretended to be one of Vidal's designers. He's awesome with accents and Margot totally fell for it!"

"Okay, so Brett's cool with our masquerade but that doesn't mean Nick will be. I mean he hardly knows me. You've spent every day with Brett while I've only spent a few hours with Nick in total!"

"Well, maybe that's what you need to do," said Lily.

"What?"

"Spend every day with Nick for the next week and get to know him."

"So first you tell me to avoid him and now you tell me to spend the week with him."

"How else will you get to know him?"

"I can't!"

"Why not?"

"Because he thinks I'm you."

"Would you get over that? Just because he calls you Lily doesn't mean it's *me* he likes. He hasn't seen me since I was five so clearly he's fallen for you, not me."

"Maybe," said Angel. Somehow Lily made it all seem so simple. And it *was* tempting to think of spending every day with Nick. "But what if it goes wrong?"

"It won't," said Lily firmly. "But if it does, I'll be right there to fix it. I *promise*."

"Really?"

"Absolutely. And if you do decide to tell Nick the truth at least you'll know for sure how he feels about you."

"It sounds terrifying."

"Spend the week with him and then decide."

"I guess," said Angel slowly.

"Do it, Angel!" exclaimed Lily. "Listen, Brett's here, so I've got to go. Ring me on Monday and tell me how it went with Nick, okay? Bye."

"Bye, Lily." Angel gazed up at her faun. Maybe Lily was right and she should give Nick a chance. If she got to know him, perhaps she could tell him the truth and he'd still like her. It seemed unlikely, but what did she have to lose? She stared at herself in the mirror. What had Lily said?

"Do it!" whispered Angel.

Chapter Twenty-Eight

Cheerful puffs of white cloud chased each other across a bright blue sky as Angel waited by the obelisk in the center of the Place de La Concorde. Nick had called that morning to invite her to spend Sunday sightseeing with him. It was their first conversation since the polo match and Angel had felt a little awkward. At first she'd been tempted to refuse but Nick had been so sincere in apologizing for the accident she hadn't had the heart.

The Comtesse was pleased by the call and had agreed to Angel going out for a couple of hours.

She'd protested that two hours wasn't nearly long enough, but the Comtesse had been resolute. "You are only recently out of bed, Lily, and it would be foolish to risk a relapse by doing too much, too soon. I am only letting you go because I trust Nicky to take care of you."

Watching him stride across the square towards her, Angel could understand the Comtesse's faith in him. Nick looked so assured, so broad-shouldered and capable. She had no doubt he'd manage to look after her for two hours on a beautiful afternoon in Paris.

He didn't seem quite so assured when he stopped in front of her.

"Hey," said Nick.

"Hey," replied Angel, wishing she knew what to say.

"Are you okay? Godmother said you'd been ill."

Angel nodded. "It was a twenty-four-hour thing. I'm fine now." She examined him for any sign of his polo accident. "What about you? How's your head?"

"Perfect. Not a scratch on me. My only real injury was to my heart."

"What?"

Nick assumed a martyred expression. "You see, you didn't visit me in the hospital," he said tragically. "But then I heard you'd been ill, so it was okay. Once I knew you'd gone out in sympathy for me—"

"I did not!"

Nick grinned. "Or maybe you were just trying to get my attention."

"Don't give yourself airs," said Angel, punching him playfully.

"Well, you've obviously got your strength back, so let's go look at some art."

"Where are we going?" asked Angel, as Nick took her hand and led her across the square.

"*L'Orangerie*," he pointed to a building. "Godmother told me I wasn't to tire you, so I thought we'd start somewhere small. It's a pity we can't do more, given that it's Sunday."

"What's so special about Sunday?"

"Nothing," replied Nick. "Only, it's the perfect day for a date."

She regarded him. "Oh?"

"Lots of Paris monuments are free on Sunday." Nick looked at her mournfully. "Think of the money I'd save if we could see more than one."

"What makes you think this is a date?" she demanded.

"Did I say 'date'? Sorry, I meant a *cheap* date."

"All right, what makes you think this is a cheap date?"

"Oh, but I don't." Nick grinned at the flash of regret on Angel's face. "At least, it *is* a date—just not a cheap date. Or it won't be by the time it's over."

"What do you mean?" asked Angel, as they entered the gallery.

"This is a week-long date," said Nick, taking her hand. "We can't do much today, but tomorrow we can do a bit more and the day after that we can have the whole afternoon and maybe the evening, which means we can go to the *Musée d'Orsay* and the artists' quarter in Montmartre. On Wednesday I'm taking you to the Ritz for lunch." He held up his hand. "It's no use arguing because lunch at *L'Espadon* is compulsory. You haven't truly experienced Paris until you've eaten at the Ritz."

Angel opened her mouth and closed it. She'd been about to tell him that she couldn't do any of these things because she didn't want to eat at the Ritz or see the *Musée d'Orsay* or Montmartre, but it wasn't true. She wanted to do all of it—especially with Nick.

"We'll go up the Arc de Triomphe and see the Louvre. On Friday night—well, I'll ask you about that later." He ushered her inside. "You can see that by week's end you'll be anything but a cheap date."

"And what about the summer season?" asked Angel.

"Oh sure, we can fit that in. Wednesday morning we're back at St. Thérèse's. Then we're bound to run into everyone at some of the museums and we'll definitely see them in the sewers."

"The sewers?" Angel wasn't sure she'd heard correctly.

"I said I'd take you off the beaten track," smiled Nick. "You'll love them, they're one of the highlights of a trip to Paris. But we won't do the sewer tour until I'm sure you're up to it."

"I'm not that delicate."

"Godmother made me promise to take care of you *and* get you home on time." He looked at his watch. "Which means we have less than two hours to absorb the magic of *l'Orangerie* before Henri collects you."

"I thought you said the gallery was small?"

"It is, but some of the paintings might take a while to see."

He led her to a doorway then whispered, "Shut your eyes." Angel closed them obediently and Nick guided her forward. A moment later he said softly, "Open."

Angel opened her eyes and gasped.

She was staring into a large oval-shaped room with just four paintings on the walls. But what paintings! Each huge, curved canvas was of a different view of a lake or a lily-pond, for these were Claude Monet's famous waterlilies.

"Incredible, aren't they?" said Nick.

"Amazing."

"And there are four more in the next room."

"You're kidding."

"Nope, I've spent hours here, just sitting and looking at them."

"I can see why."

Together they slowly circled the room. Angel had never seen anything like Monet's huge canvasses.

"It's as if he's captured the light *inside* the paint," she told Nick, as they peered at the amazing colors used by the master painter to create his famous *Nymphéas*.

The second room was every bit as breathtaking and Angel spent several minutes going back and forth trying to work out which painting she liked best.

"It's impossible to choose a favorite," she finally declared, sitting down next to Nick on the seat in the middle of the room.

"Mmm, I can't decide either. It's why I keep coming back."

"I wish I could come back."

"Why can't you?"

"Oh . . . well . . . you see . . ." Angel faltered beneath Nick's clear gaze. "This trip's a bit of a one-off. I'm not sure I can . . ."

He put his hand over hers. "Don't you want to come back?"

"Yes," replied Angel, flustered. "It's just . . . it's complicated."

"Because you live in New York and I live in London?"

"I . . . I didn't know we were talking about . . . us."

"We weren't, but maybe we should be," said Nick. "I've been wanting to ask you—"

"*Bonjour Nick!*" The words sliced the air and Angel pulled away as Marianne came towards them, the rest of the summer season gang following. The redhead stopped in front of Nick and put her hand on his shoulder. It was a possessive gesture that made Angel itch to slap her.

The group crowded around them, chattering loudly until an angry "shhh" from the museum guard reminded them of their surroundings. Several of the girls giggled, then Marianne said in French, "I thought you would be at the *Musée d'Orsay*, Nick." She pouted provocatively. "Instead you are here with the American. Why do you waste your time with her when she knows nothing of art or culture or fashion?" She curled her lip. "She will be happy to see only the Mona Lisa at the Louvre with the other American tourists."

Esmé giggled, but most of the others looked uncomfortably at Angel.

Nick rose. "May I introduce Marianne to you, Lily," he said in English.

"We've already met," said Angel.

He smiled. "So you know that Marianne has a thing for Americans."

"Is that so?" asked Angel, holding out her hand. "Well, it's a real pleasure to meet you, Marianne," she said, her American accent suddenly broad and southern. "My, but you have some pretty pictures in here."

Marianne barely touched Angel's hand as she said in English, "I'm glad you like them."

"Like 'em? I *lurve* 'em," cried Angel in a passable imitation of a southern belle.

She watched Marianne's lip curl into a sneer before saying in perfect, idiomatic French, "You see I've always wanted to see the Monet paintings that inspired Antoine Vidal's legendary collection of impressionist-inspired evening-wear."

She pointed to the painting behind Marianne. "Now that I'm here I can see how he based his evening gowns on this picture. You've probably recognized his use of Monet's celadon, peridot and emerald—all those greens in his collection that started a worldwide trend."

She turned to the others, who were staring at her open-mouthed.

"Vidal also used Monet's blue palette that year. I'm sure you all remember the incredible beaded georgette evening dress he designed for our First Lady." She waved at the painting. "But, you know, I'd never fully appreciated his use of pink and yellow in that collection, only now I've seen the original painting, I *totally* get it, don't you?"

The group nodded mutely.

Angel turned back to Marianne and said in French, "The New York Met's collection of Monet is fabulous, but," she glanced around and whispered conspiratorially, "I think what you Frenchies have here surpasses even that *American* gallery."

For a moment no one spoke and then the group converged on her, laughing and demanding to know why she hadn't let on that she spoke French as well as any of them.

But before Angel could answer the museum guard bore down on them with a look in her eye that prompted Nick to whisper urgently, "Let's go before they kick us out."

He took her hand in his and led her to the door. As they passed Marianne, Nick said loud enough for them all to hear, "I'm rather fond of Americans, you know."

Angel couldn't help smiling.

Chapter Twenty-Nine

It was at Monday's dance class that Angel discovered what Nick had been going to ask her at *l'Orangerie*. During the class he kept switching places with the other boys so he could dance every dance with her. And, far from minding, Fred had actually instructed Nick to hold Angel closer on the turns!

She'd agonized over whether she should let herself get close to him, but when he pulled her into his arms for the first dance, Angel gave in. She hated deceiving him and she didn't want to hurt him, so she decided she'd just have to find the right moment to tell him the truth.

It was during the last waltz that Nick finally asked the question he'd begun asking her that night on the *bateau-mouche*. He'd just spun Angel past Kitty and Giles, when he said, "Will you go out with me on Friday night?"

Angel grinned. "Sure. Is this to the sewers or is there a free gallery open somewhere?"

Nick laughed. "It's my birthday and my parents are hosting a dinner for me at the Hotel de Crillon. I hoped you'd be my date."

"Oh," said Angel, uncertainly. Somehow it seemed okay to go out with Nick to galleries and museums or on a sewer tour, but attending an important party as his date felt altogether different.

"My parents are dying to see you. They were awfully disappointed when you couldn't come to the ballet."

Nick's parents—that was something else bothering

Angel—something she'd been meaning to ask him . . .

"You mean Lord and Lady Langham?"

"Sure."

"British royalty?"

"Not *royalty*, Lily," said Nick, amused.

"Okay, English aristocracy then—they're Lord and Lady Langham?"

"Since my father inherited the title," Nick looked puzzled. "But it's no big deal—I mean, your dad's a comte."

"He is?" squeaked Angel, before she could stop herself. "I mean, of course, he is."

Nick looked even more puzzled. "You must know your dad inherited his title when his father died—your dad is the Comte de Tourney and your grandmother is the dowager Comtesse."

It seemed astonishing to Angel that Lily had never told her this fascinating bit of family history. On the rare occasions she mentioned her grandmother, Lily had mostly referred to her as "the Comtesse," but Angel had never thought about what it meant.

She was puzzling over it when Nick laughed.

"Stop playing games with me, Lily," he said, pulling her closer, "and tell me you'll be my date at the Crillon next Friday night."

She looked up at him. "Are you sure you want *me*?"

"Definitely!"

Angel hesitated. How could she say no? It was his birthday and he wanted her to share it with him.

"Okay," she said.

On Tuesday, Angel spent the morning with the Comtesse at a Christian Dior fashion show and the afternoon with Nick exploring the artists' quarter in Montmartre.

They caught the Metro to Anvers and, after Angel had convinced him she was well enough, began climbing the three hundred steps up the Rue Foyatier to the great church of Sacré Coeur.

Every now and then one of the funicular rail cars would glide past them carrying tourists up the steep slope.

About halfway up, Angel stopped, sighed heavily, and looked longingly at a passing rail car.

Nick halted beside her. "I knew it was too much for you," he said. "We should've taken the funicular. I can carry you the rest of the way if you're tired," he offered.

"Could you?" asked Angel, trying to keep a straight face.

"If you need—" Nick broke off as Angel burst out laughing.

"I'm sorry," she gurgled, "but the look on your face when the funicular went by!"

Nick grinned. "Very funny," he said as they began climbing again.

"Would you really have carried me?"

"Sure. That's how I got to the top on my first visit to Montmartre—my dad carried me on his back the whole way up."

"How old were you?"

"About four."

"And you still remember it?"

Nick looked at her, his face serious. "It was one of the happiest holidays of my life. Before my parents started fighting."

They climbed in silence for a while.

Then Angel said, "Marianne told me your parents had remarried."

Nick nodded. "Two years ago."

"Was it okay? I—I mean—how did you feel?"

Nick smiled reassuringly. "It's all right. I'm kind of glad you asked. I know I left you with the impression that they'd messed up my whole childhood."

"Mmm."

"Well, they did sort of mess it up—for several years, anyway. Before they grew up enough to realize that they were better together than apart." He stopped and Angel paused beside him, glad to catch her breath. They were almost at the top.

Nick looked out across the city. "How did I feel about it? Angry they'd put me through it, relieved they'd stopped all the stupid point-scoring, and incredibly happy that they'd finally figured out how much they loved each other."

"I like that last bit," said Angel.

"Me too," said Nick. "But probably the best thing was learning that even after they'd totally messed up, they still found a way to fix things."

"That's encouraging," said Angel, trying not to think about her own messed-up situation.

"I'm not even sure how they managed it. I'm just glad they did."

They reached the last step and above them the white façade of Sacré Coeur gleamed in the afternoon sunlight. Nick held out his hand. "Come on, let's get an ice-cream before we hit the tourist trail."

***

The rest of the week flew by.

On Wednesday Nick took Angel to lunch at *L'Espadon*. Angel felt like she was in seventh heaven dining in the Ritz's most beautiful restaurant. Afterwards they joined the rest of the gang on the famous sewer tour before Nick stole her away to show her the *Musée d'Orsay* and the view of Paris from the top of the Eiffel Tower.

Every night Angel stayed up a little later and every morning she woke at ten when Marie opened the curtains and put her breakfast tray on the bed. And each afternoon she found an opportunity to slip away and phone her mother.

It was wonderful to hear Simone sounding stronger and more energetic; the only drawback was that as her health improved so did her interest in Angel's daily life.

Angel longed to tell her about Paris and Nick and the summer season, but she knew that even the faintest hint that she was anywhere but Camp Wilderness would see her mother on the next plane to France—the *last* thing Simone needed when she was still recovering.

Angel made a silent promise to tell her everything the minute they were together again. By then her mother would be well enough to withstand the shock.

She couldn't imagine what Maman would say, but she knew she'd have to tell her the truth. The longer she was in Paris, the more Angel wished she could tell someone her secret. Several times she almost confided in Kitty or the Comtesse or Nick but each time she opened her mouth to confess she faltered, too afraid of how they might react.

Instead, she followed Lily's advice and spent the days with Nick. The trouble was, the more she knew him, the closer they became and the harder it was to keep letting him believe she was Lily.

***

On Thursday Nick kept his promise and took Angel to the Louvre.

It was unbelievably beautiful and Angel hardly knew whether to look at the artwork or the architecture. There was so much here to inspire her and she'd thought of half a dozen new dress designs before she'd even left the first room. After only an hour she'd run out of words to tell Nick what she thought of the wonders of the Louvre.

They walked from room to room, holding hands and arguing light-heartedly over which paintings they liked until Nick said, "We're almost there." He pointed to a wide doorway ahead of them. "That's the *Salle d'Etats*—home of the Mona Lisa."

Angel ran forward and stopped.

It was obvious which wall held the world's most famous painting because a crowd of people obscured the portrait from view. Angel and Nick waited patiently until several of them drifted away and Nick gently thrust Angel forward. "Go on, I've seen it lots of times."

She edged into the space and stared at Leonardo da Vinci's celebrated painting of *La Joconde*. It was smaller than she'd expected and far more beautiful than any print or copy she'd seen. The original had a richness and a depth she couldn't have anticipated and the colors were amazing. Angel wished she could acquire a bolt of the fabric used to make Mona Lisa's gown: what she might do with such cloth.

She stood there absorbing the portrait until Nick touched her arm.

"Want to leave the tourists to wrestle each other for photos? I'd like to show you my favorite da Vinci painting."

"Okay."

He led her out of the crowded room and into another enormous room lined with sculptures and paintings.

"The Grand Gallery," said Nick, waving his arm.

It wasn't nearly so crowded and they walked slowly along admiring the paintings. About halfway down Nick stopped. "There," he said, pointing at a large portrait of two women and a young child holding a lamb. "My favorite da Vinci."

"The Virgin and Child with Saint Anne," read Angel, translating the plaque on the wall. "It's beautiful."

"I love da Vinci's faces," said Nick. "They seem to be what an angel would look like." He smiled down at her. "They remind me of you."

"Only I'm no angel," said Angel, smiling.

"You look like an angel to me," said Nick, gently cupping her chin in his hands. "My angel," he said softly.

She looked at him and Nick gazed back with a look in his eyes that made her melt inside. Then, the gap between them was closing. Angel felt his hands tilt her chin and his lips gently brush her cheek. She trembled but didn't pull away. His mouth caressed her other cheek and then, incredibly, he turned his face to hers and found her lips.

Without thinking, Angel let herself dissolve into him as his lips pressed against hers. She lifted her arms round his neck and, caring nothing for the tourists who stopped and stared at them, she kissed him back.

Chapter Thirty

Angel woke early on Friday and lay in bed gazing at the ceiling. In less than forty-eight hours she'd be on her way back to New York. She'd miss Helios in his chariot and her favorite faun and the laughing cherubs. Maybe she could paint cherubs on her own ceiling. Or maybe not. Once she got home, she probably wouldn't want to be reminded of anything to do with Paris or the Comtesse or Nick.

Nick. Angel sighed. Tonight at the Hotel de Crillon would be her second-last night with him and tomorrow night at the Versailles Ball would be their last evening together forever.

She rolled over and buried her face in the pillow. Was it only yesterday that he'd kissed her? It had been the most amazing, unforgettable moment of her life. She'd never imagined anything so . . . so . . . delectable! And afterwards, when he'd put his arm around her and they'd wandered through the Louvre together . . .

Don't think about it, Angel told herself. Don't think about Nick's touch or his kiss or being his date at his birthday party or the awful, dreadful fact that he still thinks you're Lily. This is his big night and you're going to make it perfect for him and have one last wonderful time together.

She'd say goodbye to him at the Versailles Ball. Maybe that was when she'd tell him the truth—and the Comtesse, too.

Thinking of the Comtesse reminded Angel that she had her final fitting at Vidal's at eleven and this time the Comtesse had insisted on coming with her.

"But you needn't worry, Lily," she'd assured Angel. "I promise not to come near the fitting room until your ball gown has been safely packed into its box."

Angel was pleased. After her fitting she hoped the Comtesse would agree to a special shopping expedition.

They left straight after breakfast, the Comtesse elegant in a dove-grey Chanel suit with black trim and Angel in a pair of Calvin Klein jeans and an ivory silk Donna Karan tunic-shirt with long sleeves and French cuffs.

The Comtesse had raised her eyebrows at Angel's outfit. "So different from what I would have been allowed to wear at your age, but it is a striking ensemble."

"Do you ever wear trousers, Grandmama?"

"Occasionally, but the modern styles do not always suit me. Perhaps if I were taller."

"It's funny how wearing what suits you makes such a difference. I know I'm not nearly as tall as a Vidal model, but when I wear my ball gown I *feel* tall."

The Comtesse nodded, pleased to find such a ready understanding. "You are happy with your ball gown?"

"Oh, yes." Angel's eyes shone. "It's beyond beautiful."

"*Bon.*"

"Is your dress ready?" asked Angel. Vidal himself had designed the Comtesse's gowns for Nick's party and the Versailles Ball.

"Thankfully, yes. There was an unexpected delay last Friday and I was a little worried, but the difficulty is past and all is well."

"Was it a problem with the material or the making?" asked Angel, eager to hear more about the workings of a top fashion house like Vidal's.

"It was nothing to do with my gowns at all. There was a small crisis at the salon on Friday afternoon that unfortunately took Antoine's complete attention for a time."

"Oh?" Suddenly Angel felt uneasy.

"Poor Antoine was most distressed. The Teen Couture is as important to him as the Versailles Ball is to me. And he cannot bear anything to go wrong."

"Did something go wrong?" Angel managed to ask.

"I believe there was a problem with some missing designs. It was resolved, but Antoine was naturally upset."

"Naturally."

"He has notified the Teen Couture finalists, however, and they will be at the Versailles Ball as planned. Antoine is looking forward to announcing the winner." She saw Angel's frown and laughed. "Don't worry, Lily, the speeches will be short and your interest in fashion means that you will enjoy seeing the ball gowns."

"Are they there?" asked Angel, surprised out of silence.

"Yes, either the finalists wear their designs themselves or Vidal's models do so. It is always fascinating to see the dresses worn." The Bentley slowed. "Ah, here we are."

***

It was nerve-wracking being at Vidal's.

Angel waited nervously in the fitting room for Claudine and tried not to think about Vidal's distress over the missing drawings. Perhaps the fitters would suspect her, but when they greeted her in their usual friendly manner, Angel's pulse grew steadier.

She stepped into the black-and-crimson ball gown. Jeanne carefully tied the sash and Claudine swung the long mirror into place behind her. Angel spun slowly round and stared at her reflection.

She was wearing a perfectly fitted Vidal gown. It was an incredible feeling.

The fitters turned her this way and that, showing her the

gown from all sides and assuring her that she looked "*jolie comme un coeur*," "*très belle*" and "*comme une princesse.*"

And Angel did feel pretty and beautiful and *exactly* like a princess! Who wouldn't? Any girl who got to wear a real Antoine Vidal ball gown couldn't help feeling anything but gorgeous.

She undressed and watched in ecstasy as Jeanne swathed the dress in tissue paper before laying it in an enormous white box ready for Henri to take out to the car. Angel was pulling on her shirt when Claudine came back with another dress.

She held it out and said, "Madame la Comtesse has asked that you try this on."

"Madame—oh!" Angel gasped as Claudine let the skirt fall. It tumbled to the floor in a glorious confection of amethyst ruffles below a clinging body of lilac jersey and amethyst organza. It was the dress from Vidal's collection—the one with the skirt like whipped meringue; the one the Comtesse had described as "*la mielleure*"—the best.

She stared as the head fitter undid the zip and knelt down. Angel dropped her shirt and stepped into the dress, Claudine pulled it up over her hips, slid the straps over her shoulders and zipped it up. To Angel's astonishment it was a perfect fit.

"I don't understand," she stammered, staring at her reflection in the mirror. The dress was sleeveless with narrow straps leading down to a deep V-shaped neckline accentuated by the fitted bodice, slender waistline and the delicately layered skirt. The amethyst cloth seemed to shimmer, reminding Angel of a beautiful jewel or a delicate crystal. She stared at her reflection. The dress was utterly different to the crimson-and-black ball gown, but it was every bit as stunning.

"Does the Comtesse want me to wear this instead of the other one?"

Claudine laughed. "No, no, *pas du tout*, Madame la Comtesse wishes you to have both. This one," she indicated the amethyst dress, "is for tonight. The other is for the Versailles Ball." She smoothed a tiny wrinkle from the clinging gown and whispered, "It is for you, a gift—a surprise, *n'est-ce pas*? Madame had us work on both dresses so that each would fit you *parfaitement*."

A tear ran down Angel's cheek.

"You are not happy?" The fitter looked at her with worried eyes.

Angel gave a wobbly laugh. "I'm very happy, but the Comtesse is *too* kind."

"I think Madame has the great love for you." Claudine touched her heart. "Perhaps you will tell her your thanks?"

"I'll try," said Angel.

***

But when she met the Comtesse in the foyer and stammered her thank you, she was waved aside.

"Oh, shush, child, it is only a dress. I knew you would wish to wear something special to Nicky's birthday and it *is* your first visit to the Hotel de Crillon." She tucked Angel's hand inside her arm. "You may not know, but there are four truly great hotels in Paris—what I call *Les Quatre Grands*: the Crillon, the Ritz, the George Cinq and the Versailles. Of these, the Versailles is *le premier*, but the others also demand a certain level of dress and deportment."

As they emerged onto the street, Henri opened the car door.

Angel said hesitantly, "I wanted to ask—would it be all right if we stayed in town a bit longer? There's a shop I'd like to visit. It's not far, we could walk."

The Comtesse looked surprised, but nodded. "Wait for us please, Henri, we will be . . ." She looked inquiringly at Angel.

"Would an hour be too long?" Angel asked.

The Comtesse thought for a moment, then smiled at the chauffeur. "Go and have lunch, Henri—a *long* lunch. Mademoiselle Lily and I are going shopping."

It wasn't far to the Rue du Faubourg St. Honoré, but when they arrived at the shop it was crowded with customers.

"Oh," said Angel, disappointed. "I didn't think it'd be so busy."

"Hermès is *always* busy," replied the Comtesse calmly. "It is one of Paris's best-loved shops."

"I thought we could do this quickly," explained Angel, gazing at the customers waiting to be shown their choice of the hand-made silk scarves lying under the glass-topped counters.

"One does not choose an Hermès scarf quickly, Lily. It is an experience to be savored," said the Comtesse. "I am delighted that you wish to own such an important accessory."

"I would love to own an Hermès scarf," confessed Angel, "but that isn't why we're here." She colored and said quickly, "I want to buy *you* a scarf. To say thank you for everything you've done for me these past two weeks."

She saw the Comtesse purse her lips and rushed on, "I know you probably have heaps already, but I thought that maybe we could look at them together and find some you liked and then, I thought, perhaps you'd let me choose a scarf for you."

For one awful moment Angel thought the Comtesse was going to cry, but then she pressed her lips together and said, "That would be most delightful, Lily."

Just then a woman in a black suit wearing a discreet manager's badge swooped on the Comtesse with a cry of delight. "Madame de Tourney. What a pleasure to see you at Hermès again. Have you come to view the collection?"

"How nice to see you, Madame Dubois. I have indeed

come to see the collection, but I am happy to wait." The Comtesse nodded towards the crowded counter.

The manager looked shocked. "No, no, Madame—a valued customer such as yourself, but *naturellement*, I would be delighted to show you. If you will tell me which colors you had in mind."

The Comtesse smiled. "It is not for me to say, Madame." She beckoned to Angel. "Today, my granddaughter will select the perfect scarf for me."

***

Two hours later, Angel and the Comtesse emerged triumphantly from Hermès, Angel carrying a bag in which sat the store's trademark orange box tied up with slender brown ribbon. Inside the box reposed a beautiful three-foot-square silk scarf—the final choice after a lengthy selection process that had given them both immense pleasure.

It hadn't been easy to choose the perfect scarf, for, as Angel explained to the Comtesse while arranging yet another silken masterpiece around her neck, "How *do* you choose between exquisite and stunning?"

She'd made up her mind eventually and the Comtesse was delighted with her selection—a striking fuchsia Christine Henry *L'arbre de Vie* design. She'd have worn it out of the shop but it looked like rain and the Comtesse had said, "One *never* wears an Hermès scarf in the rain."

They wandered along the famous fashion street, stopping whenever a shop caught their eye. The Comtesse was keen to find a coat to go with her new Hermès scarf and led Angel from one designer shop to the next. Whether it was Givenchy, Valentino, Versace or Yves Saint-Laurent, the moment Elena de Tourney stepped through the door there was a flurry of activity and the instant appearance of a delighted store manager.

Angel quickly learned to appreciate her manner. The

Comtesse was shrewd and experienced with no time for flattery and no interest in gossip outside the fashion world. Her knowledge of clothes, their fabric, making and design seemed omniscient to Angel. There was not a designer whose name she did not know or a fashion house of which she was unaware. It wasn't long before Angel realized she was in the presence of a true fashion connoisseur and was content to simply watch and listen.

She wasn't allowed to stay silent, however, and as they moved from shop to shop the Comtesse became increasingly interested in Angel's opinion of the clothes. Angel answered as best she could and the Comtesse seemed satisfied with her replies. In the Rue Royale they entered Christian Dior, where the Comtesse enjoyed a vigorous discussion with the manager about the couture house's latest collection before buying a stunning pale pink and white wool coat to wear with her new scarf.

By the time they entered Chanel they were deep in conversation about the new American designer, Jason Wu, but when they stepped inside the famous shop the Comtesse broke off and said, "I sometimes think that I am never happier than when I am wearing Chanel." Her eyes held a faraway look. "I first met Madame Chanel on her return to Paris, you know, when I was about your age. I have always thought that her eye for cut and style was truly sublime." She looked at Angel. "You were probably too young to remember, but your mother also adored Chanel. I remember Catherine had a superb coral-colored suit made—"

"I love that suit!" cried Angel. "It's one of my inspirations—" Suddenly she was aware of saying too much.

The Comtesse misinterpreted her silence. "I'm sorry, Lily, I did not mean to awaken painful memories of your mother." When Angel did not answer she added, "We can do Chanel another day. It is getting late and we have

Nicky's party to prepare for. I will call Henri."

She turned away, leaving Angel to ponder on the dangers of speaking her thoughts aloud and whether it was possible for her web of deceit to become any more tangled.

They drove most of the way back to the villa in silence. They'd talked briefly about the Comtesse's new scarf (which she'd insisted on wearing as soon as they got into the car), but after that neither of them spoke. The Comtesse seemed preoccupied and Angel was busy with her own mixed-up thoughts.

It's not only my thoughts that are confused, she decided. *My whole life is just one big maze and I don't see how I'm ever going to find my way out.* She glanced at the Comtesse, who was staring out the car window. *The only real way out is to tell her the truth*, Angel decided.

If she could just explain it the right way—beginning with the Teen Couture and Clarissa's theft—then maybe Elena de Tourney would understand. If she knew about Simone's illness and Margot's threats, she might see why Angel had acted as she had and believe she'd meant no harm. She might even find it in her heart to forgive.

Of course, she might *not* understand why Angel had pretended to be her long-lost granddaughter or why she'd allowed her to lavish so much love and generosity on an imposter!

Angel's stomach clenched. Maybe she should just stick to the plan: get through the next two days, fly home to New York and leave the Comtesse with a bunch of happy memories. She'd know it all before long because Lily was coming to Paris once she'd finished in London. It could be as soon as Monday that Lily finally told her grandmother the truth.

Lily's grandmother . . .

"I wish she were mine," whispered Angel.

"Did you say something, Lily?" asked the Comtesse. "I'm sorry, my thoughts were elsewhere."

"No, Grandmama, I was just thinking aloud."

"I, too, have been thinking," she replied. "When we get home there is something I wish to ask you."

Chapter Thirty-One

Marcel met them at the door.

"We will be in the library, Marcel. Please see that we are not disturbed."

"*Oui*, Madame." The butler went away to give the order and Angel followed the Comtesse into the library. She loved the wood-panelled, book-lined room. After her bedroom, it was her favorite part of the house.

To her surprise, instead of sitting at her desk or in her favorite armchair as she usually did, the Comtesse remained standing. Unsure of whether to sit or stand, Angel stopped where she was and waited.

She didn't have to wait long.

"I want you to stay," said the Comtesse suddenly.

Angel stared at her blankly.

"I want you to stay, to spend the rest of your holidays here with me in Paris."

Angel finally found her voice. "I . . . I can't."

"Why not?" The Comtesse looked hurt.

"It's not that I don't want to," explained Angel desperately. "I love being here—you've given me the two best weeks of my life—but I have to go home."

"Could you not have two homes?" asked the Comtesse. "After this fortnight, I hoped you might have come to think of this house as your home."

"I do . . . I love it here with you in Paris and . . . everything! It's just that . . ." Angel looked at her helplessly. If ever there was a time to tell the Comtesse the truth, this was it.

She opened her mouth just as the Comtesse stepped towards her with outstretched hands. "I want you in my life again, Lily. I want my granddaughter here in this house. I know you cannot be here all the time, but I thought you might spend part of your holidays here and then—in a year or two—I thought you might like to study in Paris for a while." She caught hold of Angel's hands. "You might like to pursue a career in fashion design. You have real talent, Lily." She touched the scarf around her neck. "It is a rare gift to be able to see as you see and I thought, if you wished, that I might help you to find a place at one of the top fashion houses, if you wanted."

If she wanted! Angel was speechless. What could she say? The Comtesse was offering her a dream and she had no choice but to refuse.

She looked miserably at the Comtesse. "I'd like it more than anything in the world, but, you see, I can't." Angel squeezed the older woman's hand. "I can't stay in Paris and I can't come back. It's not that I don't want to . . . I just can't."

"I suppose I should have expected this—you are Philip's daughter after all." The Comtesse sighed. "However, while I am prepared to endure his resentment of me for past wrongs, I am *not* prepared to accept his turning you against me."

"Oh, but he didn't—"

The Comtesse interrupted. "I'm not asking you to transfer your allegiance from your father to me, but could you not find room in your heart for us both? I want you here, Lily. Surely Philip will not object? He let you come once, so he must be willing—"

"Philip doesn't know I'm here!" Angel gasped, trying to deflect the situation and realizing she'd only made things worse as the color drained from the Comtesse's face.

The Comtesse sank slowly into a chair. "Where does he think you are?" she asked at last.

"Summer camp," Angel whispered.

"And he is?"

"In South America. On business and out of contact."

The Comtesse looked up. "And so you seized the chance to come to Paris because my invitation arrived while Philip was away and you decided to come and meet your long-lost grandmother." She smiled faintly. "I'm glad you had the courage to come of your own accord." She waved Angel into the chair opposite her. "Which is why you should be able to return to Paris if you wish."

"You don't understand," said Angel, wringing her hands and wondering if she could fall any deeper into this deception. "It's *much* more complicated than that."

"At present perhaps, but it will not always be so," replied the Comtesse. "In a few years you will be of age and then you can make up your own mind." She leaned forward, her blue eyes earnest. "Whatever lies between me and Philip need not affect *us*, Lily. You must believe that."

"I do, I do," cried Angel, trying to think of how best to begin telling the Comtesse the truth.

"Is there anything I can say to persuade you?"

Angel shook her head.

There was a short silence, broken only by the steady ticking of the ormolu clock on the mantelpiece. Angel swallowed. This was it—she *had* to confess. "There's something you need to—"

"—do," finished the Comtesse. "You are right." She straightened her shoulders. "I need to tell you the truth!"

Angel stared; those were meant to be her words, not the Comtesse's. "No, I—"

"Hear me out, Lily, *please!*" begged the Comtesse. "I think it will help us both if I tell you what happened between me and your father all those years ago." Taking a small key from the gold chain around her neck, she unlocked a drawer in her desk, removed a silver frame and handed it to Angel.

It was a picture of Philip, only a much younger Philip

than the man Angel knew. He looked about twenty-one and was incredibly handsome.

"I miss him every day," said the Comtesse in a constricted voice, "and it has taken me many years to understand that what I did—that the actions I took that day—were those of a proud and unjust woman." She wiped away a tear with a lace handkerchief. "It is too late for me and Philip, but I hope it is not too late for me and you, Lily."

"I'm sure it's not."

"We shall see. Once you hear my story you may not feel so kind."

Angel hesitated. Part of her wanted to know what it was that had kept Philip de Tourney from his home and family for so many years, but another part of her whispered that it was none of her business—that she had no right to know— that if the Comtesse knew the truth of her identity she'd throw her out of the house rather than tell her what had happened with her son.

But she could see the yearning in Elena de Tourney's face—a longing to share her burden. Angel handed the photo back to her and said softly, "Tell me."

The Comtesse resumed her seat and said, "There was a girl. It sounds a hopeless cliché, does it not? But it is true. There *was* a girl. She was the daughter of our cook."

Angel smiled wryly. A cook's daughter—that was what Clarissa had called her back in New York.

The Comtesse, noticing her look, nodded. "You find it amusing that my son should have been so well-acquainted with such a person, but you see, she'd come to us as a girl and grown up in the servant's wing so Philip had known her since boyhood." She sighed. "I suppose I should have recognized the potential for danger much earlier, but I'd been brought up not to think of the staff in that way. Philip was away at school a good deal of the time, so it never occurred to me—"

"That they'd fall in love."

"No." The Comtesse plucked at her handkerchief. "When Philip told me what had happened, I was not convinced."

"Why?"

"Many reasons: he was young—practically a boy still— and inexperienced, and what does a twenty-two-year-old boy know about love?"

Angel thought of Nick—he was just nineteen but he seemed to know quite a lot about love. It didn't seem the moment to point it out to the Comtesse, however, so she said, "What about the girl? How did she feel?"

"Naturally, she, too, said she was in love—though not in so many words, for although she was only a cook's daughter, she had a remarkable pride. When I challenged her she told me that Philip had asked her to marry him, and she had said yes."

"He wanted to marry her?" asked Angel.

"That is what he said, but I was convinced she had tricked him into it. From adolescence she'd seen her chance, encouraged him through the years and refused to have him in her bed until they were married." The Comtesse's face reflected her distaste of such a ploy.

"You *know* that?" asked Angel. "It sounds so melodramatic."

The Comtesse said bitterly, "Of course she wanted marriage! She had everything to gain: wealth, power, position. But it was impossible and I told Philip so."

"What did he say?"

"He refused to listen, insisting that their love was real. That she was the only woman he would ever truly care for, there could never be anyone else and that she was his one true love—all the things a romantic boy tells his mother when she wishes him to end a relationship."

"So what happened?"

"I could not allow it to continue. You must understand,

in those days it was impossible to imagine a de Tourney married to a cook's daughter." The Comtesse pressed her handkerchief to her lips.

"What did you do?"

"I took the necessary steps."

"What were they?"

The Comtesse was silent for several moments and when she spoke again Angel could see it was an effort. "I made a mistake. I can say that now. I was proud and stubborn and I could not see—no—I *would* not see that your father truly was in love."

"So . . .?"

"So I sent him to America on business. I made sure it was an emergency so he would have no time to tell her he was leaving, and while he was gone I arranged a meeting with the girl."

"What happened?"

"I told her Philip did not love her. I told her he had gone to America to propose to Catherine—your mother—a girl of good family, old money and the right connections. A somebody. I told her that Catherine had been promised to Philip from the cradle."

"She can't have believed you! It sounds medieval."

"For most people in this modern age that is true, but she knew enough of Philip's world to know that such arrangements are still common among families such as ours. I also told her that Philip would not return to Paris until after his wedding."

"And she believed you?"

"Why not? It was a lie, but a convincing one, and I held all the cards—money, power and connections. She was poor and dependent—a student at the university. Besides, Philip had gone to America without saying goodbye. Once I had sown the seed of doubt I knew I would win." The Comtesse looked past Angel as if seeing some long-forgotten memory. "Though it was a near thing." She smiled grimly. "She was as proud and as stubborn as I was and she fought me! She told me she loved Philip and that he loved her. She stood in this room and said those exact words with such passion that she almost persuaded me."

"But not quite."

"No. Because I'd convinced myself that it was not passion but ambition that made her speak so and that the prospect of losing her chance of wealth and position *would* make her say that she loved him more than life itself."

"She said that?" Angel's eyes glowed with the romance of it all.

"She did, and in such a way. I can see her now, her head up, eyes blazing, defying me."

"What happened then?"

"I told her that Philip had always known he'd marry Catherine; that it was a perfect match and they were meant for each other."

"Did she believe you?"

The Comtesse considered the question, then said, "I don't know, she didn't say. Instead she asked me a question—she asked me if Catherine believed it."

"And you said yes."

"Yes."

"And what did she say to that?"

The Comtesse seemed to grow tired. She leaned back in her chair and put her hand over her eyes. Angel didn't move. When Elena de Tourney spoke again, her voice was so low that Angel had to lean forward to hear her.

"She said nothing. Nothing at all. She simply got up and left. But I shall never forget the look on her face. If she was defeated, it did not show—she lifted her chin, threw back her hair and walked out of this house as if she, and not I, were its owner. And she never once looked back."

No one spoke for a moment, and then Angel asked, "What about Philip?"

"Ah, yes, that is the question, isn't it?" A faint tinge of

color rose in the Comtesse's cheeks and she had the grace to look ashamed. "When Philip came home from America, I told him she had gone; that she'd left him for another man."

"He didn't believe you, did he?" cried Angel. She couldn't bear to think of Philip giving up on his true love so easily.

"Not at first. He accused me of lying, of sending her away and . . . of so many things. I begged him to listen to me, but he would not. He left the house and set about finding her. He searched for weeks, but she had left the university and no one knew where she had gone. There was no known family, apart from her mother who'd died two years earlier and a wastrel father she hadn't seen for years."

All the emotion faded from the Comtesse's voice, leaving it tired and empty. "Eventually, Philip hired a detective agency to find her. I tried to dissuade him but nothing I could say would make him believe that Simone did not love him. He—"

Angel's heart missed a beat. "What?" she cried. "*What* did you say?"

But the Comtesse wasn't listening. The years of pent-up emotion had finally found an outlet and she would not stop until she'd told it all. "He refused to believe me. He confronted me and told me that he loved Simone and was going to marry her. It was then that I realized I'd been wrong."

She raised her head and Angel saw the tears staining her cheeks. "What she'd told me that day was true—Philip truly loved her and I had destroyed his one chance at happiness." She looked at Angel with anguished eyes. "But I couldn't tell him the truth. How could I? He'd have hated me."

Angel stared at her, a hundred questions burning in her brain. Finally she found her voice. "Simone—she was the cook's daughter?"

The Comtesse nodded. "After her mother's death, she stayed on here working evenings and weekends until she finished her schooling. Then she won a scholarship to the university. Philip was already there and in that environment I think they both decided that the restrictions of their class could be thrown aside. If I had only seen the danger sooner."

"But where did she go?" interrupted Angel. She had to know, she had to be sure. "Did Philip find her?"

"The detectives found her two months later. Only it was too late."

"Too late?" cried Angel, confused. "Do you mean . . .?"

"No, no, not that! She was alive and well, but she was married."

"Married?" repeated Angel.

"Yes. Apparently she had gone to her father. He had a small farm in Brittany and Simone went there the day after our meeting. Two months later she married the owner of a neighboring vineyard and began a new life."

There it was: the final piece of the puzzle. Angel's father had owned the vineyard adjoining her grandfather's farm. She couldn't take it in: her mother had been Philip de Tourney's first great love.

Angel slumped back in her chair and asked flatly, "And Philip?"

"The day after he received the detective's report he told me I'd been right and he was leaving for America. When he arrived he went straight to Catherine and proposed. They were married two weeks later."

It was hard to focus on this part of the story for Angel's brain was seething with thoughts of her mother and Philip. It was too much. She needed to go somewhere quiet and try to make sense of it all.

Instead, she asked, "Was Philip happy?"

"Happy enough, especially after you were born. His golden Lily, he used to call you, and until your mother became ill you were all he needed to make his marriage work." The Comtesse's face took on a haunted look. "But then Catherine died and that summer your father brought you here. You were five and he thought you'd be happier in this house for a time. Nicky was also here with his parents."

"But that was the summer Philip took me to New York and never came back."

"Yes." The Comtesse smiled sadly. "I did not know then that it was to be your last summer in Paris—until now."

"What happened?"

"Philip found out what I'd done. You see, Simone had written him a letter explaining why she was going away. She told him what I'd said and that she understood his decision to marry 'one of his own class' if that was his choice. But she also told him that she truly loved him and that if he felt the same way all he had to do was write to her in Brittany and she would come to him. She said that she would live with him, with or without marriage, if that was what he wanted. All she needed to know was that he'd truly meant all the things he'd said to her."

"And did he write back?"

"No, because he never received her letter—at least, not then. He didn't find it until that last summer in Paris."

"But why?" cried Angel. "*Why* didn't he get her letter?"

"I will show you."

The Comtesse rose from her chair, crossed to one of the bookcases and pulled down an elegant volume bound in red Morocco leather. "This was their post-office: Jane Austen's novel, *Persuasion*—an ironic choice as it turned out." She let the book fall open. "They would leave their letters for each other in the back. Simone left her final letter for Philip the day after I confronted her. She returned to the house to collect her things and must have slipped in here to leave her letter in the one place she knew Philip would look."

"And did he?"

"Yes. It was the first thing he did when I told him she'd left him for another man."

"So why didn't he find it?"

"Because somehow it ended up in the wrong book." The Comtesse gestured to the bookcase. "As you can see, most of the volumes are bound in the same style. I cannot be sure, but I think that, in her haste, Simone put her letter in the wrong book. It is also possible that one of the maids let it drop when dusting the books and put it back where she thought best."

"So that summer was when Philip found the letter?"

"Yes." The Comtesse sat down again. "He confronted me with it and I had no choice but to tell him the whole story." She gazed at Angel, the lace handkerchief crushed between her fingers and the tears rolling unheeded down her cheeks. "He has never forgiven me."

Chapter Thirty-Two

Angel stared at her reflection and sighed. The dress was beautiful and the amethyst earrings and necklace lent to her by the Comtesse matched it perfectly. She was going to Nick's birthday party—she ought to feel excited. Instead, she felt strained and anxious.

It hadn't even helped that Maman had rung to say she was much better and coming home on Tuesday. Angel had been thrilled but it'd been hard to convey her excitement when all she could do was think about her mother and Philip.

It seemed to Angel as though her vision of the world had somehow rearranged itself. So much made sense to her now: Maman's cool reserve with Philip de Tourney—the man she'd once loved so desperately—and her fierce loyalty to Angel's father—the man she'd married on the rebound.

What a shock it must have been for Simone to come face-to-face with Philip in that restaurant on Times Square all those years ago. She wondered what they'd said to each other. Angel knew Maman wouldn't have told him about Papa's accident, his failed surgery or how she was working two jobs to try and make ends meet. But Philip was no fool and it wouldn't have taken much for him to see how tired she was or to figure out that she was struggling financially.

Which was probably why he'd made her such an irresistible offer.

How hard it must have been for Maman to accept it.

To accept a home and a job and a salary from the man she believed had betrayed her. Angel couldn't even begin to imagine what it must have cost her.

But she'd done it for Yves and for Angel.

If only she'd told me, thought Angel. It hurt her a little that Simone had never told her about Philip. Especially after Papa had gone. But perhaps it had been too hard. Philip had broken her mother's heart and to speak of the past or share her pain was not something Simone would ever do.

She'd married Papa and they'd had Angel and she'd chosen to look forward, not back. And she'd been happy with Yves—Angel was sure of it.

Her childhood memories were of a golden vineyard where Papa and Maman would hold her hands and swing her up to where the clusters of plump purple grapes hung on the vines. Sometimes Papa would pick a grape and put it in her mouth; Angel could still remember the sharp sweetness of the juice as it burst across her tongue.

And then the tractor had slipped its gears and everything had changed.

Maman had loved Papa so much that when she'd learned of the surgeon in America who might help him she'd sold everything and moved them to New York. She'd believed the surgery would heal his broken body and, when the first operation hadn't worked, she'd gone on believing right through the second and the third, until Papa had said "enough." He'd known the money was almost gone and he'd hated seeing Maman endlessly struggling to try and restore what they'd lost.

Simone had refused to return to France. She'd been convinced that somewhere in America there was someone who could help Papa and she'd gone on working and believing that almost to the end.

It was Papa who'd urged Simone to accept Philip's job offer. Had he known? Angel wondered suddenly.

Had Papa known that Philip de Tourney was his wife's first great love? Angel didn't think so, and even if he had, there was no doubting Simone's commitment to him and only him.

Philip must have known it too. Simone was married, for better or worse, and so he'd never told her about finding her letter five years too late.

Because it had been too late. For both of them.

And now? wondered Angel as she brushed out her hair. Would it help if her mother knew the truth? It might make her happy to know that Philip had not betrayed her. It would almost be worth the risk to see Simone truly happy again.

Perhaps when she got back to New York, she'd tell her mother everything. Angel sighed. Maybe the truth would be the best thing for everyone.

She picked up her evening bag. It was time to leave for the Crillon.

***

Angel lifted her skirts and stepped from the Bentley. It was raining lightly and Henri held the umbrella high as she shook out her amethyst ruffles before joining the Comtesse under the hotel archway.

The Hotel de Crillon was a gracious grey stone building facing the Place de la Concorde and Angel paused for a moment to admire the view across the square: the cobblestones glistening in the rain, the great obelisk pointing skywards and all around it the beautiful city of Paris.

"Come along, Lily," said the Comtesse.

As they moved through the hotel's opulent foyer, staff and guests alike stopped to stare at them: Angel, the epitome of youth and loveliness, and Elena de Tourney, looking like an empress in a high-necked emerald-green silk evening gown exquisitely embroidered with myriad tiny glass beads that winked and flashed green fire.

They joined the receiving line where Nick and his parents were greeting their guests and Angel's pulse quickened.

Nick was standing beside his father and Angel could see that it was from Lord Langham that Nick had inherited his broad shoulders, curly dark hair and engaging smile. Next to her husband, Nick's mother, Georgiana, looked tiny. She had a heavy rope of thick chestnut hair and her son's sparkling brown eyes and she smiled in delight when she saw Angel.

"Lily!" Lady Langham took her hand. "How lovely to see you at last. Nicholas has told us so much about you. How is darling Philip? Can it truly be eleven years since we were in touch? And here you are looking so grown-up." Her eyes danced. "We are going to have a wonderful talk later, so Nicholas is not to monopolize you all night."

Speechless, Angel nodded and moved down the receiving line to where Nick stood waiting.

He took her hand and said softly, "You look beautiful."

"And you look handsome," she replied, admiring his superbly cut black dinner suit.

"Thanks, I trust you noticed my tie?" He touched the elegant bow tie around his neck.

Angel stared. "But isn't that . . .?"

"Yes, exactly the same color as your dress. I asked Godmother to have it made especially."

"It's gorgeous."

He grinned. "I was worried it might end up lime-green or orange with stripes or something equally hideous."

"You obviously don't think much of my taste in clothes," retorted Angel.

"Well, you never can be sure," Nick joked.

Angel looked around the crowded room. "I think everyone looks gorgeous."

"Not as gorgeous as you." He drew her towards him. "Let's dance."

"Shouldn't you finish receiving your guests?" she asked anxiously, looking at his parents.

"I think it's okay," he replied, catching his mother's eye. She smiled and gave a tiny nod. "We have the all clear," said Nick triumphantly and swept Angel onto the dance floor.

It was a wonderful party. Angel moved through it as if in a dream and one that she was in no hurry to wake up from. Nick was in high spirits and, though mindful of his duties as host, seemed to want to spend every possible moment with her.

Everyone was there—Kitty and Giles and the rest of the summer season gang—all eager to celebrate Nick's birthday in style.

"You certainly know how to throw a party," she said, as they danced.

"I'm glad you're enjoying it."

"It's heavenly," she replied.

"Well, that's appropriate because you look like an angel."

Angel's smile faded. "Looks can be deceiving, you know."

Nick shook his head. "Not in your case—you're beautiful on the inside *and* on the outside." He groaned at himself. "It sounds so soppy when I say it out loud, but it's true." He pulled her closer. "I can't explain it, Lily, but I feel like I've known you all my life—and I don't mean because our families are friends, I mean that I feel like I *really* know you—as though you were part of me."

"If only that were true." Angel gazed up at him, her blue eyes sombre. "But there are so many things you don't know about me." She hesitated. "Things that if you *did* know, they would probably make you change your mind about me."

"Secrets, Lily?" said Nick, smiling. "I don't think there's anything you could say that would make me think badly of you."

"Do you believe that?"

"Well, I can't imagine that you've murdered anyone or robbed a bank or revealed government secrets—and I might even forgive you that last one."

She stared at him, her forehead wrinkled with uncertainty. Could she really tell him the truth: that she wasn't Lily de Tourney or even someone who belonged in his world? Would Nick still care for her if she told him that? Would he look at her with those melting brown eyes and hold her close if he knew she was a cook's daughter?

Angel wanted to believe he would.

It suddenly occurred to her that she was far more like her mother than she thought and maybe that should be a warning, because Simone had believed that Philip de Tourney would love her against all the odds and look how their love affair had ended.

She was aware of Nick watching her, obviously puzzled by her silence and wanting her to tell him whatever it was that was troubling her. Then it seemed to Angel as though he could bear it no longer. He gently lifted her face to his, bent down and kissed her.

It was sweet and perfect and it filled Angel with breathless pleasure. As his lips left hers, Nick whispered, "I love you."

A tidal wave of joy swept over her and she stared up at him in wonder. He loved her. Angel could hardly believe it was real. She hugged the words to herself and knew she had to tell him the truth. Now, before another minute passed.

"I love you, too, Nick," she said. Freeing herself from his embrace, she stepped back and took his hand. "But there's something I have to tell you."

She led him towards the Crillon's courtyard, but as she stepped through the doorway, Nick suddenly halted.

Angel turned, her gaze following Nick's, and her heart stopped beating.

Chapter Thirty-Three

Standing by the entrance were two women: one in a stunning white gown with an enormous ruby pendant at her breast and the other a dream in softest pink.

Margot and Clarissa Kane.

Still holding Nick's hand, Angel moved towards them.

As she crossed the room, she saw Margot speak to Nick's mother and Georgiana smile and nod, then escort them to the Comtesse's table.

She found her voice and managed to whisper, "Please, Nick, whatever you hear, please believe that I love you."

They reached the Comtesse's table just in time to hear her say to Margot, "May I help you?"

If it hadn't been so heart-stoppingly awful, it would have been funny to see Margot and Clarissa bob a sort of curtsey, but there was nothing comical about Margot's reply.

"Madame de Tourney, I am Margot Kane, your son Philip's fiancée, and I am here to expose an imposter." She pointed at Angel and declared dramatically, "You have been cruelly deceived."

The Comtesse raised her eyebrows. "Indeed?"

Margot tried again.

"That girl," she said, jabbing a finger in Angel's direction, "is not who she says she is."

The Comtesse looked from Margot's angry face to Angel's pale one, but said nothing.

Unable to keep silent, Clarissa cried out, "She's not your

granddaughter. Her real name is Angelique and she's a cook's daughter from New York."

Angel heard the startled whispers pass among the guests. Nick shifted slightly, but he didn't let go of her hand.

The Comtesse turned to face her. "Is this true? You are not Lily de Tourney? You are not my granddaughter?"

Angel gazed at her helplessly. She saw the certainty fade from the Comtesse's eyes and her face grow pale and in that moment she would have done anything to avoid saying the words she knew would bring nothing but pain.

"Yes, it's true. But I can explain—"

"She's been using you to get into Antoine Vidal's studio," declared Clarissa.

At her words, Vidal moved closer to the Comtesse.

"No!" cried Angel. "It's not what you think."

"She is a liar and a thief," cut in Margot. "You cannot believe anything she tells you."

"I am *not* a thief," retorted Angel.

The Comtesse turned her penetrating gaze upon Margot. "Can you prove such an extraordinary accusation, Madame?"

Angel stared at Margot. She was certain there was nothing she or Clarissa could do or say to support their claim and once they were discredited Angel could explain to the Comtesse about her mother and the Teen Couture and Lily and the London Academy.

"*I* can prove it." Clarissa's voice cut across her thoughts. Startled, Angel looked up to see her smile triumphantly, and for the first time she was assailed by doubt. A moment later her doubt turned to fear as Clarissa stepped forward and pulled a sketchbook from her bag.

"She's obsessed with the Teen Couture," proclaimed Clarissa. "We discovered she'd been copying my designs, but it was only yesterday that we learned she'd come to Paris with the intention of getting into Vidal's and swapping her signed forgeries for my original drawings."

Angel stared at her in horror. When Clarissa said it like that—with the truth mixed up with the lies—it almost sounded plausible. But there was worse to come.

Clarissa held out the sketchbook to the Comtesse, who took it and opened it. As she turned the pages, Angel's heart kicked into overdrive. It was one of her own sketchbooks filled with pictures of her Teen Couture garments in all their different stages.

Clarissa had signed every page with a flourish.

With a cry of protest Angel stepped towards the Comtesse. Nick moved with her, his hand still firmly clasping hers. "But that's mine—" began Angel.

"You would say that, wouldn't you?" Clarissa interrupted. "That's what liars do—they tell lies. Just like you've been lying about being Lily de Tourney—"

The Comtesse held up her hand. "Enough. There is one way to settle this argument. Antoine, if I might ask you to examine this sketchbook."

Vidal nodded curtly and took the sketchbook. Angel stood paralyzed as he turned the pages and examined the drawings. After what seemed like an eternity, he looked up.

"Yes, these are the designs stolen from my salon a week ago." He indicated the signature. "And this is the name of the designer whose drawings they were." He turned to Clarissa. "You are Mademoiselle Clarissa Kane?"

"I am," said Clarissa, nodding modestly.

"And you sent an entry to the Teen Couture from New York three weeks ago?"

"That's right."

"And this week you received a letter from me asking you to attend the Versailles Ball as a Teen Couture finalist?"

"I did," replied Clarissa.

Angel gasped.

Vidal spun round. "I knew I had seen you before," he said. "It came to me as you crossed the room just now. You were that waitress in New York—the one who fell."

"I was tripped—"

But Vidal was not listening. "I believe Mademoiselle Kane is who she says," he said. "Because if you, mademoiselle," he regarded Angel coldly, "were the true designer, then you would have made it known long before now."

His eyes flicked anxiously to the Comtesse's face. "The true designer would never have enacted this shameful masquerade as there would be no need for lies or theft." He turned to the Comtesse. "These designs," he tapped the sketchbook, "were stolen from my salon last Friday."

Locking her gaze onto Angel's, the Comtesse asked icily, "Did you take them?"

Angel stared at her, white-faced. She hadn't thought of this, but she could see at once how it must look.

She had to explain that she wasn't a thief, that those were *her* designs, not Clarissa's and that she'd only lied in order to right a terrible wrong.

"It's not what you think," she said, looking desperately round the room. No one moved.

The Comtesse asked again. "*Did* you take the designs from Monsieur Vidal's salon?"

"Yes!" cried Angel. "Yes, I did." She looked beseechingly at the Comtesse. "But they were mine—at least—they were *her* drawings, but of *my* designs, Grandmama."

Angel stopped, aghast, as the familiar word rolled off her tongue and appeared to strike Elena de Tourney a physical blow. "I . . . I'm sorry, Madame," she amended, wincing at the more formal title. "But if you'd just let me explain. You see, Clarissa's drawings were—"

The Comtesse cut her off. "You are *not* my granddaughter." And this time it was not a question.

"No."

"But you work for my son in New York."

"My mother does."

"And your real name is Angelique?"

Pale-faced, Angel nodded. "Though my friends call me Angel," she whispered.

The Comtesse paid no heed. "And my granddaughter— the real Lily de Tourney—is where?"

Angel hesitated, but there was no point trying to protect Lily now. "She's at the London Drama Academy," she said bleakly. "Lily won a place at their summer school. It was the same fortnight as Paris and she wouldn't give it up."

"So you thought it would be fun to swap places?" asked the Comtesse in a voice of steel.

"No!" gasped Angel. But the Comtesse was not listening.

"So everything you and I have shared this past fortnight was false." The Comtesse caught her breath. "You lied to me," she said in a voice colder than any Angel had ever heard. "You lied to us all."

"Yes," whispered Angel. She gazed helplessly around the room. There were Kitty and Giles, Rémy, Sebastian, Marianne and the rest of the gang, Señor Martinez, Lord and Lady Langham, Antoine Vidal and the Comtesse. All of them were looking at her as though seeing her for the first time.

On almost every face she saw hurt or suspicion or hostility. Only in Kitty's face was there any sign of sympathy.

Angel turned to Nick. He was still beside her, still holding her hand, his skin warm against hers.

She stared up at him pleadingly. Surely he'd believe her? Because—although it seemed like eons—only minutes ago he'd told her he *loved* her and Angel had been certain that he'd meant *her* and not Lily. They had a connection that went beyond names and families—Nick would never believe she was a liar and a thief.

Except that was exactly what she was: she'd lied to him from the beginning and she'd stolen his heart.

At the precise moment that the realization hit her, Nick let go of her hand.

The sense of loss was so great that Angel almost cried out.

She bit her lip and forced herself to turn away from him and meet the Comtesse's gaze. She wanted to look Elena de Tourney in the face and beg her one last time for the chance to explain. But all she saw was a face grown old, a face filled with doubt, regret and a deep, searing pain.

"I am *so* sorry," whispered Angel.

Suddenly, she could bear it no longer. "I'm sorry!" she cried. And before anyone could stop her, Angel picked up her skirts and ran.

She ran straight through the hotel to the Crillon's great revolving door. Blinded by tears, Angel pushed her way into it just as a figure clad in jeans and a T-shirt and carrying a duffel bag entered from the street.

Trapped on the other side of the slowly revolving door, Lily banged urgently on the glass. "Angel! Wait, please, Angel!"

But Angel didn't hear her as she ran out into the street. All she could focus on was a way to somehow escape from pain and confusion and unhappiness.

The rain had stopped and a cool breeze had blown away the clouds. A waning moon was rising but Angel saw only the open space of the Place de la Concorde and beyond it the bridge over the Seine.

Pulling off her high-heeled shoes and clasping them firmly in one hand, she lifted the beautiful amethyst dress with the other and, with tears streaming down her cheeks, fled across the cobblestones towards the river.

By the time Nick burst through the door, she was out of sight, her running form obscured by the obelisk in the middle of the square.

"Angel!" he called. "Angel!"

But there was no answer.

Chapter Thirty-Four

Angel ran blindly, with just one thought in her head: to get away. Away from the hurt and humiliation she'd wreaked on the Comtesse and Nick and everyone she'd come to care about.

She plunged into Paris's back streets, caring nothing for the hard pavement under her feet. So long as she didn't have to think about those last terrible moments, she didn't mind what physical pain she suffered.

But the images of them kept pressing on her mind: Nick with such hurt in his eyes and the Comtesse's face lined with pain.

If only she'd told them the truth, if only. Angel slowed to a walk and for the umpteenth time pushed the images away and tried to think of what to do.

She should have stayed and insisted the Comtesse hear the truth. Elena de Tourney mightn't have liked it and she probably wouldn't have forgiven her, but at least Angel would have exposed Clarissa and Margot for the frauds they were.

Why had she let them get away with such a cruel deception? Angel wondered. *Why hadn't she stood firm and answered their accusations with allegations of her own, instead of letting them convince everyone* she *was the* thief?

"Because right now I'm no better than them," whispered Angel. "Clarissa's a liar and a thief, but I'm a liar and a fraud."

It didn't matter that she'd agreed to the masquerade because Clarissa had stolen her designs and Margot had practically taken Simone hostage, because Angel could've waited until Maman was well and then told the truth.

It would have meant forgoing her entry into the Teen Couture, but at least she wouldn't have lost everything that mattered.

Even worse was that she'd repaid the Comtesse's kindness with deceit. For the past two weeks she'd let Elena de Tourney think she was her granddaughter and, although she might convince her she wasn't a thief, there was nothing she could say that would make her any less a liar.

Angel angrily dashed away a tear. How could she have been so stupid and selfish, not to have properly *considered* the consequences of her outrageous masquerade?

She'd wanted to stop Clarissa from cheating so much that she'd let herself believe Lily's blithe assurances that it would all work out. Sure, she'd never meant to hurt anyone, but she'd done it nonetheless.

If only Lily had been willing to put off the London Academy—she could have come to Paris and told everyone about Clarissa—but her acting was everything to her and Angel knew she'd stay in London until she'd fulfilled her dream.

And I totally get that, thought Angel, *because fashion design means everything to me.*

At least it used to.

Only a week ago she'd thought that seeing a haute couture fashion show and wearing a Vidal dress was the ultimate and that coming to Paris to stop Clarissa from cheating was vital.

"I was so wrong," whispered Angel, staring up at the stars. "Lily and I were both wrong." She knew that now. Because for the first time in her life she understood what it was to lose someone's love.

And in losing it she'd discovered its worth.

The price of betrayal had been too high and her deception had hurt too many people to ever make it worthwhile.

Angel turned a corner and the dome of *Les Invalides* loomed up before her. Beyond it she could see the Eiffel Tower lit up against the night sky. She wondered what Nick was doing and hoped his birthday party had continued after her dramatic departure.

She turned away. Right now, she didn't want to see anything that reminded her of him.

She passed the Rodin Museum and veered down a side street. Angel had no idea where she was going or what she was going to do. If only she had her phone she'd ring her mother and tell her everything. Simone would be furious, but Angel didn't care. Right now she'd give anything just to hear her voice.

But she couldn't ring her mother—she couldn't ring anyone! An icy invisible hand clutched Angel's heart as the reality of her situation burst upon her.

She was alone in the back streets of Paris, barefoot in an evening dress. She'd left her evening bag behind at the Crillon, which meant she had no money, no phone and no way of getting home. Her airline ticket and passport—even her designs—were all at the Comtesse's; the last person on earth who'd ever want to see her.

Angel stopped dead in the middle of the darkened street. In her headlong flight she hadn't for one moment considered what would happen to her once she was no longer Lily de Tourney.

As she stood there, staring at the stars above the Paris skyline, Angel Moncoeur shivered with cold and fright.

***

An hour later Angel dropped onto the seat beside the great

glass pyramid in front of the Louvre. Her feet were throbbing and she was so tired she could hardly think straight.

She'd never felt so alone and so utterly wretched.

At least it isn't raining, she thought, looking up at the clouds scudding across the sky. She wondered what time it was. She suspected it was nearly two, because she must have walked around for a couple of hours before coming here.

Her brain seemed to have moved beyond thinking about what had happened at the Crillon. She almost wished a policeman would come by and arrest her—at least the police station would be warm.

Angel had considered turning herself in, only she didn't relish the idea of spending the night in a cell. She'd go to the police station as soon as it got light. "Maybe they'll take me to the American embassy," she mused aloud, tucking her feet beneath her and lying down on the stone bench next to the Pyramid. She gazed up at the glass panes: hundreds of them reflecting the moon and the stars and the water in the fountain, and—

Angel yawned, and sat up. She mustn't go to sleep. Not here.

She'd think about what she was going to tell the embassy staff. That should keep her awake because the thought of telling anyone about the past two weeks was gut-wrenching. She decided she probably wouldn't mention Lily or swapping their passports or the Comtesse or the Teen Couture. Telling the embassy people the true story might see her committed or imprisoned rather than put on a plane and sent home.

Angel lay down again. She'd have to make up some story.

Great. More lies.

"Not that it matters," she told the sky. "After so many, what difference can a few more lies make?" She lay down again and stared at the Louvre.

Was it only yesterday that she'd been in there with Nick? It seemed like a lifetime ago that he'd told her she looked like an angel and kissed her for the first time . . .

A tear trickled down Angel's nose.

As the first drops of rain began to fall, Angel concluded that there was no point delaying the inevitable. She might as well be warm in a police station than soaking wet outside the Louvre with nothing to think about but Nick, the Comtesse and the mess she'd made of everything.

She slid her feet into her shoes and was doing up the buckles when she heard the sound of running footsteps and a voice calling, "Angel! Angel!"

Angel spun round to see Lily running towards her. A moment later she was being fiercely hugged.

"You're in London," said Angel, trying to breathe.

Lily laughed through her tears. "No, I'm here, just like I promised."

"But what about your play? Tonight's the dress rehearsal."

"Uh-huh and tomorrow's the play," said Lily, "but I won't be there."

"You have to be there!" cried Angel.

"No, I have to be *here*," replied Lily. "Here in Paris helping my best friend out of the rotten mess I got her into."

"Oh, Lily," said Angel, tears springing to her eyes.

Lily held out her pinky finger. "Friends?" she asked in a wobbly voice.

Angel linked her finger with Lily's. "Forever," she said firmly.

Lily hugged her again. "You didn't think I'd desert you, did you, Angel?"

"No, but—" Angel pulled free and looked Lily squarely in the face. "Things are really bad, Lily. I don't think anyone can fix them."

"It'll be okay, Angel, I promise." Lily took her hand. "Come on."

"How did you find me?" asked Angel, as they crossed the courtyard.

"I asked Nick."

"Nick?" Angel looked at her in astonishment. "But how? Where?"

"At the Crillon just after you left. I saw you in the revolving door, but you ran off before I could stop you." Lily grimaced. "I got there too late."

"But Nick can't have known where I'd be—I walked around for ages before I came here."

"Yes, but when I asked him if you'd been anywhere special together, he told me about *l'Orangerie* and the Ritz and the Eiffel Tower and the Louvre. So I just went to all of them in turn—I figured you'd go somewhere comforting."

"I'm glad you know me so well," said Angel stiffly. "And that Nick . . . Nick was kind enough to help you."

"Now don't go all uptight on me because you think it's over between you and Nick," said Lily. "Because I'm pretty sure you're wrong."

"What do you mean?" demanded Angel. "Of course, it's over. He couldn't possibly like me now. Not when he knows—when they all know—I'm an imposter."

"I don't know about that, given that he almost knocked me over running after you."

Angel turned pink. "He came after me?"

"Sure did. He's nice, Angel, and much better looking than I remember. And when he couldn't catch you, he came back to the party and tried to smooth things over with Grandmama."

For a moment hope flared in Angel's breast, before she saw the look on Lily's face.

"I'm guessing that didn't go so well?"

"You'd be right, though at least she didn't tear strips off Nick."

Angel looked at her friend in concern. "Was it bad?"

"Pretty bad. Nothing like I'd planned." Lily laughed bitterly. "I knew there was no point chasing after you until I knew what had happened so I just marched right up to her table and said, 'Hello, Grandmama, it's me, Lily.' I had this awesome speech all memorized, but I hadn't banked on Margot. I knew she'd flown to Paris, but I hadn't expected her to be sitting right there next to Grandmama oozing charm."

"What happened?"

"She played the loving mother card like you wouldn't believe." Lily mimicked Margot's voice perfectly, "Oh, don't be too hard on Lily, Elena, she just needs a little motherly guidance. It isn't her fault that she was taken in by the cook's daughter." Lily scowled. "She called you a liar and a thief and that's when I lost it."

"What did you say?"

"I yelled at her. I told her *she* was the liar and Clarissa was the thief. I said that you were the truest, bestest friend ever, but . . ." Lily's voice trailed away.

"But no one listened, did they?"

Lily shook her head. "It wasn't that. It was worse. Grandmama suddenly went ballistic—sort of icy-scary ballistic, like lava under a glacier. I was in the middle of saying for the millionth time that you weren't a thief when she cut me off mid-sentence and demanded to know if your mother's name was Simone."

"But how did she know?" Angel blanched. "What did you say about me *exactly*?"

"I don't know, something like, 'Angel Moncoeur is not a thief.' Why?"

"I'll tell you later. What happened next?"

"I said, yes, your mother was Simone and that she'd practically raised me. After that, Grandmama turned into this raging mega-empress and wouldn't let me get another word in." Lily frowned. "I tried to explain, Angel, I really did, but she wouldn't listen. She said . . ."

"Said what?" demanded Angel. "Tell me, Lily, it can't get much worse."

Lily sighed and then said heavily, "She said she never wanted to hear your name again."

They walked in silence for a minute before Angel spoke. "I think I'd better call Maman. Lend me your phone?"

"We're not calling Simone—not till we've fixed things."

"Well, I can't fix anything in this dress," declared Angel. "And I can't go back to the Comtesse's. I've got no passport, no money and no phone, so I need to call—"

"We don't need money," said Lily abruptly, digging in her duffel bag. "Not when we've got this." She held out her hand.

"But that's your platinum Visa! Emergency use only."

"What's this if it's not an emergency?" demanded Lily. "Anyway, I think we should try ringing Dad before we ring Simone."

"I guess," said Angel slowly. "But if Philip doesn't pick up, I'm ringing Maman."

"Okay."

They reached the Rue de Rivoli.

"Can you charge a cab fare and a hotel room to that thing?" asked Angel, nodding at the card.

"Definitely. We can even order room service," said Lily, smiling.

Angel looked about for a cab. "Let's wait over there," she suggested, pointing across the road at the brightly lit shop windows. "One's bound to come along soon."

As they crossed the road, Angel said suddenly, "How did you know Margot and Clarissa were in Paris?"

"Elizabeth Montague rang me."

"But how did she know?"

"A journalist from *The Times* came to my rehearsal. He was writing an article about Americans in London." Lily bit her lip. "I was so rapt that he'd mentioned me and my performance it never occurred to me that anyone back home would see it. But Elizabeth saw it online and called Clarissa."

"But Elizabeth hates Clarissa." Angel looked confused.

"Which is why she wanted to make sure Clarissa knew about my success. She had no idea I was meant to be in Paris. So when Jacqueline told her that Margot and Clarissa were a no-show at the Country Club dance because they'd flown to France, Elizabeth got worried and rang me."

"If I'd only known they were coming . . ." began Angel.

"I tried calling you, but you didn't answer, and that's when I knew I had to get to Paris."

"But when did Elizabeth call you?"

"About five minutes before I was due to go on stage," said Lily. "I left for the airport straight away."

"But what did you tell the Academy?"

For one awful moment Angel thought Lily was going to cry and then she said firmly, "Nothing. There wasn't time. I barely had time to tell the understudy." She lifted her chin. "I told Brett though."

"What did he say?"

"He was furious. He told me not to go."

"But you came anyway," said Angel.

Lily's eyes met hers. "I nearly didn't, Angel. Brett told me that if I walked out, the Academy wouldn't have me back."

Angel paled. "I never meant for you to do that," she whispered.

"You'd have done it for me, Angel."

Angel nodded. She stared down the street, trying not to think of what they'd both lost: the London Academy, the Teen Couture, Lily's friendship with Brett, and Nick.

She looked up. "After Nick told you about the Louvre, did he say anything else?"

"After he'd finished yelling at me, you mean?"

"Nick *yelled* at you?"

"Yeah, a bit, at first, but only because he was worried about you."

"Really?"

"Sure. He'd have been out looking for you except his parents told him he couldn't desert his guests and it was better to leave it to the police."

"The police!" Angel was aghast.

"Yeah, but it's okay, because I called them as soon as I saw you. By now, everyone will know you're safe—including Nick." Lily took her hand. "Don't look so miserable. If you want to know my opinion, I'm pretty sure it's not over between you two."

Angel stared at her, torn between hope and wretched disbelief. "But even if that were true," she said at last, "it'd never work. Not now that the Comtesse and Vidal and Nick's parents know the truth. They must hate me." Her face quivered. "Don't you see? I can never come to Paris again and I'll *never* be able to work in fashion." She choked back a sob. "Not when Antoine Vidal believes I'm a thief and Clarissa is the real designer."

"Well, we'll just have to prove him wrong," said Lily firmly. "Show him and everyone else that Angel Moncoeur is not only a better person than the real Lily de Tourney, but she is also one heck of a fashion designer."

"But how?" asked Angel. "It's impossible. It can't be done."

"Oh, yes it can, because there's a taxi and I have a plan."

Chapter Thirty-Five

The minute the cab door closed, Lily called her dad. "Fingers crossed he's not in some remote bit of jungle," she said, using the speaker phone so Angel could hear.

To their surprise Philip picked up after only one ring. "Hello?"

"Dad, it's me," squeaked Lily.

"Lily! I was about to call and see if you were home."

"Home?" said Lily, frowning. "But you know I'm not in New York."

"Not in New York?" Angel heard the surprise in his voice. "Where are you?"

"In Paris."

"Paris! What the devil are you doing in Paris?"

"Visiting Grandmama, like you wanted."

"I wanted?" Philip asked. "Lily, my darling daughter, what are you talking about? I never said I wanted you to go to Paris."

"But Margot told me that you—" Lily stopped and stared at Angel as the truth burst upon them.

Margot had lied that day in Philip's study. Philip hadn't rung her from an airport in South America—Margot hadn't even spoken to him. She'd received the Comtesse's invitation and, wanting Lily to accept it, had made up the whole story about Philip insisting she go to Paris. Margot had used Lily, just as she'd used Angel and Simone and Lily's dad in her march up the social ladder.

"Lily? Are you there?" Philip's voice came down the phone and Angel nudged her.

"Yes, Dad."

"Right, now tell me exactly where you are, because I'm coming to get you."

"What do you mean you're coming to get me? Where are you?"

"I'm in Paris, too."

"What? But I thought you weren't coming to Paris for another two weeks!"

"I wasn't, but the Brazilians brought the merger forward. I flew up this morning to meet the partners."

"Oh. Where are you?"

"At the Hotel Versailles," replied Philip, "on the Boulevard Haussmann."

Lily laughed. "The Versailles. Oh, that's perfect, Dad—it's almost as if you knew."

"Knew what?"

"We'll tell you everything when we see you," said Lily firmly.

"What do you mean 'we'?" demanded Philip. "It's two-thirty in the morning! Who are you with, Lily?"

"It's okay, Dad, we'll be there in five." She hung up.

When the taxi stopped outside the Hotel Versailles, Philip was already outside, pacing the pavement.

Angel saw the relief on his face as Lily got out of the cab. He bounded forward, pulled her into a fierce embrace and said, "Okay, young lady, start talking—" He broke off as Angel emerged from the cab.

"Angel!" cried Philip. "What on earth?" He looked at her damp evening dress and bedraggled hair and said abruptly, "Okay, I need to hear the whole story, but first let's get you somewhere warm." He thrust a fifty-euro note at the cab driver and ushered the girls into the hotel.

Somewhere warm turned out to be the Hotel Versailles penthouse.

It was an enormous apartment and Lily made straight for the plushest sofa, dropped onto it and pulled Angel down beside her.

Philip sat in the armchair opposite. "Right, confession time. You first, daughter of mine."

Angel felt Lily hesitate and seized the moment. "It's my fault."

Lily interrupted, "No, it isn't." She took Angel's hand. "It's nice of you, Angel, but we both know that this whole stupid plan was my idea." She met Philip's gaze. "The truth is that two weeks ago I convinced Angel to come to Paris in my place so that I could go to the London Drama Academy summer school." She saw her father frown and rushed on. "I know how you feel about me and acting and I know I shouldn't have done it and I'm sorry I deceived you." She pulled a face. "It's just that, ever since Christmas, things haven't been that great between us. So when Margot told me I had to accept Grandmama's invitation, I thought—"

"Margot did *what?*"

"Margot told me you wanted me to visit Grandmama so she could introduce me to Paris society and take me to the Versailles Ball," explained Lily. "I didn't want to go because it meant missing the London Academy and—" Lily eyed her father uncertainly. "And there were other reasons, too."

"What reasons?"

Angel could see Lily eyeing him doubtfully. "Tell him, Lily," she whispered. "It'll be okay."

Lily took a deep breath. "I didn't want to go to Paris because I thought it meant that . . ."

The frown faded from Philip's face. He leaned forward and took her hands in his. "Meant what, sweetheart?"

"That you'd discussed it all with Margot. I thought you'd rung her from South America instead of me—like she was my mother—and so I figured that you'd finally decided to marry her!"

"But I hadn't spoken to Margot," said Philip.

"No," agreed Lily, "but I didn't know that and . . ." She looked imploringly at Philip. "You *can't* marry her, Dad! Margot's not who you think she is, she's—"

"Not the right person for me," cut in Philip. He smiled ruefully at the two girls who were staring at him open-mouthed. "I know what I said last Christmas, Lily, but I've had time to think while I've been in the Amazon."

"About Margot?" asked Lily.

Philip nodded. "And about our future together."

"And?"

"And I realize we want different things. She's someone who could give me a certain kind of life and she'd be very good at it, but . . ."

"But it's not what you want," said Angel suddenly.

Philip stared at her, then shook his head. "No, it isn't."

"So what are you going to do, Dad?" demanded Lily.

He rubbed his chin thoughtfully. "I'll need to talk to Margot about a lot of things—including this business of sending you to Paris—but I'm not going to marry her, so you can stop worrying about that. As for the rest, I'll admit there's part of me that would like to be married and you certainly need someone to keep an eye on you." He looked at her sternly. "But for now, at least, I think that someone had better be me."

Lily made a sound that was somewhere between a laugh and a sob. "I promise to behave better," she cried, throwing her arms around his neck. "And I never meant to hurt anyone, not Grandmama or Angel or—"

"Which brings me to my next question," said Philip, disentangling himself from Lily's embrace. "If your grandmother thinks Angel is you, then what the devil is she doing letting Angel run round Paris by herself in the middle of the night?"

The two girls looked at each other and then Angel said firmly, "Clarissa stole my designs for the Teen Couture, so I agreed to take Lily's place at her grandmother's because that was the only way I could get into Vidal's and swap the entries without anyone knowing. I was going to tell Nick and the Comtesse the truth, only—"

"Only Margot and Clarissa showed up at Nick's party tonight," Lily interrupted, "and told everyone that Angel was our housekeeper's daughter and a thief. Grandmama wouldn't listen when she tried to tell her the truth so Angel ran away. Elizabeth Montague had rung me in London to tell me that Margot and Clarissa were in Paris so I flew straight from London, only I got here too late and—"

"We never meant it to get so complicated," interjected Angel. "And we didn't mean to hurt anyone."

"And what about Simone?" demanded Philip suddenly. "What did you tell her you were doing?"

Angel and Lily looked at each other.

"She thinks Angel's at summer camp," said Lily.

"So you lied to her too?" Philip frowned.

"We had to Dad," insisted Lily. "The whole identity swap was a total secret and Angel only agreed to it because Margot threatened not to pay Simone's medical bills unless Angel let Clarissa get away with stealing her Teen Couture designs."

"But I'd pay Simone's medical bills," interrupted Philip. "She must have known that."

Angel shook her head. "She didn't want you to." She hesitated. "I came to Paris to stop Clarissa from cheating but I never meant—"

Philip held up his hand. "Explanations can wait. Right now we have to let Simone know what's going on."

"I guess," said Lily.

"I suppose," conceded Angel.

"We must," said Philip. "You two have a lot of explaining to do but it'll have to wait until tomorrow. It's past three and high time you were in bed."

"I can't go to bed until I've told you my plan, Dad," insisted Lily.

Philip raised an eyebrow. "The only plan you need to be making, Lily, is how you're going to apologize to your grandmother when we visit her tomorrow." He sighed. "I always thought that one day I'd take you to meet your grandmother, but I never imagined this scenario."

"Well, I'm sorry about that, Dad," said Lily abruptly. "But right now, Grandmama is the least of our priorities. It's Angel we have to think of, because it's Angel who's going to suffer if we don't fix things. If you can tell me what the time is in New York, I can tell you what I need you to do."

"No, Lily—"

"*Please*, Dad," begged Lily. "I know I've messed up but I can make things right if you'll just trust me."

Philip looked at her, then Angel and then his watch. "New York time is nine yesterday evening."

Lily clapped her hands. "That means there's still time for someone to go to our house, collect Angel's ball gown and courier it to Paris."

"My gown?" exclaimed Angel. "But what are you going to do with it?"

"*I'm* not going to do anything with it," said Lily, her eyes sparkling. "You are."

She pulled Angel to her feet. "If Dad can get it onto tonight's eleven o'clock plane, it should be here by lunchtime. Which means . . ."

Angel's eyes gleamed. "Which means I can finish it and you can take it and show the Comtesse or even Monsieur Vidal."

"Even better," said Lily, grinning. "Tomorrow night, you can wear it to the Versailles Ball!"

Chapter Thirty-Six

Angel stared at her. "Wear my gown? I can't! How can I? They wouldn't let me in the door."

"They'll let you in, all right," said Lily, "because Dad will escort you." She looked questioningly at Philip, who nodded.

"But even if I dared to go, no one will listen to me. They'll—"

"They won't have to *listen*. They just have to *see*. Think about it, Angel: you in your ball gown, Clarissa in hers . . ."

"Oh," breathed Angel, a sudden vision taking hold in her mind. "Oh."

"All we need is for someone in New York to collect your dress and get it to Paris."

"What about Simone?" asked Philip. "If Angel calls her mother, I can have a car pick her up. She can bring the dress to Paris herself—" He broke off as both girls swung round to stare at him.

"You don't know . . ." began Angel.

"Oh, Dad," said Lily.

"What?" asked Philip. "What is it?"

"Maman's not there." Angel stopped, suddenly unsure of how to explain and wishing she knew whether Philip still cared for her mother in that way.

"What do you mean she isn't there?" demanded Philip. "Where is she?" A sudden thought seemed to strike him. "Has something happened to Simone?"

"She's been ill," said Angel gently.

"She nearly died," added Lily bluntly.

Both girls watched in dismay as the color drained from Philip's face. He put his head in his hands and groaned.

Lily stared at Angel in confusion but she shook her head. After a minute Philip raised a face so lined with fear that Angel's heart beat faster. Suddenly, he didn't look like an employer worried about his housekeeper, he looked like a man afraid of losing someone he loved.

He ran his hand through his hair. "Is she . . . Will she be all right?"

"Yes," said Angel, anxious to reassure him. "She had to have surgery and she's been convalescing in Florida, but she's coming home on Tuesday."

"Tuesday?" repeated Philip.

"Yes," Angel nodded. "I spoke to her today and she was planning to have a friend drive her up to see me at summer camp."

"And you're sure she's okay?"

"She said she was feeling fine," Angel assured him.

"Right," said Philip, standing up. "Go to bed both of you. No—" He silenced Lily's protests with a look. "You've done more than enough; it's my turn to make things happen." He turned to Angel. "Write a list of what you need from New York and I'll have it here by lunchtime. Lily?"

"Yes, Dad."

"We've got a lot to talk about and not all of it will be pleasant," said Philip sternly.

"No, Dad," replied Lily in a subdued voice.

"But right now it can wait." Philip's eyes glittered. "I've got some calls to make."

***

When Angel awoke it took her several minutes to work out where she was. There was no grinning faun on the ceiling and her bedroom at home didn't have a chandelier. Then she remembered.

She was in the penthouse at the Hotel Versailles and tonight was the Versailles Ball.

Angel scrambled out of bed and pulled on the satin robe supplied by the hotel. She wondered if Lily would be able to collect her clothes when she visited the Comtesse today and remembered the grubby jeans and T-shirt she'd brought to the airport two weeks earlier. It seemed like a year ago.

How naïve she'd been. And how unprepared for everything that'd happened since. She glanced at the bedside clock; it was almost one and the sun was shining.

She wondered if Philip had called Maman. Angel couldn't imagine how that conversation would have gone. Maybe it was a good thing Philip had ordered her and Lily to bed. And what about her ball gown? Could he have flown it to Paris in time for the ball?

Angel ran down the hall, pushed open the sitting-room door and stopped dead.

In the middle of the room stood a brand new dressmaker's dummy and on it, with her needle still waiting for its silver thread, was Angel's midnight-blue-and-silver ball gown.

With a cry of joy she ran across the room and caught the velvet between her hands. She rubbed it gently against her cheek and looked around. There was no sign of Philip or Lily but propped against a vase of orchids was a note:

Room service will deliver your lunch at 1:30. I've taken Lily to make peace with her grandmother. Back around 4.

Philip.

Angel considered the message. Did Philip mean that he had also gone to make peace with the Comtesse? Angel couldn't help thinking how happy his mother would be if her son would only forgive her.

And it would be better for Philip, too, Angel decided, picking up a piece of silk gauze and pinning it into place. He'd lost so much love in his life—first Simone, then his wife and finally his mother. If the Comtesse would only tell him how sorry she was, thought Angel, plying her needle carefully through the delicate fabric, surely Philip would open his heart to her.

She wondered if Philip would talk to his mother about Simone. From what Lily had said, the Comtesse had gone ballistic when she'd heard Simone's name, so it must have been a terrible shock to discover that Angel was her daughter.

Angel snipped her thread. She didn't like to imagine how the Comtesse would feel on learning that she'd treated Simone Moncoeur's child as her own granddaughter.

"Think of something else," said Angel firmly and picked up another piece of silver gauze.

It was after six when Lily returned to the hotel where Angel was anxiously waiting for her.

"Lily! Thank goodness," cried Angel, hugging her. "Are you okay?"

"I'm fine," replied Lily. "Things didn't go exactly to plan, that's all."

"What happened?" asked Angel. "Was the Comtesse mad? Did she see Philip? Did they talk? Tell me, *please.*"

"Grandmama is in the hospital," said Lily, throwing herself onto the sofa. "She'll be okay," she added quickly. "Don't look like that, Angel! I promise you, she's fine."

"What happened?"

"Apparently she's diabetic and she let her blood sugar get too low. She'd passed out just before we got there and we had to call an ambulance." Lily took Angel's hand. "I promise you she's okay. Marcel knew exactly what to do and the medics were there pronto."

"How's Philip?"

"Well, considering I left him and Grandmama almost

coming to blows over whether she'd attend the Versailles Ball tonight, I'd say they're both fighting fit."

"Thank goodness," said Angel, falling into an armchair. "I was worried they mightn't speak to each other."

"No chance of that," said Lily. "They didn't stop talking from the minute Grandmama opened her eyes in the hospital and saw Dad sitting beside her bed. It was pretty special. She took one look at Dad, cried out, 'Philip! My son!' and then burst into tears."

"Wow," said Angel, imagining the scene.

"Yeah, well, it wasn't 'wow' for very long," replied Lily, punching a cushion. "'Cause after she stopped crying and telling Dad how sorry she was for all the wasted years and he'd hugged her and told her it was all right, he went off to talk to the doctor, and left me to apologize for switching places with you."

"And?"

"And nothing," said Lily, scowling. "She might be in a hospital bed but it hasn't stopped her from being the most stubborn, pigheaded . . ." She pummelled the cushion. "I never met anyone so set on having their own way."

Angel smiled. Maybe Lily was more like her grandmother than she knew.

"Did you tell her about me?" she asked.

"I tried," replied Lily crossly. "But that's what I mean by stubborn. Like last night, when no matter how many times I tried to tell her the truth, every time I mentioned your name, she'd shut me down and refuse to listen."

Angel winced. "And today?"

"A bit better, but not much," said Lily crossly. "She still wouldn't hear a word about you, but she let me apologize, and she's invited me to stay in August before school goes back. But to be honest, she didn't seem all that enthusiastic." Lily looked sideways at Angel. "If you want to know what I think, I think she's annoyed that I'm not you."

"Don't be stupid," said Angel. "The last person the Comtesse wants in her life is me."

"I'm not so sure," said Lily, tossing her cushion onto Angel's lap. "I think she's missing you."

Chapter Thirty-Seven

It was a quarter to ten when Angel left the penthouse to go downstairs. Her heart thumped as she waited for the elevator and she touched her finger to the embroidered silver angel on the bodice of her ball gown.

She ran over the plan in her head again: Philip would meet her in the vestibule at the top of the stairs at ten and they'd enter the ballroom together—just before Vidal announced the winner of the Teen Couture.

"That way we can be sure Clarissa will be there," Lily had declared before going downstairs. "Because it'd be just like her to be late so she can make an entrance."

"And what about Margot?" Angel had asked. "Will Philip have talked to her by then?"

"I think so," said Lily. "After we'd finished at the hospital he said he had something he had to do and would meet me at the ball." She smiled gleefully. "I assumed he was going to break it off with Margot, so I didn't ask questions."

Maybe Margot will be too upset to come to the ball, thought Angel hopefully, as the elevator descended. The doors pinged and she stepped into the hall with her heart in her mouth, but the two security guards just smiled and waved her on. Trying not to run, Angel turned into the vestibule and positioned herself behind the heavy brocade curtain guarding the entrance to the ballroom.

Peeping out from behind it she could see the wide marble staircase that she'd have to go down.

The Hotel Versailles was majestic and its famous ballroom was its crown jewel. Gazing at the huge painted murals and elaborate gilt decorations, Angel was reminded of the Louvre.

Only the Louvre isn't lit by twelve huge chandeliers and filled with five hundred party guests, she thought, staring down at the men in their white ties and black tails and the women in their exquisite gowns.

She could see Kitty, gorgeous in her celestial blue satin ball gown, looking radiantly happy as she danced with Giles. And there was the Comtesse, superb in a dress of molten-gold silk with no sign she'd been ill.

Angel was relieved. She'd been worried when Lily had told her that the Comtesse was attending the ball. "Grandmama insisted. Said she'd never missed a Versailles Ball and didn't intend to start now. She wouldn't listen to the doctors—just discharged herself and went home to get ready."

Angel thought she could understand the Comtesse's decision. It wasn't just the Versailles Ball that she cared about. Last night, Elena de Tourney had suffered the humiliation of Angel's very public unmasking. To be absent from the grand occasion at which she'd hoped to introduce her granddaughter to Paris society would have been an admission of defeat.

And that was never going to happen. Not so long as the Comtesse de Tourney had breath in her body.

Angel scanned the ballroom for Philip, but she couldn't see him anywhere. She found Nick, though. He looked amazing in formal wear and she felt a pang of envy as he led Lily onto the dance floor. If only . . .

But this was no time for regret. She needed to find Philip.

She found Margot instead, looking stunning as she stalked across the ballroom in a strapless evening gown of scarlet taffeta. Angel felt her stomach clench as she watched her make straight for the Comtesse's table and sit down. She saw Margot say something to Vidal and felt a surge of disappointment when he laughed. He and the Comtesse seemed completely captivated and there was no sign that Philip had broken up with her.

Worse, there was no sign of Philip.

The great clock above the stairs struck ten and Angel's heart thumped as, around the ballroom, people turned to watch Vidal make his way to the dais.

Behind him came the Teen Couture finalists: Clarissa, striding ahead with two male contestants on her left, each escorting a Vidal model: one in gentian, the other in bridal white. While behind them came the other three finalists: a tall brunette in a black organza gown, a slender blonde in indigo silk and lace, and a raven-haired Hispanic-looking girl in pale-green tulle.

The contestants stepped onto the dais and took their places on either side of a black marble pedestal on which stood a magnificent silver trophy.

As Antoine Vidal approached the microphone, Angel saw the Comtesse rise and speak to Margot. She saw Margot nod and smile and watched in dismay as the two women—their gold and scarlet gowns almost touching—made their way to the front of the crowd.

Vidal began his speech and it was then that Angel realized: if she was going to change things she would have to do it alone.

She felt paralyzed.

Suddenly, Vidal switched from French to English, startling Angel.

"And I am delighted that this year's Teen Couture has seen the highest standard of entry since the competition began." Vidal nodded to the six finalists. "I congratulate you for your vision, your determination and for the meticulous execution of your designs. But, as always, there can only be one winner."

Angel held her breath as Vidal held aloft the shining silver trophy. "The winner of this year's Teen Couture is . . . Mademoiselle Clarissa Kane."

Any noise Angel might have made by her sudden expulsion of breath was drowned out by Clarissa's squeal of excitement as she ran towards Vidal.

In that moment, Angel felt the fear that had paralyzed her give way to a sudden rush of anger. She watched Clarissa receive the silver trophy and take the microphone.

Angel stepped forward.

She heard Clarissa say, "Monsieur Vidal, Madame de Tourney, ladies and gentlemen."

She saw Clarissa hesitate as a ripple ran through the audience and saw her shrug her smooth white shoulders, before continuing, "The Teen Couture is the most prestigious—"

Angel descended.

She saw Clarissa stop speaking and slowly turn to see what every one of the five hundred guests was staring at.

It might have been rage that had propelled Angel forward, but it faded the instant she took her first step down the great staircase. This was the moment she had visualized all those months ago and she wanted to savor it, no matter what waited for her at the bottom of the stairs.

She didn't hear the gasp that rose from the crowded ballroom as she came down the stairs. She was too busy listening to the soft whisper of the velvet and the rustle of the silk gauze behind her shoulders. She felt the embrace of the fitted blue bodice against her breasts and the delicate silver filigree straps across her shoulders and watched in ecstasy as the half-skirt of sparkling silver gauze rippled across the midnight-blue velvet of her gown like sparkles on the sea.

It was the velvet that filled her with the greatest joy. It was exactly as she'd imagined that day in the little shop in Soho: the deep blue, the pussycat softness and the sensual way it moved, pouring over her hips to embrace the floor.

As she reached the last step, it seemed to Angel as though she'd found a way to inhabit her dreams and she stood for a moment, letting herself soak up the feeling.

Then she heard the voices.

They rose up from the crowd, softly at first, then gradually louder, as the guests stared, first at her, then at Clarissa, and then back at her again: like spectators at a tennis match. Angel saw the incredulity and heard the outrage as she stood there in what appeared to be an exact replica of Clarissa's gown.

"Who is she?"

"Where does it come from?"

"Impossible!"

"*Ce n'est pas possible.*"

"*Incroyable.*"

"It's incredible!"

"How can it be?"

She moved slowly towards the stage, trying not to hear the answers.

"It is the American girl—the imposter."

"Such audacity."

"*L'audace.*"

"It is the girl who broke into Vidal's salon."

"The thief."

"*C'est la voleuse americaine.*"

The scandalized whispers swirled in an angry buzz around Angel and an insidious tingle of fear skittered across her skin. She saw the hostility in a hundred pairs of eyes and almost turned back, when a voice rose up clear and strong above the whispers.

"Go on, Angel, remember—*fortuna favet fortibus.*"

It was Nick.

She looked around and there he was, standing between his parents smiling at her, his brown eyes warm and affectionate, urging her on.

"Fortune favors the bold," whispered Angel.

Every voice fell silent as she passed through the crowd and halted in front of the girl who had so ruthlessly tried to steal her dream.

They faced each other: Clarissa, tall and elegant, a magnificent ice-queen in midnight-blue velvet and silver gauze, and Angel: soft and ethereal, an otherworldly creature in an identical gown.

Angel critically examined Clarissa's dress. Right down to the delicately embroidered silver angel on the bodice; it was a mirror image of her own.

She stared into the cat-like green eyes of her enemy.

"Hello, Clarissa."

"I have nothing to say to you," said Clarissa haughtily and turned away.

"Oh, don't go," said Angel. "Not when it's about to get interesting."

"I don't speak to thieves," said Clarissa curtly. "I don't know how you have the nerve to be here in the gown that I designed." She looked tragically around the ballroom.

Angel saw several people nod sympathetically.

As if sensing her advantage, Clarissa said, "I'm sorry for you, because I know what it is to dream. But I forgive you for stealing my design."

All around them people murmured their approval of her magnanimity.

But Angel said, "*Your* design?"

"That's right," replied Clarissa firmly.

"Then tell me, Clarissa, why the silver angel?"

To her surprise, Clarissa laughed. "Isn't it obvious?" She touched the embroidery on her bodice. "It's my logo: 'Angel Designs.' Didn't you know?"

Angel gasped. "You're lying! You—"

Clarissa interrupted, "You're the only liar here." She glanced round the ballroom. "We all know that."

Angel took a deep breath. "Okay, if the angel is your

logo then you can tell us how you made it."

"Well, duh, I embroidered it, obviously."

"Yes, but how?" persisted Angel.

"I have my methods," said Clarissa loftily.

"I'd like to hear them."

"As if I'd share confidential design information with a thief," retorted Clarissa.

"Then share it with me," said Lily, stepping out of the crowd. "I'd love to hear all about *your* design."

"Me too," called Kitty, letting go of Giles's hand and running forward to stand beside Angel. "If you're the designer, then you can tell Lily—I mean Angel—what she wants to know."

"I don't have to tell her anything," snapped Clarissa, glaring at the trio.

"Then perhaps you can tell me," said a voice. They all turned to see Antoine Vidal coming towards them. "The embroidery on this gown is of a particularly high standard and I should like to hear how you achieved it."

Clarissa paled slightly, but held her ground. "It . . . it's tambour beading."

Vidal nodded. "Yes, I see that. And what sort of implement did you use?"

Clarissa hesitated, and then said firmly, "A tambour needle."

Vidal nodded and turned to Angel. "And you, mademoiselle, how did you achieve this effect?" he asked, pointing at her silver angel.

"With a Lunéville hook," replied Angel. "My mother taught me when I was little."

"I see," said Vidal. He looked thoughtfully at Angel and then turned to Clarissa. "You have created a magnificent ball gown, mademoiselle," he said. "Perhaps you would be so kind as to tell me about the thinking behind your design?"

"My . . . my thinking?" echoed Clarissa.

"Yes. Every designer has their inspiration and I'm sure we'd all like to hear about yours. For instance, why the silver gauze?"

For a split second Clarissa's knuckles showed white as she gripped her trophy. She glanced desperately at Margot, who did not move.

"I . . . I just liked it," said Clarissa at last.

There was a sudden buzz of conversation and around her Angel could see a glimmer of doubt in people's faces.

Clarissa must have felt it because she coughed and tried again. "The silver gauze accentuated the blue velvet—the fabrics were an unusual combination and that's why I chose them."

"Yes, yes," said Vidal, a touch impatiently. "But what *inspired* you?"

Clarissa stared at him in confusion. "Winning the Teen Couture, of course."

"Ah," said Vidal, nodding. "I see." He turned to Angel. "Very well, Mademoiselle, why don't you tell us about the silver gauze?"

Angel touched the silver fabric. "Silk gauze is difficult to work with because it's slippery and it frays easily, but if you can get it to do what you want, it can be incredibly effective."

"And did you?" asked Vidal. "Did you get it to do what you wanted?"

Angel nodded. "Eventually. You see, I had a vision in my head—something I wanted to achieve."

"Ah," said Vidal, "the inspiration about which I wish so much to hear."

In a clear, carrying voice, Angel said, "My real name is Angelique, but my Papa always called me Angel—his angel. He used to tell me to figure out who I really was on the inside and to always be that person, no matter what. After he died, I'd imagine him watching over me." She touched the embroidery. "You see, it wasn't just about having an angel here, the whole dress was meant to remind me of who I am and how it feels to be loved."

And Angel smiled—at Vidal and Lily, the Comtesse, Kitty, the summer season group and Nick's parents. Last of all, she smiled at Nick, her eyes questioning.

He held her gaze for a moment, then smiled and nodded.

Angel saw him through a mist of happy tears. No matter what happened now she knew it would be all right: Nick was there for her.

She faced Vidal. "I didn't know if I could achieve my vision until just before my entry was due to leave for Paris, so I didn't draw my final sketch until three days before the competition closed. That's why Clarissa's dress only *looks* like mine. In fact, the dress she had made by Harrington's doesn't match my final drawing."

"It's not true!" shrieked Clarissa. "She stole *my* design. This is *my* ball gown." She ran over to Margot. "Tell them, mother. Tell them how I work for Miki Merua in a real fashion studio, while *she*," Clarissa spat the word, "is only a cook's daughter and—"

"Worth a dozen of you." An angry male voice cut her off.

"Dad!" cried Lily.

Angel turned to see Philip cutting through the crowd and heard Margot gasp. "Philip! You're here!" The next moment Margot had wrenched free of Clarissa's grasp and run forward to seize Philip's hand.

"I thought you were in South America," she cried. "But thank goodness you're here. I don't know what to do. Clarissa has been behaving so strangely. I had no idea about any of this." She gestured to her daughter, standing pale and furious in the middle of the ballroom.

"That's a lie!" hissed Clarissa. "You knew *all* about it— it was *your* idea!"

"It's not true," Margot argued. "Don't listen to her, Philip. You know I would never—"

"Lie?" thundered Philip. "Or send my daughter to Paris without my permission? Or threaten Angel and Simone?" He stared at Margot as though seeing her for the first time. "Get out," he said, his voice like steel. "Get out and take your daughter with you."

Margot blanched. "No, Philip, please. I did it for you, for the Comtesse . . ."

But she got no further, for the microphone suddenly squealed, drowning out every sound. As the noise faded, Vidal said, "Ladies and gentlemen, the designer of this magnificent ball gown is *not* Clarissa Kane—who has never heard of the Lunéville hook essential for tambour beading and has neither the heart nor soul essential for a great couturier. The real designer is Mademoiselle Angel Moncoeur, whose love of fashion and talent for design is evident in every detail of her dress."

He stepped down from the dais and wrested the silver trophy from Clarissa's hands. "Mademoiselle, you are a disgrace to the name of haute couture! Please leave."

Clarissa cringed, but before she could speak, Margot grabbed her hand and, looking neither right nor left, dragged her from the ballroom.

For a moment no one spoke and then Philip turned to Angel. "Go on. Show them."

She nodded and looked at Nick. He stepped forward, opened his arms and with a cry of happiness, she tumbled into them.

"Dance with me," she whispered.

He held out his hands and, as Angel raised her hands to his, the silver gauze lifted away from the midnight-blue velvet and the tiny pieces of delicate, hand-sewn fabric floated gently upwards like soft silver feathers.

And in that moment the whole room could see that her gown had wings.

Angel's wings.

Chapter Thirty-Eight

For several seconds the vision of Angel dancing with Nick, her silver wings floating behind her, held the crowd in thrall.

Then the applause began.

It swelled to a mighty crescendo as Nick lifted Angel off her feet and spun her slowly round, her silver wings rippling and dancing behind her.

"You really are an angel," he said, putting her down and watching as the silver gauze drifted down onto the velvet.

She smiled up at him and then at those around them. In almost every face Angel saw acceptance and approval; only the Comtesse stood apart, her face tense and unyielding.

Angel's heart sank.

It wasn't enough that she'd proved herself; if she couldn't win the Comtesse's forgiveness then it would be a victory forever tinged with regret.

Letting go of Nick's hand, Angel walked straight across the ballroom to where the Comtesse stood rigid beside her son.

"I am *so* sorry for the hurt I've caused you, Madame. I was wrong to deceive you. These past two weeks with you have been like a wonderful dream—*please* believe that I never meant to hurt you."

The Comtesse stood still as a stone and Angel could see the pain in her eyes. She pressed on. "I know what I did was wrong, but I only pretended to be Lily because Clarissa had stolen my designs. I know that doesn't excuse the lies I told, but I hope . . . I wish . . ." A tear ran down Angel's cheek. "Oh, Madame, won't you forgive me?"

The Comtesse gazed slowly around the ballroom at the five hundred assembled guests. Then she turned back to face the girl she had loved as her own kin.

"I accept your apology," she said at last.

Angel's heart leapt and she stepped forward eagerly, words of gratitude hovering on her lips, when the Comtesse said, "But I do not wish to see you again." She drew herself up proudly. "You are Simone Moncoeur's daughter. The child of the woman I once wronged," she declared. "Whatever your intentions and no matter how well-meant your actions, that fact cannot be altered." She stared at Angel. "I imagine your mother will be glad to know how well you deceived me. Perhaps she guessed that I would grow to care for you as my own granddaughter and know how greatly I would feel the loss when you were no longer in my life . . ." Her voice trailed away and she put a hand to her eyes.

Angel stared at her blankly, trying to make sense of her words, when a voice rang out across the ballroom.

"You are wrong, Madame!"

Angel gasped and swung round, hardly daring to believe her ears.

Coming down the staircase, looking as Angel had never seen her look, was her maman.

Simone was dazzling in a butter-yellow chiffon dress with rhinestone straps. The beautifully draped skirt rippled as she descended the stairs like a queen.

But it wasn't the dress that filled Angel with such joy; it was the sight of her mother looking so well. They reached the bottom step at the same moment and Angel flung herself into Simone's arms.

"Angel, *ma petite*, my darling girl, are you all right?" Simone hugged her. "Philip phoned me last night. I've been so worried."

"Philip phoned you?" asked Angel, myriad questions dancing in her head. Her mother and Philip had talked—*but had they talked about the past?* she wondered.

"He knew I would want to be with you, so he flew me to Paris." Simone took Angel's hand. "And now that I am here, there are things that must be said." She drew Angel across the ballroom and halted in front of the Comtesse, her soft brown eyes flashing fire as she said again, "You are wrong, Madame."

"How dare you come here," said the Comtesse, her own eyes blazing. "Because of you I was estranged from my son, and now your daughter has . . . has . . ." The Comtesse looked accusingly at Simone. "Was it your plan to make me care for her?"

"Oh," cried Angel. "No, that's not—"

"Hush, Angel, there is no need for concern, Madame la Comtesse will soon learn her mistake," Simone said.

She turned her clear gaze to the Comtesse. "Again, Madame, I tell you that you are wrong. I knew nothing of Angel's presence here in Paris until Philip phoned me last night." She smiled at Philip and added, "So you see, it was not vengeance that brought me here tonight, but your son." Simone said huskily, "I owe Philip a debt, Madame." She bowed her head for a moment, then looked up and said firmly, "Indeed, I owe him more than that—I owe him the truth."

Angel's heart skipped a beat. She stared at her mother. Was she going to tell Philip she loved him? That even though she had married Yves Moncoeur she still felt something for the man she believed had betrayed her?

She crossed her fingers, held her breath and prayed that her mother would have the courage to tell Philip what was in her heart.

But Simone's words were not what she expected.

"Seventeen years ago, after I left Paris, I went straight to my father's farm. I hadn't seen him for years, but I had nowhere else to go. Papa wasn't happy to see me, but he let me stay. I was sure it would only be for a few days because Philip would soon return from America and come for me."

Simone touched her wedding band. "My father was not easy to live with. He drank and would fall into such violent rages that I often sought refuge at the next-door farm. Yves Moncoeur and I had played together there as children and he had always been kind to me. Though I never told him Philip's name, he knew I was waiting for the man I loved."

She touched Angel's cheek. "Your papa was the kindest, most understanding man who ever lived and, as the weeks passed and I heard nothing, he told me that if my lover did not come, he would gladly marry me. He said—"

She broke off as Philip suddenly stepped forward, his face ashen. "I *would* have come, if I'd known where you were!" He held out his hands to Simone. "But I couldn't find you and the detectives found you too late. You'd married Yves and I had no choice but to believe what my mother had told me—that you'd fallen in love with someone else."

Simone stared at him in disbelief. "But my letter explained."

"I didn't receive it. Not then. I didn't find it until years later."

The words fell like a stone and the look on her mother's face made Angel want to throw her arms around her and explain what had happened to her letter all those years ago.

"But I put it in our book," said Simone. "The day after your mother—" She stopped and stared accusingly at the Comtesse.

Elena de Tourney gasped and stepped back. She stumbled and would have fallen if Vidal had not caught her. "It's all right, Elena," he said. "I am here."

She gripped his hand and Angel saw the concern on his face as he said, "You must rest. All of this," he waved his hand at Philip and Simone, "can wait. Let us go somewhere private."

"No, Antoine," said the Comtesse. "It must end here. If I am to find peace in the future then I must face my past without flinching."

Vidal hesitated, then bowed and gave her his arm. "Then let us face it together, Elena," he said. "As we have always done."

They stood together and it seemed to Angel as though the anger and bitterness faded from the Comtesse's face as she faced Simone. "Philip never received your letter. But it was a genuine mistake. It was placed in the wrong book—I honestly don't know how—but he did not find it until six years later."

Simone stifled a sob and a shadow seemed to pass over Elena de Tourney's face. "When Philip found your letter he confronted me with it and demanded to know if it was true. I told him it was too late for the two of you." Her face contorted. "My arrogance meant I lost my son that day. I lost him to the woman he had always loved—I lost him to you."

The Comtesse gazed at Simone, pain etched into her face, and Angel saw a flash of pity in her mother's eyes.

"Madame—" began Simone, but the Comtesse stopped her.

"No, let me finish. Please."

Simone fell silent.

"I have nothing but regret for the things I said to you that day seventeen years ago. I valued my pride and my heritage above my son and so he left. Until yesterday, I thought he had gone forever." She blinked away a tear. "I am sorry, Philip. Sorry for my pride and my arrogance and for refusing to accept that you truly loved Simone." She held out her hands beseechingly. "I know that what I did cannot be undone, but I beg you," she turned to Simone, "and *you* to forgive me. I was wrong about you and I was wrong about your daughter."

She turned to Angel. "It is true that I was enraged by

your deception, but it was not only because of the lies you told or because you were Simone Moncoeur's daughter. I was angry because I regretted losing you. We had shared so much these past two weeks and I felt a connection—not the tie of blood, but something even more powerful. Do you know what it was?"

Angel nodded. "It was love," she whispered.

"Yes," said the Comtesse, "it was." She stood a little straighter and said firmly, "Two days ago I made you an offer which you refused. I make you that offer again because—if your mother will allow it—I want you in my life, Angel Moncoeur."

Angel's heart leapt and then she saw the look on her mother's face.

"It's all right, Maman," whispered Angel, "the Comtesse—"

"Does not know the rest of the story," interrupted Simone. "Only Yves knew, but now he is gone. I know he would have wanted me to finally tell it all."

She stood there, pale but resolute, and suddenly Angel felt poised on the brink of something huge, something from which there'd be no turning back.

Simone continued. "I'd waited for Philip for nearly six weeks when I discovered what Yves had already suspected." She gazed imploringly at Philip. "I waited for you as long as I dared, but when I heard nothing I married Yves. He was a good man and he knew better than anyone what Papa would do if he found out I was pregnant."

Angel froze.

Eventually, she found her voice. "P—pregnant," she stammered. "But . . . but . . . did you have the baby?"

Her mother nodded.

Angel stepped back and looked from Simone to Philip. "But that . . . that means—" She struggled to speak.

Simone took her hands and said gently, "Yves was your darling Papa, but he always knew he was not your father."

"And I knew I was," said Philip, stepping towards her.

Angel stared. "You knew?" she demanded. "And you never said?"

Philip nodded. "Simone knew I would suspect you were mine as soon as I saw you, so she made sure I understood that so long as Yves was alive, he must go on being your father and never know that I was the man she had waited for." He sighed. "Your mother only agreed to become my housekeeper because she was desperate, but she made it clear from the outset that her first loyalty was to Yves and I could have no part in her personal life."

"But why would you agree to that?" cried Angel. "You knew you were my father and you had all the power—you gave us a home, you paid Maman—" She gazed at him in confusion.

"And I would have done much more," said Philip gently. "But your mother was married to a good man—a man who did not deserve to have his love for you set aside because of a chance meeting." He hesitated, and then said slowly, "Simone would never discuss the past, but she made sure she told me the one thing she knew would stop me from asserting my rights as your father—she told me how Yves had broken his back."

"No! Philip," cried Simone suddenly. "Please don't."

"Angel needs to understand," said Philip softly. "And we both owe it to Yves to tell her the truth."

"Tell me," cried Angel, and suddenly Lily was beside her, her arm around Angel's shoulders.

"Tell us both," said Lily.

Simone looked at them and sighed. "Yves was working in the vineyard. He'd got down off the tractor to fix something when it slipped its gears and began to roll. It would have been all right except that I had brought you out to the vineyard to see your papa. You were four and you'd run ahead." Her face grew grim. "One moment you were running beneath the vines and the next moment I could see the tractor heading straight towards you. Your papa—Yves—barely reached you in time. He caught you and threw you clear, but . . . but he could not escape in time."

Angel paled. "But that means Papa—"

"It means only that Papa loved you," cried Simone, hugging her tightly. "*Nothing* else."

"He was a wonderful father and he deserved your love," added Philip gruffly. "But I wish—" He took a step towards them and stopped.

Angel pulled free of her mother's embrace and gazed at her parents. Her mind was whirling but there was a look on Maman's face that made Angel catch her breath.

Philip took another step closer and held out his hands to Simone. "I know you've suffered because I got your letter years too late, and I know that Yves was a far better man than I can ever be, but if there is even the slightest chance that you still feel anything for me, then give me the chance to prove how much I love you!"

The color rose in Simone's cheeks and she looked at Philip with a light in her eyes that Angel hoped would never be extinguished.

Philip didn't hesitate. He pulled her into his arms and held her as if he'd never let her go.

A tear rolled down Angel's cheek and she realized she was smiling. Then Lily was hugging her and Kitty was jumping up and down and Nick was there, his eyes sparkling with delight.

Then Philip and Simone reached for her and Lily.

At last Angel turned to the Comtesse.

As their eyes met, Elena de Tourney said softly, "I, too, would like to be hugged. That is, if my granddaughters were willing?"

Lily ran straight into her grandmother's arms.

Angel hesitated. "Are you sure, Madame?" Then, seeing the Comtesse raise a questioning eyebrow, she laughed and said, "Are you sure, *Grandmama*?"

"Quite sure," said the Comtesse, holding out her arms.

***

It was nearly midnight when Lily found Angel sitting with Nick on a sofa in a corner of the ballroom.

"Here you are!" she said, dropping down beside them and glancing shrewdly at Nick. "I know, I know, you lovebirds want to be alone, but I've got a message for Angel so there's no use glaring at me, Nick—you should be grateful."

"I can't say that gratitude is the emotion uppermost in my mind when I think of you, Lily," said Nick darkly.

"Yeah, well, if it wasn't for me, you'd never have met my best friend and you wouldn't be here now, looking at her in that soppy way."

"And if it wasn't for you," retorted Nick, "Angel wouldn't have spent half the night alone and cold and frightened."

"I wasn't frightened," said Angel. "Well, not much. And you're not to start arguing," she declared, pretending to glare. "I met Nick because I came to Paris to get my designs back."

"Which you did," said Nick, pulling her closer, "and totally triumphed!"

"And I am *so* glad I was there to see it," crowed Lily. "The defeat of Margot and Clarissa Kane: a truly magical moment! And now our parents are getting married and everything's awesome."

"Except the London Academy," said Angel suddenly. "How do we fix that?"

Lily grinned. "Dad's so happy he'll say yes to anything, so I asked him if he could pull some strings and get me an audition."

"You're pulling strings, Lily?" said Angel mischievously. "You almost sound like Clarissa."

"I do not!" said Lily, revolted. "I'm much nicer than—" She clapped her hand to her head. "Oh, what a ditz I am! You're wanted—that's what I came to tell you."

"What's up?" asked Angel.

"It's a surprise," replied Lily, her eyes sparkling.

She led Angel across the ballroom to the dais, where Vidal was waiting.

He stepped up to the microphone. "Ladies and gentlemen," he said. "Tonight I am proud to present to you the *true* winner of this year's Teen Couture—Angel Moncoeur."

As if in a dream, Angel received the shining silver trophy from the world-famous couturier. She held it up and looked out at the crowd. There was her mother in Philip's arms laughing and crying at the same time, and Nick beside his parents, each clapping furiously, and Kitty smiling up at her with Giles at her side and the rest of the summer season group behind them.

And there was Lily, her best friend, dancing with excitement at Angel's moment of triumph.

It was Lily who reached her first. "You did it," she laughed and held out her hand.

"Friends," said Angel, extending her little finger.

"Sisters," corrected Lily, with a grin.

"Forever," agreed Angel, and smiled.

THE END

ACKNOWLEDGEMENTS

This book has been bubbling in my brain since 1997 when I came across a magazine article while at a hairdresser in the Middle East. It has been through numerous incarnations since then, although Angel and her dream of winning the Teen Couture fell into my mind fully formed. A number of loyal supporters have helped me to bring Angel's story to life and I must thank my wonderful friends: Nikola Scott, Paul Nicholls, Roy Hay, Dianne Tobias, Jenny Walshe, Helen MacDonald, Fiona Skinner, Mary Bourke, Phil Rebakis and John Nolan for their rigorous reading, helpful comments and attention to detail. Special thanks to my teen readers: Lily Pandora Fletcher Stojcevski, Emily Ezzy, Zoe Bucher-Edwards, Hannah Milligan, Rebecca Green, Hannah Roland-Kristensen, Maeve O'Callaghan, Laura Watkins, Caitlin Scally, Madeline Keegan, Morwenna Billingham, Brianna Walshe and Eden Forster. Thank you also to Dr. Claire Darby for answering my medical questions, Anne-Marie Butt for her advice and corrections of my schoolgirl French, George Mihaly for his knowledge of French vineyards, Wendy Brennan for her kindness and encouragement when I was just starting out, the inimitable Anne Gracie who said all the right things at the right time, Linda Brumley for her invaluable advice, and to Valerie, Marnie, Peter, Susan and Jon for their enthusiasm and support. A huge thank you to my brilliant editors at Penguin: Amy Thomas, Clair Hume, Sarah Fairhall and Jane Godwin, for falling in love with Angel's story and helping me to make it all it could be, and to my wonderful agent, Courtney Miller-Callihan. To my family: Ben, Christopher and Elanor – thank you for reading the final draft and for giving me your insights into the teenage mind – and to my own hero, Barry, who has waited a long time for this book and has never faltered in his love and support of its author.

Jennifer Kloester

Jennifer Kloester loves to escape into a good book. She began writing her own stories in primary school and was living in the jungle in Papua New Guinea when she discovered Georgette Heyer's wonderful historical romances. Those books took her to London, Paris and New York and inspired her to write *The Cinderella Moment*. After spending three years living in the desert in Bahrain, Jennifer now spends most days writing in a book-lined study in an old manse. She is the author of two books on Georgette Heyer: *Georgette Heyer's Regency World* and *Georgette Heyer*, the authorized biography. *The Cinderella Moment* is her first novel.

Made in the USA
San Bernardino, CA
08 January 2014